Across The Event Horizon

What the critics have said about stories in this book:

"Will stick with you… Tight, fast, dramatic, and tortuous." – *Sharon Campbell, Tangent Online*

"Rivera adds subtlety to his aliens and his world-building… Highly Recommended." – *Colin Harvey, Suite 101*

"Recommend[ed]… unreservedly… [Rivera]… is not afraid to enhance his storytelling by playing with its structure. This is excellent … SF, and a thought-provoking read…" – *Daniel Woods,* Tangent Online

"Cleverly depicted … movingly portrayed …" – *Rich Horton, Locus Magazine*

"Sure to stay with you long after the last sentence." – *Horror Scope*

"I was blown away by Mercurio D. Rivera's 'The Scent of Their Arrival'; it's the finest story I've read for some time. … stunning in its emotional impact. I shall have to read it again." -- *Gareth D. Jones, Whispers of Wickedness*

"Marvelous. … like a kick in the guts. Wonderful." – *SFCrowsnest*

"Dark and thoughtful and terrible, in the best possible way. Snatch me another story from Mercurio Rivera. " – *Scientifically Bookish*

"Thoughtful and intimate … with issues of identity and individualism coming to the fore…" – *Barking Dog*

"'Longing for Langalana' is simply stunning – one of the most moving pieces of SF I've read in a long time." – Ian Whates

"Brilliant… On my Hugo short list." – Sam Tomaino, *SF Revu*

"Very well done… packs quite a punch … To keep in mind come award-nominating time." – *Spiral Galaxy*

Across The Event Horizon

Mercurio D. Rivera

NewCon Press
England

First edition, published in the UK March 2013
by NewCon Press

NCP53 (hardback)
NCP54 (paperback)

10 9 8 7 6 5 4 3 2 1

ISBN: 978-1-907069-50-5 (hardback)
978-1-907069-51-2 (paperback)

Cover art by Edward Miller
Cover design by Kris Dikeman

Minimal editorial interference by Ian Whates
Text layout by Storm Constantine

Contents

For my dear friends in Altered Fluid (Kris Dikeman, Paul Berger, Rick Bowes, K. Tempest Bradford, Matthew Kressel, Devin Poore, Alaya Dawn Johnson, N.K. Jemisin, Rajan Khanna, Lauren McLaughlin, E.C. Myers, Lilah Wild, Greer Woodward) and Avi Kotzer, who helped me shape these stories.

Across the Event Horizon

An Introduction

Terry Bisson

He was already a storyteller; just of a different kind.

Mercurio David Rivera was writing legal briefs for a living when, taking a break, he wandered into a New School (NYC) course on *Writing SF* (disclosure: I was the instructor) to try his hand at a different sort of fiction than the kind that lawyers and litigators generally tell.

He discovered, somewhat but not entirely I suspect, to his surprise, and certainly to his delight, that he was pretty good at it.

He was also good at getting even better.

He discovered his own talent, stirred it up, and shared it with us in the workshop.

Now it's your turn to cross that event horizon. Prepare to be astonished—but only if you haven't been paying attention to what's happening in the SF field these days. For though this is his first book, Rivera has not gone unnoticed. Far from it. Published in a wide range of magazines, his stories have been anthologized, featured in several "Year's Best" collections, and nominated for a World Fantasy Award. Most distinguished (to my mind), he is a regular in England's *Interzone*, perhaps the world's most prestigious genre rag.

I like these stories a lot and here's why:

I have always (to the dismay of my colleagues) maintained that SF is not really literature. It's not about itself. It's about ideas, dramatized and put to work. Rivera got that immediately.

There are many literary pleasures in his work — nuances of character, precision of plot, prose that skitters and shines, humor and horror galore. But all are subordinate to the central agenda of classic science fiction: the presentation of weird, wonderful and thought-provoking ideas. While I hate the term "speculative fiction" when it's used to avoid the dreaded genre label SF ... in fact, it's true.

Speculative is what SF actually is.

What if.

What if the extraterrestrials we are colonizing are in fact colonizing us? What if torture were a tool for good? What if we could reach into alternate universes and pluck out the selves we wanted? What if the galaxies themselves were signals or signs? What if the internet connected with the future? What if human/alien porn went viral? What if Bargonns could swizzle?

Rivera asks and answers these questions for us. His dramatic speculations are deep and thrilling and fun; funny too, as often as not. Confident enough to be playful, he can *junot* with the best, cloaking one of his best tales in NY street Spanglish.

Though considered a New Star, Rivera is Old School in the most important way. This is classic SF in post-modern dress, more quantum than Newtonian, but always ringing the old bell that Wells hung for us a hundred years ago. It makes you think. Of new things in new ways.

Lots of people hate that, of course. But this book is not for them.

It's for you.

Terry Bisson
January 2013

Dance of the Kawkawroons

Windswept confetti.

That's how Annie had described the Kawkawroons when she first spotted them hovering miles away against the white sky, bookended by the twin suns.

We crouched low on the edge of the cliff while hundreds of feet below us the blue waves of the Equatorial Sea crashed against the pebbled shore. In the distance, the rust-red peak of a derelict tower broke the surface of the ocean. Built by a long-extinct civilization before sea levels had risen, tens of thousands of these submerged skeletal spires dotted this alien waterworld.

Our transport ship sat behind us in a patch of flatland atop this butte. After swallowing a thimbleful of Inspiration a few months ago, I'd invented the shipcloaker, which allowed us to sneak past the quarantine patrols in orbit.

Annie handed me the binoculars and I trained them on the Kawkawroons. The creatures' fluorescent plumage blazed in the sunlight. "It's not too late to turn around and forget about all this," she said.

Typical of her, pretending to try to talk me out of a course of action only after she was certain I had fully committed to it. This then gave her license to say "I told you so" later. I completed our little dance by making a sour face and shaking my head as I handed the binoculars back.

One sun was setting behind us while another was rising ahead above the cobalt horizon. The winds whipped so hard that my yellow parka flapped noisily, and I had to tighten the hood on my jacket.

With their keen vision, the Kawkawroons would have

spotted us by now, despite the enormous distance. When the winds let up for a moment, I stood up and waved my arms over my head. Two of the Kawkawroons settled on top of the distant tower; perhaps they had established nests in the abandoned steel structure before sea levels had risen. One of the others, however, separated from the flock and honed in on us, expanding its wings, riding the gusts until it hovered just feet from the edge of the cliff.

Strangers. From the angle at which the worldbreath carried me I could make out the two strangers on the edge of the rocky perch. One of them waved its naked wings – was it a mere chick? – signaling that it wanted to play with me. I circled and circled but they refused my invitation to race.

Why did they tease me so?

Below me, Great Mother's blue-green waters churned and slapped against the cliffside as if She played her own special game. Half of me still slept after the weeks-long journey across the ocean. I did not want to wake my self, because then I might want to rest instead of play.

The strangers huddled together and pressed circular stones to their eyes. They swayed their featherless wings left and right.

Fine, I thought. I will approach. But if I set down how can we chase each other through the clouds and fly upside down and dive into Great Mother to hunt salty eels? How can we sing within stony outcrops to create clever echoes? Perhaps the strangers wanted to roll in the dust and bathe with me?

I got as close as possible without landing – *careful, careful* – so that my other half might stay sound asleep.

The Kawkawroon floated in the air with almost no wing movement. Its large bulbous head wobbled, as if too heavy for its thin neck. Bright yellow and aquamarine feathers sheathed its angular torso, which was twice the size of a human body. It had two exposed bones like forearms folded beneath expanded wings, and its face looked frighteningly proto-human; sharp-chinned, with a protruding blue beak instead of a nose just atop a lipless orifice. A perfectly round left pupil tracked our movements while the right eye gazed blankly in a different direction.

"This is insane," Annie said. Despite her words, I could sense her excitement. She was simply looking for reassurance.

"No, everything's okay. It's just observing us. The Kawks tend to be tame after their migration across the ocean."

"How do you even know...?" She closed her mouth. "Oh."

Inspiration.

Annie's question reminded me to activate my earpiece translator. *The translator she'd invented,* I reminded myself. Annie, who had trouble with high school Spanish. Annie, who had zero tech experience and tended bar with me at Norton's for as long as we'd been together.

She poked at her ear, triggering her own translator.

Holding my hands at my side, I raised my left knee as high as I could. Then I extended my right arm, palm up. But when I went to bend my right knee, a blast of wind made me lose my balance and stumble backwards.

"No!" Annie said. "It has to be precise!"

"I know that!" Although how I knew it – how Annie knew it – I couldn't say. It was Inspired.

I began again: two lifts of the left leg; three lifts of the right leg. A twirl. I extended my right arm and wiggled my fingers. Bent at my waist.

"Slower," Annie whispered in my ear.

She shot me an exasperated look, one I'd seen too many times before. "Let me," she said. With a shake of her head and a cluck of disapproval, she set to the task at hand, starting the dance from scratch.

In five minutes, she completed the Invitation to Speak.

The Kawk hooted and mimicked her precise movements, completing the elaborate dance while riding the wind. Then it further extended its multi-jointed stick-legs, as if about to land.

But it remained airborne.

"Friends?" it said. Its voice was an extended coo, even through the translator.

"Friends," I said.

It did a midair spin. "Let's play, friends! Let's chase each other through the clouds and dive for –"

"Can you help us?" Annie said. "Where is your nest?"

So much for careful diplomacy. After we'd traveled so many light years, I guess Annie wasn't about to pussyfoot around the subject now.

My breastbone thudded rapidly when I realized these were not chicks. The strangers displayed the colors of our people, but they were not Kawkawroons! I screeched at the sight of their flat faces and featherless bodies, so startled that my other half almost woke up. One of the strangers approached as if to play with me, and started to signal that it wanted to speak. Then it changed its mind. Maybe it was shy. The second stranger – much friendlier than the first – completed the invitation. But could they even speak Kawkawroonese? The strangers had called to one another in a language I had never heard before. Low-pitched growls like those of the mimisets.

The one nearest to me reached into its strange coverings – which I had mistaken for feathers – and pulled out a glinting pebble that it slotted into the side of its head. The rock flashed like lightning, startling me, and their language changed from gargling nonsense to the soothing squeaks and chirps of Kawkawroonese.

"Can you help us?" the stranger said. "Where is your nest?"

I skipped in the air, delighted that the strangers could speak. They wanted to be my friends! Only friends asked each other for help. I stopped. But why did they want to see my nest?

I could feel my other half stir.

"Come, friends," I said.

I dropped from the edge of the perch and swooped to the

cave a hundred feet below us where I had built a nest months ago. Worldbreath held me aloft while I waited and waited for the strangers to follow. Finally, I flew back to see what had delayed them.

I found them doing a very odd thing.

They molted! They shed their coverings – revealing more of the same feather-like material underneath, only hideously black. If they had looked like this when I first saw them, I would never have wanted to play with them. In the back of my mind, before I knew they were strangers, I had hoped we might even frolic above the clouds and bask in the sunlight. But no more.

Rather than fly, they lowered long strings, like vines, over the edge of the cliff, and clutched them tightly. I hovered beside them as they squirmed down the cord – like the cancapikas of the Green Islets, inching down towering trees. I trilled at the rocks and made magnificent echoes. But the strangers remained silent.

They were no fun at all.

Instead, they gathered food from between the rocks. Perhaps they did not want to play because they were hungry? But rather than eat the food, they cawed, and then let it drop to Great Mother, which made no sense at all.

I clutched the rope and rappelled down the cliff face another five yards. Annie followed a few feet above me.

We'd stripped off our blue-sleeved yellow parkas to avoid attracting the attention of any more of these creatures. One would do for our purposes.

The Kawk screeched louder as we descended. "There's no damn way that thing is tame," Annie shouted. I could barely hear her in the yowling wind.

Now she's cautious, I thought, after telling the creature point-blank we were interested in its nest. My friend Gilbride, the xenobiologist who'd allowed us to sip the Inspiration back on Earth, had warned us that these creatures had complex dance rituals, and moods that could shift from docility to aggression at a moment's notice. The Kawks were genderless and all of them could lay eggs, but we knew few other hard facts about them. We knew even less about the extinct aliens whose civilization once thrived on this world. Intelligent life was rare enough that ExoGov had declared Kawkworld off-limits to everyone but anthropologists and xenobiologists, of which we were neither.

Dark spots speckled the rocky outcrops of the cliff. The cavern into which the Kawk had flown earlier opened up about two hundred feet below us. The creature sounded so child-like. Hopefully it was mature enough to have a nest.

The Kawk moved dangerously closer, fluttering less than two feet away from me. I pulled my gun from its holster and waved it at the creature, but it didn't back off.

Annie shrieked suddenly, her voice disappearing in the howling wind. Holding on to the swaying rope with one hand, she swatted at her arms, her head, and pulled down her hood.

Pain shot through my arm. When I looked down, something the size of a crab, an insectoid, sat on my wrist, antennae squiggling. I swiped at it and sent it hurtling into the ocean.

Another sting on my leg. My back.

I lost my grip and fell. I swung in circles, suspended by the harness around my waist.

The scorpion-like specks that dotted the cliff wall swarmed towards us.

I continued to swat the insects off my arms and legs, sending them plummeting to the waters below. Some had found their way underneath my backpack, and I couldn't reach them.

A squawk.

The Kawk swooped in and plucked the bugs off of me with its beak, throwing its head back, swallowing them whole. It darted back and forth from me to Annie, gorging itself on the black insects. Soon the wave of specks on the wall abated, disappearing into crevices in the bluff.

"Are you okay?" I shouted.

"Oh God, oh God, oh God..." Annie continued to swat at

the insects though they were no longer there. Her blond ponytail draped over her left eye.

"We're not far from the cavern." I tried my best to calm her, though I think I was really trying to calm myself. Eventually I started to edge downwards again, and she followed. As I released some of the rope with my right hand, I rappelled down the wall, avoiding the overhanging rocks.

The Kawk, now quiet and seemingly bloated, remained at our side in the swirling air currents.

We reached the aerie an hour later.

The strangers hid in my nesting den and refused to come out to play. Maybe they were hoping I would go look for them? But that meant I would have to land, and that would wake up my other half. I had no choice.

I unbent my legs and wiggled my toeclaws. Then I swooped into the entranceway. The strangers, who had been crouched in the rear of the den, scrambled away from me and held their hands over their face. They were very funny. I spread my wings wide and set down.

And as my bare feet felt cold stone, I woke up.

Like the suns emerging from behind a cloud cover, my head cleared and I felt whole again.

I retracted my wings into my back-pouch and stretched my legs. After so many weeks of flight, it felt unnatural to walk again. I rubbed the plumes on my left ribcage, which were caked with sea salt; that side of my body felt weary after so many days of wakefulness. Each of my halves had taken turns sleeping during the great migration.

Then my other self reminded me: I had strangers in my midst. I should not have been surprised, I supposed. These were not the first visitors to show an interest in a Kawkawroon brood, if the myths were to be believed. But I had doubted such tales were true until now.

The creatures had placed a triangular blue covering over the center of their faces in an attempt to simulate a beak. A sign of respect, no doubt. They had somehow restored their handsome blue-and-yellow appearance, and approached tentatively. Each of them placed a hand to the repulsive flap of flesh on the side of its head, where a shiny substance glittered. They then performed the lifefont dance in a methodical if awkward fashion, moving with precise arm and leg motions. These creatures were small but quite heavy given the sound of their stomps. Amazing. The legends spoke of strangers who undertook voyages that made our own migrations pale by comparison – voyages from islands beyond the clouds, places so distant it would take an entire lifetime to fly there – and that our destiny would forever be tied to theirs. It had been said that such visitors had delivered our people to Great Mother at the dawn of time. But *these* flat-faced wingless creatures looked like no strangers I had ever heard described before.

I decided to join their lifefont dance. They faced me and I mirrored their precise movements--or did they mirror mine?--and we lost ourselves in the motion. I extended a leg, swept open a wing, puffed my chest. I danced not merely out of courtesy, but out of a genuine fascination with these creatures.

When we finished, one of them stepped toward me. As before, the glittering objects in their skin flaps blinked red and their vulgar growls morphed into the familiar high-pitched whistles of civilized language.

"Thank you for directing us here," the stranger said.

"But of course," I responded. "How could I deny shelter for the wind-weary?"

"You sound... different." I could not read the expressions on the speaker's flat face – how could it even defend itself without the sharp edge of a real beak? – but the tone of its voice reflected surprise.

"Than when we spoke before?" I laughed. "What did you expect?" Part of me, after all, had been asleep earlier. Both my halves were fully awake now.

The creatures repeatedly looked at each other before addressing me, part of their bizarre foreign rituals no doubt.

"I don't understand," one of them said.

Perhaps I had given the strangers more credit than they deserved. I tried to hide my disdain but it whistled through. "The great migration here from our southern nest took eighteen days of flight. Completing such a long voyage would have proved impossible unless we took turns sleeping."

"We?"

"Of course, both of us." I pointed to my left side and my right side, wanderlust and nest-making, frivolity and solemnity, passion and aloofness. Did the strangers even know the difference between up and down?

They flicked their ears and spoke to each other in their guttural growls and moans so that I could not understand them. I found this ill-mannered. On the other hand, it occurred to me that I had not shown much courtesy myself. As tired as I was, they must have been even wearier given the distance of their migration. And I had neglected to offer them food or drink.

I made the proffer, regurgitating a dollop of sweet sanlop at my feet, but the creatures declined.

I should not have been surprised given the churlish manner in which they discarded food during their climb down the cliffside. They moved like mudworms, these strangers, like crippled Kawkawroons on their deathbeds. How did they traverse Great Mother? And how could they travel without wings to the islands beyond the clouds, if such stories were to be believed?

"You desire one of my brood, do you not?" I said. Kawkawroonese tradition required me to tender one of the lifefonts in exchange for their dance. But the creatures had already declined food, so I expected them to turn down the offer. Imagine my surprise, when they bobbed their hideous heads and said, "Yes! Yes!" like stunted chicks.

I moved to the rear of the cavern and stepped into the nest. And as they watched, I crouched in the mound of weeds and wet soil and laid a dozen lifefonts. I cupped one.

When I turned to hand it to them, one of the strangers pointed an object at me that shined like quartz. This must have been their way of reciprocating for my gift of the lifefont. Perhaps the creatures were more polite than I thought.

One of the strangers carefully took the lifefont from my hand, cradling it as if it had already hatched.

I, in turn, stepped forward to retrieve the shiny object the other one was offering to me.

Thunder.

Pain.

Terrible agony.

I dropped to the floor, writhing, clutching my left side.

"Did you have to shoot it?" Annie said.

"It came at me, goddamn it!" Why did she always have to second-guess my every move? So much had changed in the months since we'd consumed the Inspiration, but our parrying remained the same.

"I'm just saying. These are *intelligent* beings. And we're not even supposed to be here." She cradled an egg against her chest while pressing the blue breathing mask over her face to try to tolerate this cavern's unbearable stench. "Then you go and shoot one down like it's a pheasant or something."

The Kawk lay on its side, hooting pitifully. I'd blown a hole clear through the left side of its torso and wing pouch.

I took a misstep and slipped in the puddle of black vomit it had left. It had obviously made itself sick from eating too many of those insects.

"What if those bugs were venomous?" Annie said. The red welt on the side of her face had grown to the size of an apple. My own arms were numb and swelling up where I'd been stung.

"Hopefully the ship's medbot can treat –"

"Hopefully?" she said. "Look at us! What are we doing? *We weren't supposed to shoot it!*"

"It's done! There's nothing we can do now." When I removed another egg from the nest, the Kawk let out a pathetic screech. I held up the egg against the light of the cavern entryway. Perfectly round. Crystalline. Transparent. The yellow sac had a green spot at its center: Inspiration.

Annie's eyes gleamed and I could see that her qualms about hurting the Kawk had instantly evaporated at the sight of the yolk. It was enough Inspiration to last us for years to come. We might even sell some of it; there was certainly high demand for the substance in the black market on Earth.

"Do you realize how much this can change our lives?" I said.

She paused for an extended moment. Then she silently zipped open her backpack and made room for the eggs. Between our two bags we had enough room to clear the nest and take all twelve eggs with us.

The Kawk squawked ferociously as we removed each additional egg. Who knew what drove the creature to hand over one of its eggs after our Inspired dance, but it sought now to protect the remainder of its brood, an understandable reaction. I'm sorry, I thought. You encountered a more advanced alien civilization and paid the price. How many species in the universe have met the same fate?

I craned my neck out of the cavern inlet, and looked up. The insects had re-gathered on the cliff wall so I retrieved the electroprod from my backpack to clear the path for our climb to the landing spot above, where our transport ship awaited us. With any luck, we'd be back on Earth in a month.

My left side floated in and out of consciousness.

How I wanted to make the vile creatures pay. If I could have moved right then, I would have taken out their eyes with my beak.

Why did they have to hurt me? Vicious, ungrateful walkers!

But when the strangers crouched down and began to empty my nest, removing lifefont after lifefont, I forgot my pain and yawped with delight! Kawkawroon legend spoke of so many other strangers of different shapes and forms who had followed this same path. I did not understand it entirely, but I knew this was all part of the prophecies, part of the sacred, unknowable plan.

I was dying.

In my final moments I yearned to take that final dive into Great Mother's embrace. If only I could move; I could not move....

Warm worldbreath. Cradle me; carry me on my final sojourn toward sweet-smelling perches beyond the endless white clouds....

The sun set over the Maui coast while I sat at my desk poring over the latest reports. Still no progress in replicating Inspiration in a lab setting.

I smiled and rubbed my eyes, turning away from the screen to take in the sunset. To think that a few years ago I'd been tending bar at Norton's Pub across the way from the Honolulu Xenobiology Institute, and now I was an actual member of HXI's R&D staff. In the year since Annie and I had returned, how many other human beings had benefited from tasting Inspiration? I had let a few close friends try it, though I hadn't told Annie. The truth was that I'd fought a constant temptation to share it with everyone I knew. How many others had experienced that amazing rush, that thrill of Inspiration? Quite a few, judging from the number of revolutionary discoveries exploding across the globe.

Construction of the island tower was almost complete.

A knock on the office door. Annie glided into the room wearing yellow sweatpants and a tight T-shirt, sipping bottled water. From her movements, her expression, I could tell she had good news.

"Spill it," I said.

"It's official. Moscow, London, Shanghai, Sydney..." She counted on her fingers. "Towers are going up in all the major cities. With the quarantine lifted, we won't have to worry about our Inspiration supply any more." She did a little twirl. "Thousands of Kawks are being shipped over."

"I don't know." I scratched my chin. "Are we sure they'll produce eggs here?"

"If we perform the ritual dance..." She shrugged. "It wasn't just my idea, you know. Dozens of Inspired people independently came up with the same plan. Have you heard about this month's other inventions?" she said.

I shook my head.

"A synthetic compound that provides all the nutrients that the Kawks need." She started counting on her fingers again. "A chemical bath that simulates the composition of their ocean so they can stay healthy and disease-free. An AI-driven communicator that allows us more nuanced interactions with them so we can follow their complex rituals and maximize egg production."

"Wow, that's great news."

"Can you imagine what else lies ahead with the help of Inspiration once the Kawks are settled here? Cold fusion, AI tech, genetic engineering... Who knows?" She paused, staring sideways out the window.

"What's the matter?"

"Do you ever feel, I don't know, a little guilty about all this? About what we've done to the Kawks?"

"Guilty? Not really. We're treating them well." I understood what she meant, but it was just the natural order, a pattern repeated throughout human history. Cultures colliding. Conquest. Yes, we had conquered the Kawks, but it wasn't as if we'd *really* enslaved them. The creatures would be given free rein here as long as they continued to supply us with Inspiration.

"How about we stay home tonight?" I said, putting my arm around her waist. Annie's tight sweatsuit usually revved me up, and she knew it, but I made the half-hearted offer more out of habit than any real desire. It had been months since we'd slept together.

"I have another idea," she said, wiggling free. And I knew immediately what she had in mind: something better than sex.

"Let me guess. Inspiration?"

She smiled. "Just a teensy bit. I'm close to finishing a force field that can regulate temperatures to make it more comfortable for the Kawks to lay eggs."

"So you'd rather work than make love? I'm hurt." I jutted my lower lip in a pretend pout.

"Aw, poor baby." She kissed the tip of my nose. "Join me?"

I nodded. The truth was that I had my own project I wanted to complete – a sonic amplifier that generated complex echoes that pleased the Kawks.

As we headed out of the office toward the lab, I stopped at the window and stared at the skeletal spire that had been rising higher and higher into the grey sky.

A feeling nagged at me that I was missing something.

"So how long do you think before construction of the tower is complete?" I said.

"Not long at all," she said.

And at that moment, an image struck me. An image of countless Kawkawroons perched atop tens of thousands of towers across the globe, the human throngs staring up at them, blank-eyed, dancing at their feet.

"What's wrong?" she said.

I froze, struggling to retain the thought, but just like that, it disappeared like daylight behind a pulled window shade, eclipsed by a burst of sudden Inspiration.

"Nothing," I said, itching to get to work. "Nothing at all."

Longing for Langalana

I wince at the intensity of the Earth Emissary's beauty, and take a step backward. Despite my decades of exposure to his people, the mere sight of this uniformed young man, this stranger, still causes powerful feelings to bubble to the surface reflexively. As he strides into the room, his emerald-green eyes glitter. The resemblance to Phinny is uncanny. He nods a greeting and sits down at the conference room table. His pink, smooth-skinned brilliance makes me squint, and I have to turn my back to him to combat the giddiness. Facing the thick-plated window, I observe the dull, grey moonscape, the dead dust dunes stretching off into the horizon, softly lit by the indigo glow of Langalana overhead.

I struggle against the urge to stare at his hazy reflection in the glass.

"An Emissary, eh?" I say, leaning heavily on my red-furred cane. "Your father would be proud." Peeking over my shoulder, I point to the wicker bowl on the glass table, my finger trembling ever so slightly. "Please, help yourself to some *chapra*. But chew the leaf slowly. Its nectar is very, very sweet. Your father used to love it when he was a boy, you know."

I slowly rub the scales on my chin and gesture toward the massive, reddish planet that fills half the black sky. "Magnificent, eh?" Mauve clouds encircle its equator and dark purplish seas stand out starkly between three large landmasses.

"To think, our peoples traveled so far, endured so much. But in the end, Langalana spurned us," I say. "And so, we've been left to pine from afar, to dream about what could have been."

I turn around and dare to look directly at him again.

The young man sucks gingerly on the tip of the red-leafed *chapra*. Like his father, a majestic swath of thick, yellow fibers sheathes his closed cranium and falls to his shoulders. A profound love causes me to ache and shudder; I shake my head and avert my gaze again.

"I know why you're here," I say.

From my sleeping quarters I spied the silver landbuzzer – a glinting pinprick in the distance – speeding toward us. As if riding choppy waves, it skimmed atop the undulating, scarlet-furred grasslands that stretched in every direction. The buzzer clattered up to the reed fence that surrounded our hearth and two humans – an older female and a young boy not much taller than me – clambered out of its sidecars.

I froze, open-mouthed, for I had never seen an actual alien before. In the weeks since landfall – when our Wergen brethren left us and continued onward to the Northern Continent – these were the first pilgrims we had encountered. I'd been told that they came in magnificent shades of pink and brown and yellow, like the Visian demigods of our mythology, but to actually see them with my own eyes... Rather than a single breathing canal, they bore two tiny holes in the center of their faces beneath a protruding skin-covered bone. Tossed, colored fibers covered the tops of their rounded heads. But most striking of all, a rainbow-colored aura that I can only describe as a coating of pure, unadulterated beauty shimmered about them. I bent down and peeped at them over the windowsill as they approached our front yard. The old female conversed casually with Father and Elkah, both of whom worked the fields with the bots. Although I longed to see the aliens up close, I felt paralyzed by a sudden overwhelming shyness.

"Shimera!" Father called out. His voice, though loud, sounded shaky.

I hesitated for just an instant before bolting through the central fireroom to the hearth's front archway. Father and Elkah stood side by side, both clutching their bunched-up tether – for when they stood so close together there was a chance that one of them might stumble over it or become entangled.

"Shimera, these are our new neighbors, Dr. Zooey Crest and her nephew, Phineas." As he spoke to me, Father kept his eyes fixed on the humans.

When I tried to return the aliens' greeting, I found myself breathless. I could only nod.

"I was hoping, young lady," Dr. Crest said, "that you might be able to tutor my nephew in the Wergen tongue." She said this in perfect, unaccented Wergenese. "I'm inundated with lab work, and Phinny could really benefit from some personal instruction. He knows just a few words and phrases."

As Dr. Crest spoke, the boy, Phinny, stood behind her, gawking at the tether that connected Father and Elkah's craniums.

"Say hello to our neighbors, Phinny," Dr. Crest instructed the boy, switching to Earthen. "In Wergenese."

The boy stayed hidden behind his aunt's pleated, white skirt and shouted out a badly accented "hello." While the adults continued speaking, he shifted his gaze to me and stuck out his dark pink tongue. I smiled, marveling at this strange and wonderful human greeting.

"Shimera would be honored to tutor the boy," Elkah said.

When Phinny looked at me again, I bashfully stuck out my own colorless tongue, which couldn't extend nearly as far as the human's.

The boy laughed delightedly and Dr. Crest glanced at me, raising an eyebrow. "Yes, well… Phinny will come by around midday tomorrow."

"You really must visit for dinner," Father said.

"Yes, please, we insist," Elkah added.

Dr. Crest shot us a strange look, one I had difficulty reading, and shook her head slowly. "That's very kind of you, but I'm afraid we're going to have to pass. Some urgent gengineering experiments require my attention."

"Can we come by and help clear your fields?" Father asked.

"Perhaps assist you with your lab work?" Elkah said. "Really, there must be some way we can help."

Several lines appeared across Dr. Crest's forehead. "That's quite all right. The Wergen bots are managing the fieldwork just fine, thank you. And I work best alone."

"Are you sure —?"

Her glare cut Father off in mid-sentence. "Good day." She grabbed the boy's hand, turned, and marched off.

Father and Elkah bowed their heads, embarrassed that they'd been too forward.

And as the landbuzzer receded into the distance Phinny looked over his shoulder, and I thought I saw his long, pink tongue stick out once again, greeting me in his special way.

"We were planetary pioneers, the 'heroic trailblazers' of Langalana," I say, my voice tinged with bitterness. "My father and Elkah performed the traditional Wergen function: maintenance of the fieldbots used by the pilgrims to clear large patches of the grasslands in preparation for the settlement's expansion. And Dr. Crest studied soil samples and, months later, headed up a team of human gengineers responsible for crop production. This was years before the construction of the Science Institute, Emissary, years before the devastation had begun, before the landfall of hundreds of human exobiologists, anthropologists, entomologists."

I pace slowly, shifting my weight to my cane, and rub the scales on my chin.

The young man stares at me silently, impassively.

"But what did Phinny and I care about the logistics of settlement? We were just children, children exploring a vast new playground." I can't help it; my voice becomes wistful now. "Every morning Phinny came to my hearth for his lesson in Wergenese. Our conversations in those first few days – in

Earthen, of course – were formal and very brief for, you see, I was still painfully shy around him.

"And as the days passed we became more comfortable in our surroundings, more comfortable around each other. Oh, the afternoons Phinny and I spent in those breathtaking grasslands! How many games we played! How many secrets we shared! One day, he told me he'd discovered a natural trail through the grasslands, a trail that twisted out towards the Purple Sea."

Elkah oversaw the skittering bots that cleared the growing grass in front of our hearth while Father prepared the meals inside. At that time, their cranial cord extended for almost a full ten meters and still sported the great elasticity so typical of the recently-tethered.

When we strolled past Elkah, her head jerked upward and her white eyes zoomed in on Phinny. "Where are you going, Phineas?" she asked.

"To the overlook," he replied in slightly accented Wergenese. "For my lesson."

"*Very* well spoken," Elkah gushed. She patted his head and her fingers lingered in his yellow tresses. "You're an excellent student." At that very instant Father must have moved toward the rear of the hearth because Elkah's tether pulled slightly, causing her to take two steps backwards. "Olbodo!" she shouted over her shoulder. "What is *wrong* with you?"

Phinny grabbed my hand – which pulsed with pleasure at his touch – and pulled me along to the recently discovered path that snaked in a southwesterly direction. Because the blue sun hovered directly over us, we cast no shadows as we wandered through the trail. The grasslands resembled nothing on Werg – or Earth apparently, judging from Phinny's wide-eyed reaction every time we moved through them. A deep crimson fur lined each blade of grass, and the fields literally swayed – not from the warm wind, but of their own volition – left, then right, in perfect rhythm.

From the twisting dirt path, the fields fell away and we emerged onto a jutting, rocky overlook. Shielding our eyes, we stood at the lip and marveled at the glorious, placid Purple Sea, kilometers below, lapping against the crystalline cliff side. A steady breeze blew, warm and silky and impossibly salty.

We set down our blankets and I began Phinny's lesson, instructing him on the nasal twangs that punctuate Wergenese verbs. I found that Phinny had an impressive facility for languages, so much so that his skills approached Wergen levels. He always picked up the nuances quickly, biting his lip and concentrating intensely. Before long, however, a dam seemed to burst in his head – he'd hurl stones into the sea, or recite the Wergenese alphabet while standing on his head, or break off a reed and challenge me to a duel, or lay on his stomach and spew a dewy substance from his mouth over the edge of the overlook – signaling the end of the lesson.

As we began our long hike back I could sense he had something on his mind he wanted to ask me. His reluctance to do so surprised me, for Phinny had questions and opinions about everything and in the weeks that I'd been tutoring him never once hesitated to voice them:

"Do you have any brothers or sisters?" he had asked.

"I had two sisters who died at birth," I replied.

"Why do fieldbots look like giant spiders? The Wergens should make them look, I don't know... friendlier," he said.

"The bots are modeled after Scythians – our pets on Werg."

His barrage had continued: "I wish I had those white Wergen scales. You shouldn't say you're 'colorless' – you're white, like chalk;" "The math and science holoprograms are boring, don't you think?" "I'm glad Aunt Zooey got assigned to Argenta rather than Inlandia;" "We're the luckiest kids ever, to be the first pilgrims on this continent." "They say you can fit a hundred Earths into Langalana, but I don't believe it!" And so on.

I always answered in Wergenese and we spent hours on that

overlook, the afternoons vanishing into the sun's blue blaze as we chatted and played.

As was our practice, I walked him back to his habitation. Sometimes I would wander inside to catch a glimpse of Dr. Crest in her spacious laboratory, the rectangular gene-splicers lying on long tables and humming in the background. But today she stood at the entranceway in her white lab coat and waved for us to enter when she saw us approach.

Phinny and I entered the lab where Dr. Crest stood in front of a table with a microscope, a blue syringe and odd-shaped metallic devices that scurried about the table on their own. "Did you have a good lesson, Phineas?"

"Yes, Aunt Zooey," Phinny said in Wergenese. "Learned a lot."

"The watermelon is ready, if you'd like to try some."

Phinny jumped up and down and let out a whoop. Dr. Crest had been trying for some time to gengineer Earthen fruits and vegetables to grow in the garden behind their habitation.

"Can we have some right now?" Phinny said.

She hesitated. "Come here, Shimera."

Despite her wrinkled dermis, she radiated waves of beauty — like all humans — that made me feel tingly and happy to be alive. She gently grabbed my hand — an electric tickle buzzed through me — and placed it on the table, palm up. Her five fingers, so pink and dainty and dexterous, brushed my three digits with a sandpapery substance. "Let me do a quick run of your cell samples to make sure it's safe for you to eat these fruits," she said. "Phinny, why don't you run outside and cut up a melon."

Phinny scrambled out the door.

"Shimera, I've received Elkah and Olbodoh's daily dinner invitations, their notes and e-messages." Dr. Crest removed a bundle of red slips of paper from her lab coat jacket and dangled them in front of me. "Tell them to stop it." She crumpled the invitations in her five-fingered, white-knuckled fist and tossed them into the waste bin. "You Wergens can be so goddamned

31

overbearing."

The scanner beeped and Dr. Crest stared into a monitor and made a peculiar gesture, raising her opposable digit in the air. "All clear. Enjoy the watermelon."

I face the Emissary, but make a conscious effort not to look him in the eye. He has finished the *chapra* and fingers the edges of the empty wicker bowl.

"From that brief exchange with Dr. Crest, I learned at a very early age how important it was to suppress our feelings around humans, how our emotions make them uncomfortable, and can potentially drive them away. I promised myself at that moment that I would never make Phinny feel awkward around me. I would bottle up my feelings for him deep inside me rather than ever risk losing him," I say, my voice trembling.

"Keeping that promise proved more difficult than I could ever imagine. Your father's kindnesses, his generosity, his humor, all touched me deeply. I tried my best to contain myself around him, mind you, just not always with success."

I limp over to the window and press both my hands against it.

Following Phinny's lessons, he and I would sit in Dr. Crest's garden in what he called the "watermelon patch." He'd split the melons with a long blade and we'd lifted out the pink centers eating them heartily, juice dribbling down our chins. We also occasionally sampled the succulent *chapra* that grew on the reeds of grass, a much sweeter food than the melons. As I've said, I preferred the taste and texture of the watermelons while Phinny loved the *chapra*.

One day, intoxicated with sugary *chapra*, Phinny finally blurted out the questions that I sensed had been weighing on his mind.

"Shim, why do Wergens love humans?"

His directness frazzled me and I found it difficult to

respond.

"What makes *us* so special?" he asked.

"Well... I mean, you're all so... beautiful." I blushed.

"You think so? Aunt Zooey thinks that it might be biological. Maybe the way we smell or something."

I didn't know what to say.

"Your father? And Elkah? Why are they, you know, tied together that way?" he asked. And from the look in his eyes I could sense that this subject, the tethering of Father and Elkah, was what interested him most of all. But I was painfully shy about the subject.

"They're tethered," I said, embarrassed.

After a few seconds, when he realized I would volunteer no more information, he asked, "Are your scales soft?"

I shrugged.

Phinny shyly reached out to me. "Is it okay if I...?"

I nodded, and he gently brushed his hand along my cheekbone.

I know it's silly, but, sometimes, all of these decades later, I can still feel the warmth of his fingers tracing the crevices between my scales.

"They feel... rubbery, nice," he said. "On Earth only reptiles have scales." His gaze shifted to the *coronatis*, the leafy headdress that covered my cranium. "And what about your head..."

"That's personal," I said quickly, and he withdrew his hand sheepishly.

"Why do Wergens wear those things? Those leaf-hats?"

"To cover our... areas." I looked away from him again. "That's where our cords emerge. When it's time."

He digested this information. "Shim, do you think a Wergen could ever tether with a human?"

My hearts skipped. I shrugged.

"Do all of you get tethered?" he asked.

"After the tests are done, yes, for the most part."

"Tests?"

"Our medics always test our genes to make sure we're... compatible. Some persons have diseases that don't let them tether. And some people just choose not to," I said, looking downward. "That's not a good thing."

"Oh." And just like that, Phinny jumped to his feet and sprinted in the direction of my hearth. "Race you!"

I leapt to my feet and chased after him, laughing. "Wait! Wait!"

Perhaps it was because I stood slightly taller than Phinny, or because he constantly took instruction from me on Wergenese, but he resented whenever I told him what to do outside of our lessons. Looking back, I suppose I did sometimes take a superior tone with him, but you have to understand, this sprung from my desire to protect him from the dangers that existed alongside Langalana's natural wonders.

All of that changed on one cool day, a day just like any other with magenta clouds looming overhead in the pink-tinted sky and the smell of snow in the air, the day that Dr. Crest sent Phinny to my hearth to obtain an extension blade – one of the fieldbots had damaged a claw and she needed to replace it – and I decided to accompany him on his walk back home. The truth is, I not only wanted to be with Phinny, I also wanted to experience soaring over the grasslands in his landbuzzer, which his aunt had let him borrow.

As we accelerated away, Elkah and Father waved goodbye to Phinny from a window. "Goodbye, Father!" I shouted, smiling broadly, one hand on the handgrip and the other holding my headdress in place. "Goodbye, Elkah!"

"Why don't you call Elkah 'mother'?" Phinny asked.

"Elkah isn't my mother, silly," I said, tittering at the absurdity of his comment. "Elkah is Father's second mate."

"So your parents are divorced?"

"Divorced?"

"Yeah, divorced. Like mine. They separated when they

realized that they couldn't get along any more."

"Separated mates?" I shuddered. I had never heard anything more horrible, more... alien.

"Mom decided that it would be best for me to stay with Dad," he said. "She's a really important person on EarthCouncil and doesn't have time for kids. But then Dad enrolled in the Delta Expedition. So he left me with Aunt Zooey." Phinny had a sad, faraway look in his eye I had never seen before.

I didn't know what to say, so I simply stared ahead.

We said nothing for a while. The buzzer skimmed the apex of the red blades, and we both held on to the handlegrips as we surfed the waves of grass.

"So. Where *is* your mom?" he said. "On the Northern Continent?"

"Hah! She's here, just encorporated, Phinny!"

"What do you mean?"

"Don't you know what encorporation is, silly?"

Phinny straightened up. "Well, I've heard of it..."

"Oh, look! A manticola!" I shrieked. "Stop for a second."

I jumped off the sidecar and pushed my way through the tall, feathery grass to the bright yellow-and-white petals of the budding manticola stem. When I stooped down to take in its scent, I heard Phinny scream.

He shoved me hard from behind, sending me sprawling to the ground.

As I tumbled, I saw it, there on a patch of grassless sand, emerging from a shadowy burrow. With a clicking sound, the thing twitched and unfolded its carapace segment by segment until it stood at eye level with Phinny. It was as thick as my leg, with a lightning-bolt shaped torso. Thorns covered its muscular chitinous sections, and it bore the same deep-red color as the surrounding grasslands. As I tried to figure out whether this was plant or insect, the creature screeched. It seemed poised to sink its sharp teeth into Phinny when he pulled the extension-blade from his pocket and lunged. He drove the blade right between the thing's four black, bulbous eyes, pounding the creature again and again, even after it had slumped to the ground.

I watched from ground level as Phinny flattened the creature's head with his blows until it lay in a red pool of viscous fluid. Only then did he stop.

I walked behind him and placed my hand on his back. "Did it bite you?" I asked.

In response, Phinny made a bizarre choking sound and disgorged chunks of semi-digested food onto the ground.

"Are you ill?"

He wiped his mouth. "Why did you run into the grass blades?" he shouted. "There's no path here! You *know* it's dangerous." He stomped off toward the landbuzzer.

I ran after him. "I can't wait to tell everyone, Phinny. You saved me. What *was* that thing? Weren't you even a little afraid? The way you struck it down, why, I've never seen such courage!"

He ignored me.

But as we rode back and I chattered on and on about his bravery Phinny's mood seemed to brighten. He stood straighter, with his chest puffed.

Following the incident, we were both so excited and flustered we got turned around without even realizing it and wound up back at my hearth. As we approached, I saw Elkah tending the fields and I leapt off the landbuzzer as it slowed – this time carefully staying on the sandy walking path – and shouted out what had happened as I ran toward her.

"That sounds like a grubber! There've only been a few of them spotted on the Northern Continent – uncommon, but dangerous creatures – but I didn't know we had them here. How'd you know its weak spot, boy? Right between the eyes! I certainly wouldn't want to be fighting off one of those things with nothing but a blade." She patted Phinny on the back and shoulders. "Shimera, you have to be more careful. The boy could have been hurt."

From that day, the dynamic changed between us. It's hard to

explain, but I no longer felt the same need to protect Phinny. I knew that he could take care of himself. Not only that, I knew that he could protect me too.

I slowly circle the table. The young Emissary looks at me curiously, as if staring at an experiment gone awry.

"Despite the large number of incoming human pilgrims over the years, Argenta's population grew only slightly. Most arrivals settled in Inlandia or in provinces in the Northern and Western Continents.

"As for my people, you have to understand, Emissary, the Joint Venture Agreement provides that only five percent of the population can be Wergen. Given Langalana's sheer size, we were spread thin, to put it mildly. No Wergens lived in Inlandia. Our arriving pilgrims lived solely on the large continent in the north – an inconceivable distance from Argenta. As a result, I went almost a decade without seeing another of my kind – except for Father and Elkah, of course. A decade! Nevertheless, surrounded by beautiful humans – most importantly, in the company of Phinny – I consider these days on Langalana, these halcyon days of my childhood, the happiest moments of my life."

The Earth Emissary opens his mouth as if to say something.

I saw Phinny less frequently when he began to spend much of his time assisting other pilgrims with the construction of the farmhouses and plantations. Most often I would visit him at the work site where he helped Aunt Zooey's team with the irrigation system. We would eat together at midday and discuss the latest developments on Langalana.

He stopped by my hearth one morning to share the news that another starship jammed with over ten thousand humans was expected to arrive early next year. The plans to expand Inlandia to accommodate them needed to be expedited.

"I'm going to be working twelve-hour days, Shim: programming the bots to process grassland reeds, working with the engineers to diagram the city layout."

"Phineas!" Father shouted, lumbering closely ahead of Elkah. With the cord fully extended, they could now walk only several feet apart. "My, but you've sprouted. What broad shoulders! You've been working the crop fields, eh?"

And, indeed, Phinny's transformation had been dramatic. He'd grown much taller and his yellow fibers seemed paled by the sun to an almost golden white. His skin had browned and his body had become lean and taut.

After I guided him away – his beauty mesmerized Elkah and Father and prompted them to earwig him far beyond the point of rudeness – he turned to me and whispered confidentially. "I never noticed before, but their tether... It seems to have shrunk."

I blushed. Of course their tether had constricted. Father and Elkah had been mated for quite some time now. "I-I..."

"It's okay, Shim. I know you don't feel comfortable talking about it." He turned to me. "It's going to happen. I'm moving to Inlandia."

"Really?"

"Aunt Zooey's getting older. She needs to continue her research in a less challenging environment. With the grubber swarms and the constant evacuations, it's getting to be too much for her."

I heard the words, but had trouble registering their meaning. "I think your loyalty to Dr. Crest is admirable."

"It's the least I can do after everything she's done for me."

My spirit sank as the reality set in. Although he'd been talking about this for some time, I never thought that the day would actually come. "When?"

"Next week. The bots need major reprogramming to assist with the construction of the highways and office buildings and sewage systems. And we need to clear several more miles of Inlandia's grasslands."

As we walked our familiar path to the overlook, the field's color seemed to shift from red to purple.

"What about you, Shim? There's plenty of opportunity in Inlandia, you know. The grubber infestation here has only gotten worse. And with your language skills —"

"I can't leave my hearth, Phinny. Not yet. Not until my Passage."

"Your 'Passage'?" He raised an eyebrow. "Isn't it time you finally told me what this is all about?"

I hesitated, for our rituals are sacred, personal. But then again, this was Phinny. "When a Wergen reaches the age of maturity, there's a Passage ceremony," I explained. "A male stands with the female through the rites. But in my case... the nearest Wergen is on the other side of the planet. What am I to do, Phinny, swim across the ocean?"

"Well, it's just a matter of time before we have the parts for the bots to construct spaceplanes —"

"It doesn't matter. I couldn't perform the rites with a stranger."

"I'll stand with you," Phinny said, just like that, his green eyes aglitter.

I felt like flut-fluts flew circles in my stomachs. "You *would*?"

"Hey, I'd do anything for you, Shim. You know that." He reached out and caressed my cheek with the back of his hand, tracing the lines of my scales.

My hearts were so full that they seemed to expand into my throat and choke off my voice.

When we reached the overlook, he bent down to pick up a stone, which he shucked sidearm into the coruscating waters below. How many times had he done this over the years? Something about the familiarity of this act made my hearts swell even more.

And so on a chilly day, with the rising sun peeking from behind an amethyst cloudbank, we stood atop Piner's Peak, the highest point nearest Argenta, and performed the rites. For as far as I could see, the grasslands shone like a vast coverlet of scarlet, shimmering in the indigo sunlight. On Werg, my closest friends would have attended the Passage Ceremony; here, just Phinny, Dr. Crest, Elkah and Father stood by me. On Werg, my companion would have been a potential tethering mate; here, my sweet Phinny accompanied me, wearing the *coronatis* and ivy-laced ceremonial garb traditionally worn by Wergen males.

Father and Elkah — thrilled at Phinny's participation — presided over the ceremony. They moved awkwardly, their tether now not more than six inches long and so taut that Elkah's head leaned slightly to the left and Father's tilted slightly to the right. By this time, Father had attained dominance so Elkah rarely spoke. As Father sang the Old Words, I removed my headdress, exposing my cranial cavity, and sang the song of adulthood.

I caught Phinny peeking for a second before averting his eyes.

My cheeks flushed and I felt my cranium moisten.

Father raised his arms and said the final words. And then chaos erupted.

Father drew his sidearm and a laser pulse fired. Phinny yanked on my arm as he stumbled, pulling me away from the sudden movement behind us. When I turned, a grubber's carcass lay on the ground, steaming. Another one sprung at us, and Father fired again. At the same time, a purple-thorned grubber loomed over Dr. Crest, who held her hand over her face. Everything was happening in a heartbeat, and the shock rendered Dr. Crest – indeed, all of us – silent. Unable to move quickly, Father and Elkah stumbled over each other and fell to the ground, the sidearm dropping out of Father's hand. Without thinking, I hurled myself at the creature before it could strike at Dr. Crest. As I collided with it, the grubber turned, a blurry streak, and clamped onto my upper leg with its mandibles. While I rolled on the ground, the creature on top of me, a shot rang out and I found myself staring at the grubber's headless carapace.

"Are you all right?" Phinny asked, clutching Father's smoking firearm. But I could barely hear him over the scream —

my own scream, I came to realize – as I spotted the thorns embedded in my thigh and the clear blood streaming from my shredded leg.

I lift my cane in the air and waggle it, shifting all my weight to my healthy leg trunk. "A memento."

The Emissary scratches his chin.

"Phinny and Dr. Crest delayed their relocation to Inlandia for several weeks during my slow and painful recovery while Father and Elkah programmed the medibots to tend to me. But the venom proved beyond the bots' ability to treat. In fact, Father initially feared that the bots might find it necessary to amputate my leg, but Dr. Crest intervened and worked to develop what we then thought would be an all-purpose anti-venom. You have to realize, Emissary, this was before we understood the true nature of the grubbers."

He stares blankly at me.

"Eventually the infection waned and my fever subsided," I explain. "Although my body ached during this period, my spirit soared for every night your father sat with me and held my hand and read to me. In truth, I dreaded my recovery, for I knew that once my condition had improved, Phinny would be leaving me."

I fell into a deep depression after Phinny's relocation to Inlandia. I couldn't bring myself to get out of bed to attend the scheduled tutorial sessions in Wergenese – or even to help Father and Elkah with the clearing of the grasslands. Phinny must have sensed the impact his departure had on me, because he made an effort to call and visit regularly. Over time, though, the bi-weekly visits became monthly trips, then just random stop-bys on business outings several times a year. But we would still speak just about everyday. During our holo-chats he would confide in me about his problems, about his adjustment to life Inland: how the grasslands had been cleared away and glass towers erected, how he'd obtained a position as an intern on the recently formed

Settlement Council. He told me in great detail about debates with his new friends and co-workers, which ranged from political discourse about settlement policy to petty squabbles about who got the offices with the best views. Some of the councilmen had strongly supported the Growth for Humanity Bill pending on Earth, which pushed for more profitable alliances with other alien species at the expense of current Human-Wergen joint ventures. Phinny told me that even though it wasn't his place to do so, he'd passionately defended the Wergen alliance, invoking loyalty, the deep friendship that had developed between our species, the vast amount of knowledge and philosophy that humanity still had to learn from the Wergens.

During these years that Phinny lived in Inlandia, I lived my days waiting for his projection to appear on my holo-monitor. I longed to hear his gentle voice, to laugh at his self-deprecating humor. These chats became more difficult to schedule, however, as the grubber infestations increased. It seemed that every few days the evacuation sirens blared and full-blown laserfire blasted on the outskirts of Argenta.

At the time, a personal matter also concerned me. My body ached to tether, but being isolated from my own kind made this impossible. By then – although I had not discussed it with Father or Elkah – I had already made my decision. I would not tether. More than anything, I wanted to commit myself to the person I cared for more than anyone else in the universe. I wanted to spend my life – in the way that humans share their lives – with Phinny.

Phinny knew about my dilemma; I had confided in him about my need to tether, but not about the decision I had made. During one of his unexpected visits, we took our familiar walk together. A bioelectrical field – quite effective at the time – kept the trail and the overlook clear of grubbers. During this walk, I confessed my intentions.

"I don't plan to tether," I said to him.

"You're just saying that because of your circumstances. I'm

sure that if there were others of your kind among us you'd feel differently."

"Maybe I'll just get 'married'," I said playfully. "I've practically lived my life like a human anyway. After reading up on it, I must say, Phinny, there's something quite intriguing about the marriage ritual."

"When do I get to read the book on Wergen mating customs?"

"Phinny, you *know* we wouldn't write about such things…" But when I saw his warm smile I realized he'd just been teasing.

"I know, I know," he said, holding his hands up as if surrendering. "Shim, I have something in mind." And it was at that moment – I don't know what gave it away, really – that it finally dawned on me: Phinny had been planning to 'propose' to me. I tried then – as I had on so many prior occasions – to imagine our lives together once we formally committed to each other. Human marriage was such a pale shadow of tethering. But if it was with Phinny, with my sweet Phinny, it would suffice.

"Why Phineas Crest, I can't imagine what it might be," I said, mimicking his teasing tone. Then I spoke seriously. "Thank you, Phinny. Thank you for always being there for me." I kissed him on the cheek.

He hugged me, and I felt a buzz surge through my body.

"Phinny!" a familiar voice shouted. Father and Elkah lumbered toward us.

Phinny took a step backward, a look of horror etched across his face. In hindsight, I suppose I should have realized that he would react this way, never having seen this stage of encorporation before.

Father plodded on four legs, his and Elkah's. Elkah's left arm protruded from Father's midsection. Their two torsos were pressed so tightly together that Elkah's left side melded into Father's right side. Another sign that Father had established dominance was that Elkah's head had disappeared within his, save for her right ear, which still remained visible. In several months, all traces of her body would vanish.

"Don't be afraid, Phinny," Father said, skittering towards us, a magnificent tumbleweed of extremities. "It's still us."

Phinny stood silently, his mouth agape, his eyes bulging.

Father chattered away for a long time while Phinny gawked. Finally, I grabbed Phinny's arm and gently led him away.

"So *that's* encorporation!" he said. "But... Elkah?"

"She'll be encorporated completely within Father. Like my mother. Oh, some of Elkah's skills and random memories will survive. And when encorporation is complete, Father – the new Father – will be impregnated with a brood."

"That's how your people...?"

"Phinny, I can't believe you didn't know. You've been seeing this with your own eyes for years." I placed my hand on his shoulder. He flinched.

"I've never heard of anything more horrific. Wergen females die when they mate?"

"Not necessarily. The dominant partner – male or female – encorporates the weaker one and then propagates. Father's genetic dominance was determined long ago when he and Elkah first tethered. In the same way, my genotype is such that I would surely be dominant if I ever tethered."

"I see," he said. Wrinkled lines formed across his forehead. He folded his arms across his chest and walked a few strides ahead of me. "Poor Elkah."

"It's part of nature, Phinny. Part of who we are. Trust me, Elkah looked forward to the day when she could pass on her best qualities to Father, when she could provide the raw materials necessary for the birthing of a healthy brood."

He said nothing for a long while. During this interminable silence I cursed Father's unbelievably poor timing. His appearance had upset Phinny just at the moment when he was about to "propose" to me, I was sure of it.

"Phinny, what were you going to ask me?" I finally said, breaking the silence.

He shook his head slowly. "Encorporation. I'm surprised Aunt Zooey didn't tell me about it, or that it hasn't appeared in the xenobiology literature."

"You know it's something we don't talk about. It's very... personal to us. So much so that it's an express condition of the Joint Venture Agreement that humans not write about it or discuss it."

He smiled now, that wide angelic smile that could light up all of Langalana. "Nature is marvelous, wondrous, isn't it?"

I exhaled loudly and returned his smile. Phinny was so gentle, so broad-minded. Of course he understood. Of course he accepted our ways.

"Tomorrow," he said, "I want you to wait for me at our special place."

"Oh?" I felt weightless. "Whatever it is, can't you tell me now?"

"No, no." He shook his head and smiled bashfully.

"Please, Phinny?"

"Don't make me ruin it!"

He squeezed my hands and kissed them. "My dear loyal, Shim. I have so much I've wanted to tell you. *Tomorrow.*"

"Tomorrow, then," I said.

I arrived at the overlook almost an hour early, dressed in the shimmering golden robes that Phinny had purchased for me in Inlandia. I brought blankets and sat down in the same spot where I had first begun Phinny's lessons in Wergenese. In my mind's eye, a ghostly version of that rambunctious boy from long ago sat on the blanket next to me, concentrating intensely then jumping to his feet to toss a rock into the ocean.

From the position of the sun, I could see that Phinny had scheduled this moment to coincide perfectly with the sunset.

Where would we live? Phinny had mentioned the spaciousness of his Inlandian apartment. But we had not spoken about children. Although biological procreation could never

45

happen, Phinny had often mentioned the numerous orphaned children left behind by pilgrims killed by the grubber locusts.

I heard the rustling blades of grass and turned around. Phinny stood there. His face glowed with joy to see me; his long yellow fibers ruffled in the ocean breeze. I rose to my feet and he came to me, held my outstretched hands in his. My entire body tingled; I felt incandescent.

"This is my gift to you, Shim," he said, his voice hoarse with emotion.

How many times had I dreamt of this moment?

And how many times in the hundred years since have I relived that moment, a moment forever preserved in my synaptic amber.

He released my hands and swept his arm backwards as if clearing a messy table, as if avoiding a charging grubber.

I followed the direction of his hand, which pointed to the grasslands behind him, to the squat silhouette of a male figure. A figure unmistakably Wergen. He stepped toward us, emerging into the light of dusk.

"Remember when we were children, when Aunt Zooey took your cell samples?" Phinny said. "I transmitted your samples to the Northern Continent. They ran the normal genetic tests and found a perfect match. When the last human starship arrived, I arranged... Well, it doesn't matter. Shim, this is Korte. Korte, Shim."

Confusion overwhelmed me. Phinny's words initially registered as gibberish. But as their meaning sank in, a wave of vertigo caused me to stagger sideways and backwards.

The Wergen knelt and bowed his head. "A profound honor, Lady Shimera."

I turned and bolted into the grasslands as quickly as my legs would carry me, dashing through the chest-high blades into denser brush that rose higher and higher over my head. "Shim! What's wrong?" Phinny called out behind me.

Running blindly through the fields I heard Phinny's voice

become fainter and fainter. "Shim! Shim!"

I lost all sense of time racing through the grasslands, the blades' gentle fur brushing against my skin. Had seconds passed? Hours? I dropped to my knees and heaved suffocating sobs. My breathing canal begged for oxygen but my body shuddered with each spastic sob. I rolled to the ground and hugged my knees. What had happened? I couldn't understand what had happened. Rocking myself, I wept uncontrollably.

When I finally opened my eyes, the twilight had faded and the stars had blinked on. Occasionally I heard a buzzer whiz over my head and voices calling out my name. But I only wanted the grubbers to appear and end my agony, to seize me in their mandibles and mercifully rip me to shreds.

A knock on the door of my room woke me up the next morning. Sitting up, I looked around and found myself in my hearth. A dream. Yes, it had all been a horrific dream.

Phinny entered. And all at once I knew that yesterday had really happened. His disheveled appearance and the creased semi-circles under his eyes suggested that he had been part of the search party.

"Shim. What happened? Why did you run away like that?" He sat beside me on the edge of my bed. "Don't you know that the grubbers are everywhere now? It's a miracle we found you in one piece."

I glared at him.

"I thought you'd be happy. Korte is a perfect genetic match; he'll make an exceptional tethering mate."

My eyes brimmed with angry tears.

"What is it?"

"Oh, Phinny, you idiot. Don't you realize that I'm in love with you?" I said, the words finally pouring out of me. "That I've been in love with you from the first day we met? That you mean everything to me, that I can't imagine a life without you?" The tears stung my eyes. "I couldn't care less about tethering."

He seemed stunned. "Shim... I understand," he said. "You're Wergen. Of course you love me."

"No, you don't understand. You don't understand at all. This goes beyond that. I don't love you because you're human. I love you... because you're you!"

He shook his head. "How can you say that? You know that every Wergen feels that way about every human." His face filled with unmistakable pity.

"I don't feel this way about any other human!"

"That's because you've spent more time with me than you have with anyone else. It's only natural that you would have a stronger attraction toward me."

"Your kindness, your humor, your generosity, those are the things that I love... not your beauty."

"Shim..."

"How can I convince you?" I clutched his hands. "How can I make you understand that what I feel for you... It's real. *I swear it.*"

"On a rational level, you have to know that this just isn't true. You're too intelligent not to realize that the biological impulse that drives your species to be attracted to mine... It's affecting you."

"Fine." I let go of his hands and crossed my arms. "So you've known how I felt about you all these years? It must have provided you with such amusement."

"Shim, I need you to understand," he said. He gently ran his hand across my cheek.

I slapped his hand away. "Don't you dare touch me!"

"You're like a dear sister to me..." he said, his voice cracking.

"Leave!" I jumped out of bed and shoved him.

"Shim..." He hung his head and walked toward the door.

"Don't you care that the very sight of you tortures me? That your touch is agony to me? You're a monster!"

"You have to understand..." He turned and grabbed my shoulders.

"Get out! Get out!" I slapped him hard. He took a few steps back, his hand over his red cheek, and I slammed the door in his face. "Leave me alone! I don't ever want to see you again. Do you hear me? Let me live my life in peace." But even as I said the words, I longed for him to break down the door, to take me in his arms and beg my forgiveness, to kiss me and hold me tight, and tether with me in the fleeting, short-lived way of his people, were it possible. My back to the door, I slid to the floor and stifled the sobs with my hands. After several interminable seconds, I heard him retreat, his footsteps like daggers in my hearts.

"Don't look at me that way, Emissary," I say. The look of pity – even after all these years – still stings. "It wasn't easy, but I eventually got over your father."

The Emissary nods his head slowly.

"I redirected my energies towards... more productive endeavors. I taught classes in Wergenese to thousands of arriving humans. And years later, I turned my attention to politics. I traveled to Inlandia every month and sat on the Settlement Council as Argenta's elected representative. And eventually, with the development of spaceplanes and other forms of intercontinental travel, the World Council was established. Remarkably – even though I remained untethered – my people selected me to serve as Langalana's Wergen Ambassadrix.

"My feelings for your father have been dead and buried long, long ago. The way we'd left things, the truth is I never thought I'd see him again."

Against the advice of my military advisers, the remains of Father and my half-siblings, Lyrra, Olsinore, and Vergo were set ablaze on the summit of Piner's Peak. An entire platoon of armed soldiers surrounded the procession, on the lookout for grubbers. Blue-tinted snow fell around us in sheets, forming a covering that made the grasslands appear tired and aged. The pyre still smoked

– the final words having been spoken – and, out of respect, the humans and Wergens congregated around me to sing a brooding threnody.

That's when I saw him, standing off in the distance, his face covered by a scarf, his yellow tresses blowing in the wind. Ten years later and I recognized him instantly. It seemed like only yesterday since we'd spoken for what I thought was the final time.

When Phinny realized that I'd spotted him, he approached, accompanied by an obese female human wearing a fur-lined hooded coat.

"Shimera," he said, hugging me. "I'm so sorry about your family."

"Phinny? It's really you! I'd heard that you relocated to Earth."

"Yes, I was near the system when I got word of Olbodoh's passing."

"The grubbers are everywhere, Phinny. *Everywhere*. The swarms now overwhelm our strongest biolelectric force fields. When I found Father and the children... it was too late..."

Phinny embraced me again and this time I fell into his arms. After a few seconds, he pulled away and gestured to the pot-bellied female. "Shimera, this is my wife, Lois."

"Your wife?" I shook her hand in the way that humans greet one another, and my hand tingled. How I hated myself in that instant; how I hated that this woman's touch brought me pleasure. "I'm honored," I said.

After we exchanged pleasantries, Phinny whispered something into his wife's ear and she nodded. A Wergen patrolman took Lois's arm to help her with the slippery footing.

Phinny hooked his arm with mine, and I handed my cane to the patrolman. We walked several steps ahead of them, our footsteps crunching in the snow. "Wergen ambassadrix?" he said. "My, my, my. What happened to the farmgirl and teacher I knew?"

"Without distractions, she found she could expand her horizons."

Phinny looked away from me uncomfortably.

This sounded bitterer than I intended so I changed the subject. "How's Dr. Crest?"

"Aunt Zooey died about five years ago. She stayed in Inlandia, convinced to the very end that the solution to the grubber problem lay in gengineering. When the locust storm hit."

"We lost so many good people that day. I didn't realize she was one of them."

"Shimera, isn't it time for you to abandon this world? It isn't safe here."

"I can't give up on Langalana, Phinny. I just can't," I said. "Remember how easy we all thought this was going to be? Simply power up my people's fieldbots and welcome the arriving starships, right?" I shook my head and smiled. "Well, just because things have gotten difficult is no reason to quit. I have responsibilities here."

The snow had intensified as we walked toward the settlement, but I could still make out the Wergen security forces in our perimeter, following with their weapons drawn.

"Shim, about the way we left things all those years ago... I'm sorry. It was wrong not to stay in touch."

I stopped. "Does she love you, Phinny?" I whispered.

He nodded.

"Let me ask you something," I said under my breath with a ferocity that surprised even me. "How do you know?"

"Excuse me?"

"How do you know? How do you know she isn't just physically attracted to you, that she isn't just driven by a biological compulsion to propagate your species, to combine her DNA with yours?"

"Shim..."

"How do you know it's true love?"

Flakes of blue snow hung on his hair, and he looked like he

carried a great weight on his shoulders. "I suppose I don't. But I know this much: she doesn't *have* to love me."

His words deflated me. We took a few more steps in silence before I answered. "I've read medical journals about your species' state of 'love': the increased dopamine levels, the heightened neural activity in the ventral tegmental area of your mammalian brains. It's all chemical, you know. All driven by the evolutionary urge to breed. You look down on us, but I don't think your kind is *capable* of true love."

"I don't look down on you," he said. But he gave me the look again. The look of unmistakable pity.

Lois and the patrolman had caught up to us so we started to walk again. I coughed and cleared my throat. "As I was saying, Phinny, we're not giving up on the grasslands. We'll figure out some way to drive back the grubbers. I have absolute faith in that. Tell me, can you and Lois stay a few days?"

Phinny looked back at his wife who gave a small, near-imperceptible shake of her head. "No, I'm afraid not. We're on our way to visit Lois's parents in the Scornian system. Plus, Lois is pregnant and it's not really safe for us to stay here too long."

"Oh?" I stared at her midsection and tried to recollect my lessons in human procreation.

We stopped in front of the row of hearths of my neighborhood.

"Well, things have certainly changed here," he observed.

"Yes, a lot more Wergens, eh? Can you and Lois come in for a few minutes? Perhaps have a bowl of *chapra*? Or maybe some preserved watermelon? For old time's sake."

He looked at Lois again and this time she rolled her eyes and tilted her head back slightly. I could have sworn that this caused Phinny to take a step backward, as if an invisible tether pulled at him. "No, no, we really have to be going." He placed his hands in mind. "I promise, I'll keep in touch this time."

"That's good," I said. But as I gauged Lois's expression I thought I saw another near-undetectable headshake. And I realized that this would be the last time I would ever see Phinny again.

I slowly circle the table.

"Langalana rejected all of our efforts to tame her, Emissary. We had to evacuate the settlements three sun-cycles ago and relocate here. The grubbers kept multiplying exponentially. We've concluded that they're a form of biospheric antibody, keyed in to our alien DNA. The grasslands became uninhabitable. Then Inlandia fell. The Northern and Western Continents fared no better. Eventually we tried relocating to the frigid peaks of Langalana's highest mountains – but the grubbers followed, scaling the vertical walls unimaginable heights to pursue us. We even tried constructing new settlements on remote islands, but in time the grubbers honed in on us, swam across the vast oceans to find us. For a few years we thought we'd found a solution when the gengineers developed chemicals signatures that camouflaged our alien DNA. The grubbers actually stopped attacking and multiplying, then disappeared altogether. One day, however, they suddenly saw past the chemical mask, and the swarming recommenced. Hundreds of thousands of pilgrims have since been killed.

"We have no choice. It's time for us to move on, Emissary. For all of our dreams of settling Langalana – so many starships traveling such vast distances – we're not welcome here. So I've given the order," I say. "The Wergen contingency will be moving out of this system, joining humanity on some other new world. Glitteria, perhaps? That's why you're here, isn't it? To coordinate our relocation to the next human colony?"

The Emissary stands up and clears his throat. "Thank you for telling me about my father's childhood. The truth is, we had a falling out a long time ago and we were never as close as I would have liked... Before he died, my father heard I had business on Langalana. He asked to see me and requested that I seek you out, to give you a message."

"A message?"

He reaches into the inside pocket of his blue uniform jacket and pulls out an envelope. I look at the extended hand and, shivering slightly, take it from him.

The Emissary pauses. "As for the business I have here..."

"Eh?"

"Yes, we'd heard about the decision to move your people." He rubs his hand over his mouth. "I realize that with your displacement to this satellite you may be unaware of recent developments." He hesitates. "I'm here to inform you that the Growth for Humanity Bill finally passed."

"Excuse me?"

"EarthCouncil has decided that our most profitable joint ventures with the Wergens are behind us. We've learned a lot from your people, Ambassadrix, for which we're deeply, deeply grateful. But we're now able to produce high-quality bots on par with the best that the Wergens can produce... And the Eremites have offered us new technologies, new opportunities."

"I... I understand." I feel numb. "Well... at least there will be ongoing cultural exchanges between our peoples. We still have much to learn from one another."

"I'm afraid I haven't made myself clear. Our disassociation must be total. You have to understand, Ambassadrix. My people have difficulty coping with the Wergens'... deep, unconditional adoration. I'm afraid that it's brought out the worst in a certain segment of our population. There have been some... abuses... on other colonies. No, I'm afraid that it's not in anyone's interests for our worlds to interact any further." He stands at the window and stares at Langalana. "So many precious resources. What a shame." He turns. "In any event, I really must be going."

I clench my fists. "What about the contracts in place between our people? The Joint Venture Agreements that have been signed?"

The Emissary walks to the door and pauses at the threshold. "I'm sorry. If you wish to file a grievance, I'm sure some financial settlement can be reached."

After a long pause, I answer. "I'm sorry too, Emissary."

"Yes, well... Good luck to you," he replies awkwardly, and nods goodbye.

As he turns the corner and his footsteps fade down the hall, I hold up the yellowed envelope in my hand. I don't need to open it; I know what it says: Phinny loved me. He came to realize over the years that he'd made a terrible mistake not asking me to marry him, that the love that we shared was pure, genuine. But once he'd realized his terrible mistake, circumstances had conspired against him. By then he had responsibilities to Lois and to his son.

Ah, Phinny, I've been over you for so long now. It doesn't matter any more.

I fold the envelope, unopened.

Leaning against the window, I focus intensely on the cold beauty of Langalana. The planet hangs there, so close, so close that I can almost snatch it out of the sky and cradle it in my bosom. I reach for it, but find the glass thick and impenetrable, and the proximity only an illusion.

I sigh and slowly run my hand along my cheek, tracing the crevices between my scales.

Missionaries

I teeter on the edge of the precipice. The yawning gulf is so vast, so dark, like an infinite black sea.

The alien hovers in front of me. Released from its shell, it's too beautiful, too hideous for me to fathom.

"Take the leap, Cassie," it says/thinks/sings.

I extend my trembling foot forward and breathe deeply, but I can't do it. I'm afraid. "No!"

I turn and run.

Shhhhh.

The ritual requires us to approach the Outpost on our knees, crawling across a frigid, rocky terrain. The thin band of light that skims the horizon creates the illusion that the sun has just set. Except there is no sun here. Even in my safesuit, my back aches and my legs burn from shuffling forward in the kneeling position. God give me strength. My tongue is sandpaper-dry. Bodhi Bendito had directed us to turn off our suit's hydration system at the commencement of the Crawl. "Challenging tasks lie ahead of us," he had said. "Our agony must prove worthy."

I can't see him, but Bodhi's mantra pipes over the commlink. I try to focus on his humming and to contemplate God's plan for us but my mind wanders instead to Mom and Dad. What would they have thought if they could see me now? How would Thomas have reacted to the sight of his twin sister scrabbling across an alien landscape?

As we drag ourselves over a ridge, a valley opens up below us and the Outpost comes into view. It shines so brilliantly against the backdrop of the tar-black sky that I have to blink away tears and tint my helmet plate blue.

Behind me, the Saved One floats in its lead-lined sphere, basking in a cloud of Bose-Einstein condensates. It seems unfair that it can't share in our physical pain. At least I don't think it can. During the months of this mission the Saved One has produced an increasing number of gurgles and grunts – and occasional piercing screams – through the sphere's voice-generator, but since landfall it has lapsed into an ominous silence.

"It's glorious," Nicolai whispers over the commlink. He shuffles on his knees to my left.

And next to him, as always, crawls his lover Antonio.

Their silver safesuits gleam in the light of the Outpost. The station's phosphorescent polyplastics cast a bright orange glow that fools my brain into believing, if only momentarily, we are on the shore of a beach rather than the dry terrain of a rogue planet that millennia ago escaped Cancri 55's orbit and now roams the universe in perpetual darkness.

"Mind-boggling. They exist in places we could never even dream of," Nicolai says. "Isn't that right, Saved One?"

The Saved One floats silently.

Antonio opens up a private link with me and Nicolai. "Couldn't Bodhi have landed us a bit closer? Maybe downhill? This is beginning to smart."

"Wouldn't that defeat the purpose of the Crawl?" I say.

"You think?" Antonio says. "Lighten up, Cassandra. I'm kidding."

I have to admit that my sense of humor isn't what it once was. The extended pause that follows makes me think that he and Nicolai have continued their banter over a private commlink.

Bodhi's mantra stops.

Two specks emerge from the Outpost's docking doors. They wave us forward, flashing beams crisscrossing in our direction. Their red suits identify them as members of the exploration team that discovered this hotspot, this free-floating planetoid where aliens like the Saved One lurk.

Mom and Dad call us into the kitchen and break the news. Thomas and I are taking a year off to travel – three Jovian moons in one whirlwind trip – before beginning university next year. They think this is an opportune time for a family vacation.

"We booked tickets on the lunar shuttle for next week," Mom says. She pauses. "The Reverie departs to the A'burain Shrine on Monday."

"A pilgrimage?" Thomas throws his hands up.

"And I don't want to hear any whining about it!" Dad adds, just as I'm about to voice my own objection.

I can't believe it. Mom has been a Savior for as long as I can remember, but she's always been discreet about it. The last thing I need is for my friends to think I'm religious too.

"Look, I'm financing your road-trips over the next year," Dad says. "The least you can do is show a little respect, and give up one week of your life for something that's very important to your mother."

Mom puts her hands on Thomas's shoulders. "Open your mind, Tommy. Every able-bodied person should expand their horizons and go on a pilgrimage at least once in their lives. Don't you want that unique experience? To feel that you're part of something that's bigger than all of us?"

"That's right," Dad says. He nods his head vigorously as if he believes every word of Mom's nonsense. Even though I'm sure he finds the idea of a pilgrimage as silly as Thomas and I do, he always makes a point of supporting Mom's beliefs, which I've heard him describe at different times and in various states of sobriety as 'quaint', 'adorably earnest' and – this I really didn't need to hear – 'mysteriously sexy'.

"What if my friends find out about this?" Thomas says. "I'll never live it down."

"Do you have to report your every bowel movement to your friends?" Dad says.

Great. Dad's familiar 'bowel movement' remark means that he's serious about this. So we're going on a pilgrimage to the

A'burain Shrine on the dark side of the moon, where visions of the Virgin Mary, Mahatma Ghandi – and probably Santa friggin' Claus, for all I know – were all said to have appeared at different times to oxygen-deprived believers searching for the meaning of life in the lunar debris.

"And what do you have to say, Cassie?" Mom says to me.

I run through a laundry list of smart-aleck responses before settling on, "Should I bring my bathing suit?"

Mom smiles and gives me a hug.

I slip into my black tunic and pantaloons and run a towel over my bald scalp. My knees still ache from the Crawl and my lower back throbs. The cancer has spread to my spine so I'm supposed to avoid physical exertion. But God will protect me.

I'm tracing my index finger along the jagged purple scar that runs down my right cheek when a knock on the door startles me. A doctor enters the changing room. He's in his mid-twenties, with a toothy smile and the dark complexion of someone who's grown up far away from here. Something about his grin reminds me of Thomas. He pulls out a water canister from the pocket of his white lab coat. "Here, drink some more. You've been through quite the ordeal."

I rub my sore knees. "I've had my fill, thanks."

"Dr. Michael Byars." He sets down the flask and extends his hand. From his sideways glance at me, I can tell that he's trying not to stare at the scar on my face.

"Cassandra Quiles." I hold onto his hand for a bit longer than I should and say, "You've got a lot of faith in your decontamination showers, I see."

He stares at his open palm for a long second and chuckles, taken aback by my joke. Not what he expected of a Savior, I'm sure. Antonio would be proud of me.

"Bodhi Bendito and the others are finished with their chem-showers. If you're ready, I can take you to them."

He doesn't mention the Saved One. Outpost security had

demanded that it remain in a lead-lined holding cell, though in truth there's no way to know whether anything could stop it from escaping if it wanted to. I have no doubt they are running every conceivable scan on it. No matter, it won't make a difference. Teams of astrobiologists, linguists and physicists had spun their wheels for years trying to communicate with its kind at Sagittarius A, the black hole at the center of the Milky Way.

Yet we had managed to break the aliens' century-long silence in just a few days, prompting the Saved One to splinter off from its kind and join us. In the process, we'd made a name for ourselves. The Outpost's interstellar signal inviting us to this rogue planet referred to us as the legendary 'Saviors of Sagittarius A'.

I follow Dr. Byars out of the changing room.

"Are you sure you've had enough water? Dehydration isn't good for someone in your... condition," he says, and I feel the air rush out of me as if I've been sucker-punched. He knows my medical history. That means he would've read all about the accident, about Mom, Dad and Thomas. My hands turn into fists. I suppose it made sense that they'd researched our personal backgrounds given what we'd accomplished with the Sagittarians.

As I trail him, the ache in my left knee intensifies and I limp slightly.

"I should take a look at that."

"Let's not waste any more time," I say.

Dr. Byars's smile fades and he escorts me through a web of corridors until we reach a large circular door that irises open. We step onto a balcony overlooking the station's ground floor, which extends a quarter mile across and teems with activity. Thousands of monitors glow green and red inside an endless catacomb of cubbyholes. In an open area in the center of the floor a massive telescanner points up at the glass-domed ceiling. Bots scurry about and scores of workers in red jumpsuits tinker with an array of metal pipes that stretch hundreds of feet from floor to ceiling. The nearest workers stop what they're doing to observe us.

I'm relieved to see Bodhi waiting for me with Suri Chandra, a short squat woman who is the head of the Outpost. I'd read about her. Once we'd come through the wormhole-stretch, the Outpost's decades of datafiles streamed into our ship's computers and became accessible to us. Nicolai and Antonio join us a few moments later.

"Welcome," Chandra says. "Shall we get started?" The wall behind us shimmers into transparency, revealing that the Outpost sits on the edge of a great, bottomless gulch. I suppress a gasp. The canyon spans so many miles that the other side isn't visible. It's a bottomless pit. A precipice to infinity.

"We discovered them here about five years ago," Chandra says. "Invisible, intangible, detectable only by the faintest traces of radiation and the familiar etchings they leave on baryonic matter."

Etchings? And then it occurs to me. The great gulch. The Sagittarians have sculpted this vast global canyon, just like they had shaped the dust clouds that orbited the black hole of Sagittarius A into planet-sized pyramids and octagons and endless geometric designs.

Chandra continues. "Their radiation signature is identical to that of your 'Saved One'. And they've ignored all our entreaties, just as their kind did at Sagittarius A. It's as though we don't exist to them. We've tried every conceivable strategy to get their attention without success: laser pulses, radio transmissions, nanobeams. Yet they did show an interest in you at Sag-A." She wears a mask of befuddlement, as if she's been contemplating this particular riddle for years and the answer now lies within her grasp. "How? How did you do it?"

"You've uploaded our files. You know precisely how we made contact," Bodhi says.

"Yes, prayer," Chandra says. "Rituals." There's a desperate edge to her voice that makes me think that they've tried replicating those rituals without any luck.

"We would like to open a dialogue with them, Bodhisatva,"

she says.

"As would we," Bodhi says with a smile. "But, to be clear, my brothers and sister and I have traveled all this way for a very specific reason. The same reason we went to Sag-A. To help the Sagittarians commune with God."

"I see." Chandra purses her lips. "And has the 'Saved One' lived up to its moniker? Has it benefited from the wisdom of your teachings?" Just for a microsecond, her mask dissolves and she and Dr. Byars make brief eye contact, exchanging a dismissive and contemptuous look. I'm not surprised by her condescension; we're under no illusions. We're just a silly cult in their eyes, a remnant of the final gasps of organized theistic religion from planet Earth.

"Well, I suppose that remains to be seen," Bodhi says.

"You haven't been able to communicate with your so-called 'Saved One,' have you?"

"We don't understand it, true," Bodhi says. "But who's to say whether it can comprehend us?"

She paces along the railing, staring into the great gulch. "I know that your order holds certain... beliefs about a supposed personal deity. Which is all fine and good. Who am I to judge?" Chandra says. "But we've sought a dialogue with the aliens for almost a century now. Most everyone has given up hope."

A century? I keep forgetting about realtime and relativity. We'd lost nearly eighty years during our mission to Sagittarius-A.

"We want to learn about their culture, their science," Chandra says, "while you want to save their 'souls.' I believe we share common ground. We both need to find a way to communicate with them if we're to achieve our respective goals. And since you've already had some success in drawing their attention, and the environs here, harsh though they may be, are less hostile than at Sag-A, it might make sense to pool our efforts."

Pool our efforts? I'm tempted to remind her that they're the ones seeking our help, but Bodhi has counseled me to be tolerant above all else, to avoid reacting, so I keep my mouth shut.

Bodhi bows his head. "We would welcome your assistance."

I awaken with a start, sitting up and gasping for air. I've just had a nightmare that I can't remember. I look around me. Where am I? It hurts to breathe. My arms and legs are bandaged.

My bed has safety rails and dimmed fluorescent bulbs light the room.

I surrender to the panic as if I'm a little girl again, and scream.

I expect Mom and Dad to come racing into the room, but instead a man enters. He's bald and wears teardrop earrings and a black tunic cinched with a red belt. A Savior. I recognize him. He had come to me a few days ago, when I was drifting in and out of consciousness and had requested, of all things, religious counsel. What was I thinking? What had happened to me? I couldn't remember.

Long pink scars brand his forearms like tattoos. His face is smooth and clean-cut – he can't be more than thirty years old – and his eyes have a warmness in them that instills immediate trust. His soft voice and gentle manner immediately calm me.

"It's okay, child." He sits on my bed and pushes me back down. "It's okay. I'm here."

"Where am I? Where's my mother, my father?"

"You're in the Armstrong Hospital on Luna. Don't you remember the accident?"

The memories flood back. Hysterical passengers stampeding through the Reverie's corridors in search of lead-lined bunkers. Bodies trampling me. Chaos. Across from me, a woman calmly staring out the plexi, a beatific grin plastered on her face, welcoming death. I couldn't breathe.

"A solar flare," the Savior says. "The ship's shields failed. I'm sorry, Cassandra. Your parents and your brother are dead."

"No!" I whisper. "No!" The whisper grows into a sob.

"I'm sorry. I'm so sorry, child."

I don't want his sympathy. I want my parents; I want Thomas. I slap his face and claw at his chest. I try pushing him away but he holds my arms tight. Then he pauses and releases my arms and allows me to strike him again and again until I press my face into his shoulder and shriek and shriek until the nurses arrive and administer a sedative.

We sit at ridiculously long tables with over fifty members of the Outpost's exploration team, including Chandra and Dr. Byars, for our final meal before commencement of the fast.

Nicolai and Antonio sit across from me, Dr. Byars to my left and Bodhi to my right.

Bodhi had insisted on the Saved One's presence for the meal – not that it could eat or speak or do anything but hover in its sphere and emit an occasional gurgle or bloodcurdling scream through the voice generator. From her expression it is clear Chandra does not approve of the Saved One being here. I find it ironic that someone so desperate to communicate with the Sagittarians can disapprove of sitting down to dinner with one of them.

Bodhi asks for a moment of silence while we pray. We clutch the medallions of truth that dangle from the end of our beaded necklaces. Soon our murmurs become a mantra. When we finish, we leave our seats and crouch low to the ground while facing in the general direction of Earth.

I catch a glimpse of Dr. Byars and Chandra from the corner of my eye, pity and disgust etched across their faces.

When we return to our seats an awkward silence follows. Bodhi says warmly, "You've prepared quite the feast for us. We're grateful."

Everyone begins eating. Knives and forks clank against dishes and I direct the bots to fill my plate with stewed spinach and broccoli. All eyes at the table are fixed on the Saved One, which hovers at the head of the table. Its silver ovular shell sparkles in the bright lights. Its center band remains translucent, the churning gases within visible.

"So it's never spoken to you?" Chandra asks, raising her chin toward the Saved One.

"Only occasional sounds," I answer.

"What exactly is inside the sphere?" Dr. Byars says.

"Don't be coy, doctor," Nicolai says. "Surely you've run your scans by now. They're Bose-Einstein condensates, sodium atoms so cold that they can slow a beam of light to a fraction of its velocity."

"Don't look so surprised," Antonio adds. "We're astrophysicists, Nicolai and I. We met on Southern Titan at Singleton."

"I'm well aware of your credentials," Dr. Byars says. "I was just surprised —"

"That men of science could be so foolish as to go on a religious mission?" Nicolai says.

"Is there much of a difference between science and religion?" Antonio says. "At the quantum level, I mean. Even at the macro level, we live in a universe with physical laws fine-tuned precisely 'so', to allow life to exist. Some might consider the Big Bang a —"

Byars raises his hands. "There's no need to be defensive. We're all religious people here."

I'm taken aback. When I left Earth, religion was condemned as the reason-killer, the root of prejudice and narrow-minded thinking. Had the pendulum swung back in the other direction over the past eighty years?

"Oh?" I say. "Religious scientists?"

"Well, perhaps not religion as you know it," Chandra says, smiling. She sips a glass of wine. "We're Quantists. Closely knit communities that explore the mysteries of existence together. Hardly mystics."

"Quantists?" I say.

Dr. Byars smiles. "You've missed a lot."

"So you believe in God?" Bodhi says.

"Not in the simplistic way – I'm sorry, no offense intended, Bodhisatva – that you do. We don't believe in a personal deity, but in a unifying theory of reality – rooted in quantum phenomena beyond our ability to understand. Something we call the Creative Force."

"You have proof of this... Creative Force?" I say.

Chandra laughs. "It's not something that can ever be definitively proved. But we have absolute faith in its existence. And through our exploration of the universe and an immersion in physics we hope we can grasp a tiny piece of that Creative Force. Doing so as part of a community. It drives home the fact that we're part of something larger than ourselves."

"Well, at least on that we can agree, Doctor," Bodhi says.

"Even if we can't agree on..." Chandra struggles for the word. "A 'God.'"

"So the B-E condensates worked to attract the alien?" Dr. Byars says, changing the subject.

"We know that the Sagittarians are a form of dark energy," Nicolai says. "A self-aware aspect of the quintessence field concentrated in complex patterns we never thought possible. We also know that they can interact with matter. So it made sense to provide them with a medium that would allow them to slow down to a level where they might be able to communicate with us."

Dr. Byars crunches on a large carrot. "We have about a hundred chambers on this station filled with every imaginable type of B-E condensate. Yet no alien ever jumped into one of them."

The Saved One shrieks. It's a bone-chilling howl that reminds me of a dog caught under the grav-field of a transport vehicle.

Several workers drop their utensils and a half-dozen jump up and flee the table.

I struggle not to laugh at their reaction. I suppose I've grown accustomed to the Saved One's sporadic wailing and burbling.

"What the hell...?" Dr. Byars says.

"Why does it do that?" Chandra says.

"We don't know for sure," Nicolai says. "Personally, I think it's experimenting with the voice generator, trying to learn human language."

"It sounds like it's in agony," a red-bearded man at the far end of the table says. He's standing, ready to run at the slightest movement by the Saved One.

"'Show me a life with no suffering'," Bodhi says, "and I'll show you a life not lived to its fullest.'" Bodhi looks at me out of the corner of his eye when he speaks these words, one of the central tenets of our faith.

"In that case, I'm not so sure I want to live life so... fully," Dr. Byars says with a smile. Several people laugh softly and others take their seats again.

"What about you, Miss Quiles?" Chandra says to me. "You're the most recent member of this clique, aren't you? Do you believe in this philosophy of suffering, of communing with a personal... God?"

I gulp down a string bean and meet her stare. Then I roll up both my sleeves and show her my other scars.

When the doctor enters the room accompanied by Bodhi Bendito, I know the news can't be good.

"I'm sorry, Cassandra," the doctor says. "As with the other survivors of the Reverie disaster, you have terminal cancer..."

I'm only able to register random phrases after the word 'terminal': "Nanotherapy can help... Another year and a half, two years perhaps, if you're lucky... Other experimental treatments are in development... A positive attitude is important."

Bodhi Bendito walks past the doctor and puts his arm around my shoulders. "You're not alone, child. I'm here. The Saviors are here."

After the oncologist leaves, I sit cross-legged on the floor with Bodhi for a long while without saying a word. When he speaks again, he says, "Your personal agony is beautiful, child. With every ache, every jab of pain, you're living. Never forget that." And then he rolls up his two sleeves and displays the scars on his arms. They start at his elbow and run all the way to his wrists, overlapping purple marks, hideous upraised tissue in lieu of normal skin. "There have been so many times in my life when I felt... inconsequential. There's nothing worse than that. Pain is God's way of reminding us that we matter, child." He runs his index finger across each scar and I wonder how many other wounds are hidden beneath his tunic. "My father was a Savior priest, and his father before him. They taught me about the Prophet Merkel's moment of enlightenment atop Olympus Mons, about his great vision of truth. That our suffering allows God to take measure of our sacrifice and bestow his blessing on us. It is a great honor, Cassandra, to take on that pain. It's perhaps the greatest honor a person can know."

"So by hurting yourself, you think you're helping others?" I say. He sounds insane, but I have no doubt about his sincerity, his kindness.

He laughs softly. "I know so, child. I believe it with every fiber of my being. And my father and grandfather also understood this truth. At a point in both their lives, each of them undertook missions to commune with God."

Missions? My heart skips at the word.

"My grandfather traveled to the ancient colonies on Southern Mars, and my father to the domed cities of Titan to spread the Prophet's message. I've reached that juncture in my life, Cassandra, when I too need to go on my great mission. I'd been planning this for some time when I was called to the hospital to help you. So far there are three of us in our conclave. I believe you are destined to be our fourth, Cassandra."

I'm struck by the irony. Mom also dreamt of a great trip, a pilgrimage. I miss her so much. And I think about dying alone in a hospital. It isn't fair. I haven't had a chance to do anything important with my life.

"Where are you going?" I say.

"It's an ambitious mission, Cassandra. We're traveling to Sagittarius A, the center of the Milky Way, to commune with the aliens."

"The aliens?" I was seven years old when the discovery of the alien 'sculptors' – a form of living, sentient radiation – had shaken the world to its foundation, finally proving once and for all that humanity was not alone in the universe. They were said to live at the center of the galaxy in a dust cloud that swirled on the edge of an event horizon, and they had ignored all our attempts at communication.

"This mission will allow us to spread our teachings to other beings." His face is glowing. "Join us, Cassandra."

It all sounds crazy. But I could spend my final days doing something Mom would approve of, something of consequence. I think again of how little time I have left, of being alone.

"There are Savior conclaves visiting human colonies across the cosmos," Bodhi says, "trying to make them remember what it is that makes us human. What they've lost amidst all the so-called advancements. The sense of the sacred. Of being part of something. Something greater than ourselves. God teaches us that suffering shared is suffering assuaged."

Something greater than ourselves. Like Mom said. And as he sits there and brushes a strand of hair out of my eyes, I tell him that I'm not sure about any of this, but I already know that I'm going with him. Mom would have wanted me to. I do want to be part of something bigger than myself in the time I have left. I need this. But most of all I need Bodhi.

Chandra and Dr. Byars have agreed to allow us to proceed with our ceremony. We prostrate ourselves in a central room that faces out into the great abyss through a plate-glassed window. Each of us sleeps on the cold metal floor and we pray all day and night. Three times a day we drink from a tin cup of water that washes down the stims that keep us awake. We eat nothing.

Within two hours my back aches from lying on the floor. On the second day I don't feel hunger any more, just a constant vertigo that makes it impossible to stand. By the fourth I don't know whether it is the advancing cancer or the effects of fasting, but I feel weaker than I ever have before. I can only pray silently, though strangely the Saved One makes more noise than usual, squeaking and buzzing and hiccupping. Nicolai and Antonio place a second sphere next to it, hoping this will invite another of its kind to join us.

On the eighth day of fasting, Dr. Byars intervenes. Two bots move me onto a gurney and lift me out of the room. My fellow Saviors protest, but there is nothing they can do in their weakened state.

I try to object, but the world spins so furiously when I attempt to speak that I have to close my eyes, just for a second.

I empty out the drawers and pile Thomas' clothes in a big stack along with Mom and Dad's. Bodhi plans to donate them to the poor.

Antonio activates the autovacuumers that scuttle back and forth, sucking up dust.

"Do you need any help over there?" Nicolai says. He has thick blond eyebrows and dimples that magically appear when he smiles. As a result, ever since I met him I've found myself trying to make him laugh. He's about twenty years too old for me – even if he weren't married and gay. Maybe that accounts for Antonio's acerbic humor. He always manages to find a way to get the usually taciturn Nicolai to muster a smile.

"If surrounding me with handsome men is Bodhi's way to get me join the Saviors, I have to confess it's working," I say.

Dimples appear.

"Do you have everything you need?" Antonio says.

All I care about is the dataspeck I carry in my earring, which contains family photos and videos.

Thomas kept a jar full of holodots from the performances

we'd attended, and as I pull them out one at a time and activate them, the title of each play rotates in the air and music gently echoes. I think of all the Thursday nights we'd spent at the theater together. He was born exactly four-and-a-half minutes before me, but he always treated me like a much younger kid sister. I trigger another holodot and a mournful ballad from *Delightful Introspection* plays. I recall the time Thomas and I ditched our skimmer and ran through the traffic in a heavy downpour, just making the curtain call. I open another and remember the time we'd stayed in our seats debating the ending of *The Epiphany*, and whether it was intended to be literal or metaphorical, until the ushers shooed us out of the theater.

I squeeze the holodot and don't want to let it go.

Nicolai puts his hand on my shoulder.

Antonio pulls open the disposal drawer and I tilt the jar so that the holodots spill over the edge and disappear into its gullet. There's no room for extra possessions on our upcoming mission.

When I finish, Nicolai takes my left hand and Antonio the right. I pray, the way that Mom used to. I pray for the strength to get me past this. For the clarity of vision to see the new path that lies before me. For the fortitude to commit myself fully to the Saviors on our upcoming mission to Sagittarius A.

And then, after a lifetime of denying God, after weeks in the hospital mourning my family, I finally open my heart and let Him in. I thank Him. I thank Him for the support, the love, afforded to me by my new family.

When I awaken, I'm in the infirmary, a cutaneous nutrient patch attached just below my left clavicle. Dr. Byars sits at my bedside and offers me a cup of juice. "Here, drink this. You've been unconscious for the past forty-eight hours, Cassandra."

I slap the plastic cup out of his hands.

"What did you do? You've jeopardized our mission!" I say.

"And you were jeopardizing your life. You said that the Sagittarians had previously responded within seven days after you started your little ceremony," he says. "I waited until the eighth day. In your already-weakened condition you were in serious danger."

"I'm dying! Who are you to decide how I choose to live my final days?

"Listen to me," Dr. Byars says. "Listen carefully. In the time that you've lost in interstellar travel, there have been advancements, Cassandra. The form of cancer you developed from the solar flare is treatable now."

I'm so surprised I don't know what to say.

"Chandra didn't want me to tell you. She didn't want to do anything that might undermine your... commitment to our project."

There's a long pause. I've become so used to the idea of dying that I still can't process his words.

When he turns around, he has a square, black tablet in the palm of his hand. "These will eradicate the cancer from your system. A steady dosage can cure you in about thirty days."

I stare at it. I'm at a loss.

He grabs my hand, places the tablet in my palm and closes my fingers over it. "Whatever hold that man has over you no longer exists." He leans closer. "I know the way his kind operates. Lurking in hospitals, seeking out those who are sick and most susceptible to his unique propaganda."

"You're wrong."

"He's exploited you. He's preyed on your vulnerability to get you to join his cult."

"You don't know what you're talking about! The Saviors go to hospitals because that's where we can help most. It's where people are hurting, where they need the comfort of prayer, where they most need God. Yes, 'God.' Do you have to flinch every time I say the word?"

He shakes his head and smiles sadly. "The concept of a personal God is silly, Cassie. Primitive. The Creative Force that shaped our universe, that reveals itself through quantum

73

phenomena, that's real."

"Can't you even conceive that there might be a different way of viewing the universe?" I say. "That we might play a bigger role than that?"

He pauses. "Have you had sex with him?"

I slap him hard.

He raises his hand to the red mark I've left on his cheek. "You need time away from the man, Cassandra. After you've undergone treatment, if you still want to roam the universe saving alien 'souls,' that's your prerogative."

"You have no right..."

"On the contrary, I have an ethical duty to treat you given your diminished mental capacity. You're staying here."

"Damn you," I say. But even as I curse him, I stare at the bottle of black pills he's left on the stand next to my bed and wonder whether this man has saved my life. Maybe God doesn't intend for me to die yet? Maybe I'm not meant to spend my life with the Saviors. I push away the thought and silently curse him again, this devil who has poisoned my heart with doubt.

I must be hallucinating.

These can't be dust clouds! They're too magnificent, too wondrous, to be real. Planet-sized sculptures: triple-helixes, an electron orbiting an atom, honey-combed concentric circles like a bull's eye, a replica of the Pillars of Creation! The endless designs are staggering, and they stand out starkly against the absolute darkness of the black hole.

"How can they maintain those elaborate shapes while in the orbit of a singularity?" Nicolai says.

Antonio focuses on navigating the ship while Nicolai tends to the various instruments that measure radiation and gravity.

Bodhi continues humming, like he has for so many days. His throat must be raw.

Our ship streaks in the direction of five pyramids – the first the size of Jupiter, and each subsequent one double the size of the preceding one. Along the sides are etchings of patterned geometric shapes, decahedrons, rectangles, circles and occasional mountain-sized protuberances along its base that resemble fingers.

Antonio and Nicolai have placed the B-E sphere in the center of the praying room and Bodhi and I sit cross-legged to one side of it. The top hatch of the sphere is open.

We're all weak from hunger. Bodhi runs the sterilized blade into his forearms and thighs, slicing through scar tissue. He grits his teeth. For a moment I don't know whether I can go through with this. I hold a lancet in my shaky hand and look over to Bodhi for reassurance. He nods.

I plunge it into my left arm and split open the pink skin, which gushes blood. The excruciating pain almost makes me stop the mantra.

He pats my shoulder and then I stare into his loving eyes. Blood is splattering onto the holy mat we'd laid down beforehand.

My head is spinning. I lean into Bodhi and kiss him. He returns my kiss for just a second and then puts his hands on my shoulders and pushes me away.

I'm too embarrassed to even mutter a response. He stares at me more intensely than anyone ever has before in my life. "Saying no to you, Cassie... Now I know what it is to suffer. Now I truly know agony."

His gaze holds mine and with my heart bursting with love, with total devotion, I run the blade from my forehead to my right cheek causing blood to stream down my face.

Bodhi flinches.

"There's an energy fluctuation," Nicolai announces. "The radiation signature matches that of the Sculptors."

"It peaks further ahead. I'm taking us five kilo-kliks closer to the event horizon," Antonio says.

"We'll lose significant realtime," Nicolai says. "Decades."

"Just for a few seconds."

"Careful, Toño, careful…"

"We're in," Antonio says. "Ten seconds, fifteen seconds…"

The ship shakes violently and the lights blink and all at once the B-E sphere shudders and glows. A loud static emanates from its speakers. It sounds at first like a soft groan, then like the agonizing scream of childbirth.

I leap to my feet and wipe the blood out of my eyes.

Bodhi stands shakily, totters toward the orb, and seals the top hatch.

"Contact!" Nicolai says. "We've made contact! Get us the hell out of here, Toño."

Shhhh.

A woman sticks her head into the room. "Can I have a word, Dr. Byars?"

"What is it?"

"We have a situation. One of the missionaries, the one called Antonio, donned his safesuit and went outside."

"In his weakened condition?"

"Yes, and… we can't be certain… but it appears he's taken his own life. He hurled himself into the great gulch."

What? Vertigo hits me again.

"The other one, Nicolai, has also left the Outpost and is following the same path. The Bodhisatva is talking with Chandra. He's preparing to go after them."

Dr. Byars turns to leave, then stops at the doorway. "I'll let you know what's going on as soon as I find out."

I hear the security guards racing in the same general direction as Dr. Byars.

The minute the footsteps recede, I drag myself out of bed. My head still spins but I know that my safesuit is stored separately from the men's suits not far from here.

I chase Thomas around the acacia tree, and he stumbles and falls and scrapes his knee.

He's sobbing, pressing both his hands against his right leg. Fat tears roll down his cheek and he's blubbering.

"Shut up, Thomas!" I hiss. I look around. No sign or Mom. "Don't be such a baby!"

He bawls more loudly.

"Shut up! Shut up! Shut up!""

Bodhi breathes heavily through the commlink. He trails far behind me as I sprint ahead, the Outpost's glow lighting the terrain. My safesuit targets Nicolai about fifty meters in front of me. There. In the distance. He stands at the very edge of the precipice.

As I close ground, Nicolai turns to face me. Then he leans back and drops over the side of the cliff.

"No!" I scream.

I run to the gravelly ledge and lean precariously over the side. It is as if I'm dangling off the edge of a flat world, over an infinite abyss. There's no sign of him.

Then I hear it. A voice. A voice that echoes all around me and penetrates the marrow of my bones.

"Cassie? Can you hear me?"

My heart stops. It's Thomas's voice.

That's when I see it hovering over the void.

A blur, a micro-rip in space and time that fills me with both dread and wonder. Although my mind can't make sense of what I'm seeing, I instinctively recognize it, even outside of its shell.

The Saved One.

Although it floats directly ahead, the voice it's using, Thomas's voice, comes from all around me, from inside me. It resounds in my temples.

"You can speak?" I say.

"Not really. But what's important is that you can finally hear me." He giggles. "I was rescued by another of my kind who noticed my pain and lifted the veil."

"The veil?"

"Yeah, silly. The veil. You know, the substance in here."

"The Bose-Einstein condensates?"

"Uh-huh. I decided to experience life as you do, in this slow, limited manner and sort of lost myself in the process."

I still can't believe I'm hearing Thomas' voice. But it's Thomas' voice from when we were much younger.

"Why are you ... here?" I point to the yawning chasm.

"Your kind is, well, crippled, Cassandra. But don't you worry, I'm here to help."

"I don't understand."

"Precisely!" He titters. "See, you're unable to grasp reality. Your senses are warped, kiddo."

"What did you do to Antonio and Nicolai?"

"They've seen the light, so to speak. I saved them. Transformed them."

I take a step back. "You're scaring me."

"Don't be afraid, Cassie. Hmm, how can I put this so you understand? You know how a light particle flits around in a fuzzy state, everywhere at once, until the moment you observe it?"

Yes, basic high school physics. The uncertainty principle. The observer effect. Any particle, until observed, exists in all possible states simultaneously. But what does this have to do with anything? I once overheard Nicolai and Antonio discussing the wave function of photons and wondered what that concept might mean to aliens that consist of dark energy.

"Open your mind, Cassie."

I stand in front of the full-length mirror dressed in a black tunic with red slippers and Bodhi Bendito hands me the shears. I cut off my ponytail at its base. And I keep on cutting until I have only half an inch of hair shorn close the scalp. I hand the shears back and he places the electric razor in my other hand. I push it down the center of my scalp, leaving a wake of white flesh.

"Imagining a possibility is enough to collapse a wave function, to cause a reality to fluctuate into existence," the Saved One says, only now it sounds like a more mature, teenaged Thomas. "You see, there is no actual, objective universe, Cassie. There is no physical reality, at least not in any meaningful sense, without consciousness, without observation."

I'm standing in front of a mirror again, but I'm not me. I have a different face. I'm taller. My hair is honey-brown and falls past my shoulders.

Who am I?

My very being is the end product of uncertainty. I'm the outcome of a random spermatozoa – one of millions – fertilizing an egg. Random genes in a random combination.

I embody uncertainty.

Dr. Byars and Bodhi lean over the edge of the precipice as my body plummets. Bodhi's outstretched hand reaches for me.

They aren't listening to the Saved One. The man of science. The man of faith. Both too afraid to take the ultimate leap.

Have faith, Bodhi! Jump!

His eyes widen and he takes a step back from the edge.

"The flow of time isn't real, Cassie." The Saved One laughs. "Your perception of the 'past' and 'future' is generated by the filter of your unevolved senses. You delude yourselves into believing that the individual moments you experience come and go, swept away in an endless stream of such moments. But in actuality, Cassie, the sea of time is frozen and every instant that has ever been or ever will be, every ripple, every wave, stretches out before you forever preserved, right here, right now.

"Do you follow?"

We're dodging traffic, racing through the streets in the heavy rain. Thomas is holding on to my hand, and pulling me along. I'm laughing, out of breath. My hair is drenched.

"The fundamental truth is that the universe didn't create life. It is life that spawned the cosmos. You're both the particle and the observer, Cassie. Do you understand? Do you?" It sounds excited.

"Yes, I – I think so."

I allow myself to fall backwards over the edge into the abyss. Wasn't I already falling? No.

I never stepped off the precipice. No one did.

I rejected Dr. Byars' nanomeds and embraced my faith.

Nicolai sits at my bedside. My entire body feels numb. I can't speak. I reach up to touch my face and I trace jutting cheekbones and eye sockets.

Antonio anxiously faces out the window of the hospital room as if he can't bear to look at me.

Nicolai reaches out and holds my claw of a hand.

I try speaking but the only sound I can generate is a raspy inhuman moan. I'm struck by the fact that I sound like the Saved One, trapped inside the B-E sphere.

"It's okay, Cassie. It's okay. We're here."

And as I take my final breath it dawns upon me with the last electrical impulse that courses through my grey matter: it isn't suffering that brings us closer to God; it's compassion. But how can there be compassion without suffering?

"Why us? Why did you choose to speak to us?" I say.

"Because your pain, Cassie, is so pure, so sincere that it shines like a beacon, beckoning for compassion."

"So then God exists?" I say.

"Everything and nothing exists! Haven't you understood what I've been telling you? When you conceive of Him, you collapse a wave function and make it so. God is real. And you created Him."

"I didn't know. I couldn't know," I say. "Your people..." I'm so overwhelmed I start to cry. "Your people must truly care about us."

A pause.

"My people... No, they care nothing about stunted life-forms like you. But I felt the need to help you. I felt the calling to ease your suffering and open your minds to the light. That's why I came to you when I sensed your pain. To bring you the truth."

There's something so familiar about its words. And that's when it hits me. The Saved One.

My God, it's a missionary.

Thomas stuck bubble gum in my hair.

Tears run down my cheeks as Mom pours oil onto the brush and pushes it through my hair. It catches and pulls, and I sob more loudly. "Shh, it's okay sweetie. I know it hurts." Mom holds my hair at the roots and brushes the tangled ends with quick strokes. "Shhhh."

Epiphany. Transcendence.

I was. And I could be. I am. And I will be.

"It's okay, Cassie. It's okay," Dad says. "We're right here. We never left."

Snatch Me Another

Lindy sat in her compact pickup truck, took a deep whiff of In-Bliss, and tossed aside the spent plastic inhaler. She rested her forehead against the cold steering wheel.

A blue-tinted circular portal the size of a manhole cover opened over the passenger seat, and a thin bare arm descended from it. She recognized the limb's freckled, pale skin, the small scar on the inner wrist. Her own arm. The hand groped blindly until it grabbed the inhaler, then retracted. The portal disc closed with a "pop."

"Ah, take it," Lindy muttered. "It's empty anyway." She stared at the front door of her red-brick Colonial. The buzz started to kick in, and calm fell over her like a warm shawl. She left the truck door open and staggered down the gravel pathway and up the porch stairs. Lindy jammed her hand into the pocket of her jeans, fumbling for the house key. As she stood on the welcome mat, she heard the television blasting – frenetic Munchkins singing "Follow the Yellow Brick Road" – and the white noise of chattering children. She stabbed at the keyhole and missed three times, but the door swung open.

"Mommy!" Tommy said. He wore a bright blue birthday hat over a patch of curly, red hair. "Look what I got!" He held up two identical GI Joe dolls.

For a second, Lindy felt nothing but pure love. But then the glow faded to a muted sadness. "That's nice, dear," she mumbled. "Go play with your friends." She stepped around him through the throng of shouting six-year-olds, beyond the swinging door that led from the shag-carpeted living room to the bright kitchen. She leaned against the Formica counter to regain her balance.

Kristina sat at the table, scooping strawberry ice cream onto white paper plates. She paused, blew a dangling strand of brown hair out of her eyes, and glanced at Lindy warily. "Nice of you to show up," Kristina said. "Tommy's been asking for you."

How did she slip back into the role of housemom without missing a goddamned beat? Lindy thought. How could it be so easy for her?

"Are you okay?" Kristina asked.

"Just peachy."

"We need some more plates. Could you snatch me some?" Kristina grabbed a dirty paper dish with a curlicued "Happy Birthday" emblazoned on it, tore off a clean edge, and handed her the slip of cardboard.

Lindy took long, deep breaths.

"You sure you're okay?" Kristina said.

She snorted her assent. "Why wouldn't I be? It's a party! Let's wear our hats and sing happy birthday until our throats hurt. And let's not forget to pin the tail on the goddamned donkey."

Kristina looked away and continued scooping ice cream out of the frosty carton.

Clutching the sliver of cardboard, Lindy lurched through the doorway that led from the kitchen into the garage. The Snatcher sat next to the washing machine. Wide-mouthed and waist-high, it resembled a barrel with a glistening silver coating. If it didn't weigh so much, if it weren't so sturdy, she would've kicked the goddamned thing on its side and taken an axe to it. But what difference would that have made? Over the past six months, the Black Market had exploded. With a single phone call to Senecal, Kristina could have it replaced within twenty-four hours.

Lindy lifted the heavy metal lid and leaned in, placing the piece of the paper plate – the honing sample – at the bottom of the Snatcher. She placed the cover back on and rotated a red dial on the device's side. Then she heard the familiar rumbling deep inside, like distant thunder and whooshing wind gusts, the sounds of dimensional walls crumbling. Lindy lifted the cover. The Snatcher's maw released a thick, blue mist. She rolled up her sleeve and bent down, sticking her arm in up to her shoulder, groping blindly until she felt the paper plate. She pulled out a whole white plate with the same orange-lettered "Happy Birthday" on it. Placing and removing the lid over and over, she continued reaching in and snatching out one after another. Cake crumbs coated one plate so she let it fall back through the base of the Snatcher. When she reached in again, she felt someone slap her hand. She withdrew her arm and tried again until she had a dozen dishes in hand, perfect replicas, except for a single one with an off-white color. She imagined the reactions in the alternate dimensions. Ruining a few of these parties, she had to admit – albeit in different universes – wouldn't make her lose any sleep.

When she returned to the kitchen, Tommy burst through the swinging door and hugged her leg. "Mommy, Mommy, will you play musical chairs with us?"

The plates fluttered to the floor.

"Mommy? Will you –"

"Listen, I told you to go play with your friends, okay?" She pushed past the boy and trudged up the stairs.

"Lindy!" Kristina shouted after her.

She paused at the top of the staircase and looked over her shoulder. Kristina crouched down and comforted the crying boy. At that moment, Lindy thought she felt something again – the remnants of a maternal love so raw, so deep, it threatened to paralyze her, drown her.

She reached into her jacket pocket for another inhaler and slammed the bedroom door behind her.

One week earlier, on a chilly September morning, Lindy had leaned against a tree at the summit of a grassy hill while Father DeMichael delivered a prayer over the white oak casket, which lay wrapped in red roses and white tulips. Across from her, on the other side of the casket, Kristina stood between her mother and a second Father DeMichael, who held her hand and bowed his head. No one could distinguish the 'original' Joseph E.

DeMichael, the one who had counseled Kristina all her life, from the one pulled over from another reality. Lindy shivered. She'd heard rumors of *people* crossing over, but she'd never seen these 'variants' before. A dozen colleagues from the car shop where Lindy worked surrounded them. Half stared at the casket while the other half raised their eyebrows and whispered to each other, gawking at the two Father DeMichaels.

Lindy turned her attention to Kristina. During their intimate moments together, Lindy always playfully referred to Kristina's simple, girl-next-door looks as 'domestic sexiness'. But on this day Kristina's blank, bloodshot eyes peered out from behind her tangled and unwashed hair. Until that moment, Lindy hadn't noticed her pallid face had a too-thoughtful expression, a look with just a slight hint of madness. At home, she'd remained mute and blank-faced, on the prescribed inhalers they were both taking, sleepwalking through her daily routines.

A blue, circular portal appeared in midair over the coffin, and a long bare arm reached down and plucked away a white tulip.

Everyone pretended it hadn't happened. The Father DeMichael presiding over the service cleared his throat and continued with the prayer.

Lindy gazed up at two enormous, looming thunderclouds that seemed identical, with just a slit of blue sky separating them. Both appeared thick and dark gray. She focused, trying to detect a difference in the clouds' size or shape or respective shades of gray, with no success, as they converged.

A light drizzle began to fall. Umbrellas sprouted up around her. She continued looking skyward, enjoying the feel of the cold rain on her face.

After the last of the children left the party and Kristina came to bed, Lindy went into the bathroom and inhaled more In-Bliss. She tried to maintain her equilibrium as she wobbled back to the bed. Kristina lay there with the pillow propped against her back, her reading glasses on the edge of her nose, riffling through the newspaper. "Did you kiss Tommy goodnight?"

Lindy didn't reply. She pulled back the covers on her side of the bed and lay down.

After a few minutes, Kristina spoke again. "Did you read today's 'Dear Annabehl' column? Apparently someone stole a tiny fragment of Van Gogh's *Starry Night*." She placed the open newspaper on her lap. "There are now over a thousand originals, and the prices are plummeting with each new one that's retrieved."

"And what did Dear Annabehl have to say about this?"

"To relax, that we're living in a brand new world and have to learn to redefine our moral boundaries."

Lindy grunted.

"Should I call Senecal and order a *Starry Night*? We can have it delivered first thing in the morning."

"I suppose it's irrelevant that Senecal is an illegal dealer or that the Snatcher is illegal or that every damned thing we pull out of the Snatcher is illegal."

"I think the painting would look fabulous in the living room, centered over the sofa, don't you?"

"Ever since we got the Snatcher nothing seems to matter any more."

"Senecal won't take money any more, by the way. They want unique items they can use as honing samples."

"Are you even listening?" Lindy asked.

Kristina sighed and pushed her reading glasses up the bridge of her nose. "Look, there's no point fighting it. Legal or not, everyone has one by now. Even cops have their own Snatchers."

"We don't need a snatched painting. There are sometimes slight... differences."

"Imperceptible, usually."

"Doesn't it bother you that in a thousand alternate universes, Van Gogh's original *Starry Night* is now missing?"

"Why do you have to think about these things?" Kristina

frowned. "This is... bigger than us. And all I know is we're losing things left and right in this house. This morning, my earrings got snatched. And just this afternoon an arm swiped a twenty-dollar bill off my dresser. If other realities steal from us..."

"Then why shouldn't we steal from them?"

"Plus, haven't you read the newspaper?" Kristina said. She lifted the paper from her lap. "We now have all the simian flu vaccine we'll ever need, and an endless food supply to feed the hungry..."

"What about all the other craziness, the economic crisis? It's only been six months since the first Snatcher prototype was stolen, and now... everything's spinning out of control. Can't you see that?"

"Lindy..." Kristina sighed and put her hand on her shoulder, but Lindy rolled over and wrapped the covers around herself.

After a long pause, Lindy whispered, "How'd the kids' parents react today?"

"They seemed fine. They were just happy to see Tommy's feeling better."

"Don't kid yourself. They knew. They knew and they were just being polite."

Kristina turned off the reading light. They lay there, back-to-back, in the darkness, an awkward silence filling the air before Lindy spoke again.

"No *Starry Night*, okay?"

Kristina inhaled as if to respond.

"Mommy," Tommy's voice squeaked from the doorway. "I had a bad dream."

Kristina turned on the nightstand lamp and sat up. "Come here, baby."

Tommy ran to her, and she lifted him up onto her lap. "I was lost," he said, "and I couldn't find you."

"It's okay. You're safe," she said, snuggling him.

Lindy stood up and grabbed her pillow.

After a few seconds, Kristina said, "Mommy's going to read

you a story, just like she always does, so you can fall back asleep."
Her eyes drilled into Lindy's. "Aren't you, Mommy?"

Lindy nodded.

"Can we read *Thunder Bear Adventures*?" Tommy asked.

"Honey, there's no book with that title," Kristina said.

"But it's my *favorite* one! Mommy always reads it to me."

Lindy and Kristina locked eyes again.

When they had returned from the cemetery Kristina changed into
her white nightgown, even though it was the middle of the
afternoon. She hovered about the house aimlessly. And there was
a lag in her responses to Lindy's questions, as if communicating
via satellite. In a strange, flat voice, Kristina announced she was
going upstairs to take a nap.

Lindy sat down on the living room sofa and turned on the
news telecast. None of the stories registered – only random
words and phrases penetrated her consciousness: 'Snatcher',
'pandemonium', 'markets crashing', 'war', 'variant'. Lindy could
only think of those final moments in the hospital, Tommy lying
there unconscious, his head wrapped in bandages, his shallow
breathing becoming labored and then raspy before finally ceasing.
Given the circumstances – the surgeons' inability to reach the
brain tumor, the odds they'd been given, the potent
chemotherapy treatments he'd undergone – his death shouldn't
have come as a surprise, but at that moment the world had settled
into a dull, steady gray that had yet to fade.

An hour later, Kristina stomped down the stairs faster than
she had moved the entire day, brandishing a hairbrush like a
conductor's baton.

"What's the matter?" Lindy asked.

"Tommy was so excited about next week's birthday party.
Kool Aid, cake, ice cream, games, okay? Friday afternoon." She
continued vocalizing scattershot thoughts; her eyes snapped left
and right. "Let's have the party, okay, Lindy? I don't know why
we never thought of it before! The solution is so obvious!" She'd

fallen asleep crying; smudged tracks of mascara stained her cheeks. "Let's celebrate Tommy's birthday, okay, Lindy? Okay?"

"What are you talking about?"

"It doesn't have to be... this way..." She waved her hands in the air.

"Honey, he's gone." Lindy swept Kristina's hair back from her forehead.

"But he doesn't *have* to be." She pulled a patch of Tommy's red hair from the brush and held it between her thumb and index finger.

"Don't say it," Lindy said. "Don't even think it." She put her hands on Kristina's shoulders and looked her in the eye. "Listen to me. We'll get past this, I promise."

Kristina pushed her hands away and turned around, looking out the window. "I'm not 'getting past' anything. We're bringing him back." As her determination set in, her shaky voice sounded more coherent. "Don't you think others have done this? The obituary column gets shorter every day." She spun around and faced her again. "For his birthday, Lindy. So we can throw him the party he wanted." Black rivulets began to run down her cheeks again. "What kind of parents are we? We can save him, Lindy! We can save him! How can we not...?" She choked on the final word and sobbed into her hands.

"It wouldn't be our Tommy," she replied. Although Lindy had steeled herself during Tommy's illness and the burial, she found her lower lip quivering. "And we couldn't do that to another child's parents."

"With their Snatcher, they could snatch themselves another Tommy –"

"He's dead. *That's it.*"

Kristina's face grew stern, and she paused for a long while before speaking again. Then all at once, her grave expression melted. "I'm sorry, Lindy." She sighed and collapsed onto the living room couch. "It's just so hard."

Lindy sat down next to her. "I understand."

"I know you're right," Kristina said. "I know we'll find a way to get past this." She wiped at the corner of her eyes with the sleeve of her flannel nightgown.

Lindy patted her thigh.

"Do you want anything?" Kristina asked. She stood up and headed toward the swinging door to the kitchen.

Lindy shook her head and stared at the framed picture on the coffee table of the three of them in Maui, she and Kristina and Tommy, all in their bathing suits, sporting yellow leis and broad smiles. Tommy wore Lindy's sunglasses. She felt like an overstretched rubber band; a minute ago she'd been on the verge of tears, but now she found herself smiling.

A blue disc materialized in midair, and a tanned arm with blood-red fingernails snaked out of it. It snatched the framed photograph and retreated back into the portal.

Goddamn it, not that picture, Lindy thought. If she'd just had another second to react, she would have stabbed the goddamned hand with a fork.

A shriek cut through the silence.

Lindy leapt from the couch and ran into the kitchen. The door to the garage was wide open. No... she hadn't... Lindy thought, she didn't....

Lindy ran to the garage and was confronted with the sight of Kristina leaning over the Snatcher. She had pulled Tommy halfway out. His skin was blue-white and he wore the navy-blue suit in which they had buried him. He was unmistakably dead.

Kristina continued to wail.

"Let go!" Lindy grabbed her arms. "Let him go!"

Kristina released her grip and the cadaver dropped, disappearing into the ethereal blue mist that wafted out of the Snatcher. Her hands shaking, Kristina placed the metal lid back on the Snatcher and then removed it again.

Lindy tried to pull her away from the device, but Kristina surprised her with a shove that sent her sprawling to the floor. Kristina reached into the Snatcher and soon had another variant of Tommy in her grasp, which she tugged upwards. Before long, she cradled another corpse – this one more decomposed than the first, but still outfitted in the same navy-blue suit – and let out a high-pitched screech.

"For God's sake, stop it!" Lindy said.

Kristina dropped the body back into the Snatcher, and turned the red dial on the side all the way right. On her third attempt, she leaned in and pulled out a red-faced Tommy clad in polka-dotted pajamas.

"What's happening?" he screamed, slapping at her arms. Kristina laughed and kissed his cheeks and hugged him tight. Tommy began to cry. "It's okay, baby. Your mommies are here." Kristina rocked him in her arms in an exaggerated motion.

Lindy moved toward them and grabbed the boy around the waist, prying him from Kristina's embrace.

"What are you doing?" Kristina said.

Lindy carried him back over the mouth of the Snatcher and tried to jam him back in. The boy wailed and splayed his legs, his feet catching on the sides of the Snatcher.

"Mommy!" he sobbed. He wrapped his arms around Lindy's neck. "Mommy!"

She stopped struggling.

"Tommy," Lindy said. She hugged him back. "Shhh. It's okay, it's okay."

As Lindy led him back to his room for the bedtime story, Tommy stopped to put on a stray birthday hat, then diverted them to the bathroom. He insisted on brushing his teeth again before going back to sleep – a classic stalling tactic, for sure – but she saw no harm in it. She held Tommy from behind while he perched on a stool and brushed his teeth, peering into the bathroom mirror. She took the toothbrush out of his left hand and moved it to his right hand.

"Why can't we read *Thunder Bears?*" He drooled toothpaste into the sink when he spoke.

"We'll read it another night," she lied. "Just pick another book."

He shifted the toothbrush back into his left hand and continued brushing.

"Use your other hand, honey. It'll be easier." But when Lindy tried to remove the toothbrush from his left hand again, he pulled away and continued brushing. "No, Mommy!"

Lindy focused on the smooth, effortless movements as Tommy brushed up and down with his left hand. And all at once, the hairs on her arms stood on end. She had allowed herself to forget, just for a few minutes, that this boy was not her son. Tommy – *her* Tommy – was right-handed.

She took a step backward.

He rinsed and raced to his bedroom. "I'll get the book!"

Lindy felt dizzy. Her heart raced; she needed another whiff of In-Bliss. Staggering after the boy, she stood at the doorway to his bedroom – Tommy's bedroom – and watched the imposter sort through the books – Tommy's books – on the bottom shelf.

"I can't find *Thunder Bears*," he whined.

"Huh?" The words barely registered. Her Tommy deserved better than this, she thought. He deserved to be remembered, to be mourned.

"I want you to read me *Thunder Bears*."

"Look, just go to sleep!" she said.

"You promised!" He started to cry. "I want *Thunder Bears!*"

For a split-second, the boy stopped weeping. He winced and brought his hands to his temples. Then the bawling grew louder.

"What's the matter?"

"My head hurts," he said, sobbing.

Lindy gasped. Her heart pounded. She leaned back against the wall and found herself sliding to the floor. She stared up at the light fixtures on the ceiling, which were spinning, spinning.

Tommy continued crying for his book, his hands on the sides of his head, until Lindy crawled over to him. She lifted him up and lay him down in the bed.

"Shh. It's okay, baby. Mommy's here." She held him in her arms, massaging his forehead. No, no, no, she thought. We can't go through this again. Not again.

After a minute, he cried himself to sleep.

She set him down on the bed. The entire room was spinning now.

She stared at her hands. They seemed to move independently from her body, clutching the soft pillow. She moved it an inch away from his face and held it there for a few seconds.

"What are you doing?" Kristina said from the doorway.

Lindy jumped to her feet, dropping the pillow.

Kristina's eyes widened; her face flushed.

Lindy staggered past her and down the stairs. As she opened the front door, Kristina shouted from the top of the stairway: *"What were you doing?"*

Lindy slammed the door behind her.

Lindy drove several blocks to the beach and stayed awake all night in the pick-up truck, staring at the ink-black sky. Not a single star was visible behind the dark thundercloud cover. The rhythmic swoosh of the distant waves reminded her of Tommy's final raspy breaths at the hospital. She blinked and the sky suddenly grayed. A sickly dawn had arrived, illuminating the garbage-strewn sands.

She drove back home and parked at the curbside. After half an hour, she found the energy to sleepwalk down the gravel pathway to the porch of their house, ice-cold, numb.

What had she almost done?

Kristina would forgive her anything, she always thought, but *this...*

As Lindy moved past the living room window she caught a glimpse of two figures inside. There, on the couch, watching cartoons, lay Tommy. And Kristina sat next to him. Van Gogh's *Starry Night* hung on the wall behind them.

And all at once a tremendous wave of relief washed over her, as if yesterday had been nothing more than a drug-induced nightmare, and today she'd been slapped awake to a brand-new, shiny reality. Maybe Kristina felt the same way. Maybe they could both find a way to get past this. This time, she thought, the doctors would catch the tumor early. This time he'd be okay. She'd be a good mother to him. Lindy knew now she'd somehow find a way to adjust, to accept the new Tommy as her own. Dear Annabehl was right; they lived in a different world now.

As she walked toward the front door, Lindy got a full view of the living room. Her heart froze. A third person, a woman, sat next to Kristina, thigh against thigh, laughing along with them. The woman got up and walked behind the couch and tickled Tommy from behind, catching him off guard. As Tommy squealed, Kristina also shrieked with laughter.

The woman was Lindy.

Lindy stepped back from the window and staggered down the walkway. She tripped and fell to her knees, crawling to the pickup truck. There, she fumbled for the inhaler in the glove compartment and took a hit. The sky, the world, was spinning. And as quietude gradually enveloped her, she imagined an outstretched arm appearing in midair, white and smooth and smelling of Kristina's perfume, reaching down to take her hand and pull her up through a patch of cobalt-blue sky to a different place, a place where she belonged.

She took another deep whiff.

Dear Annabehls

== 1. ==

Dear Annabehl:

I'm concerned about the inordinate amount of time that my 13-year-old son 'Jeff' spends with himself. A boy his age should be out and about, playing with friends, participating in sports and other after-school activities. I come from a very traditional family, and I have to confess that I'm concerned that this behavior suggests that Jeff may be gay.

My husband thinks I'm overreacting. What do you think?

Concerned Tuscaloosa Mom

Dear Concerned:

Generally, a boy Jeff's age spending time with himself is perfectly normal. The question I would pose is: how *many* of his selves does he spend time with? Attachment to any particular self might prove to be unhealthy. If your son's behavior persists for more than a few weeks, you need to revoke his Snatcher privileges and take him in for some psiprobing. If it's of any comfort, this sounds more like classic narcissism than homosexuality. However, should your son be gay, you need to learn to love him for who he is. Alternatively, search for a heterosexual replacement. I recommend that you swallow two Validums, and pick up the recently published *Bonds Between Multiple Me's* by Dr. Gregory Byars for an excellent discussion of this subject.

== 2. ==

Dear Annabehl:

I'm going through the most difficult period of my life. I caught my husband Robbie cheating on me. The thing is, he's cheating on me – with me. He insists that as long as the person he's

97

sleeping with *is* me, he isn't technically cheating. That's BS! I say that he exchanged his vows with *me*, not with skinnier, stringy-haired, slutty versions of me. He's being immoral and unfaithful, isn't he, Annabehl? I just don't get it. What does he see in other me's that he doesn't see in me? I'm hurt, lonely and frustrated.

Dora/Memphis, TN

Dear Dora:

Take a deep breath and a Xantax, dear. It's all a matter of perspective. That Robbie chooses to spend his time away from you *with you* is actually quite romantic. In fact, one might say he's exceedingly faithful and truly devoted. You should be flattered as heck. What strikes me as odd is that while Robbie is off enjoying you, you're 'lonely and frustrated'. Get up off your derriere, girl, and kwitcherwhining! You should be spending time with other Robbies. You'll find that doing so will strengthen your marriage and make both of you much happier in the long run.

== 3. ==

Dear Annabehl:

We lost our son Tommy to an inoperable brain tumor, just a few days before his sixth birthday. My wife got it into her head that we should go forward with the birthday party with another version of Tommy as a way to say our final goodbyes. We set the Snatcher to a high-end frequency and nabbed another Tommy, who was none the wiser about his displacement. Well, you guessed it. The birthday party came and went and now 'Tommy' is still with us. What about 'Tommy's' real parents? They must be going through hell. And what about our Tommy? Doesn't he deserve to be mourned?

Whenever I raise this issue with my wife, she gets angry and changes the subject. She pretends that nothing ever happened. I know I should love the new Tommy, but all I feel is numb. What should I do?

L.P./Chicago, Illinois

Dear L.P.:
I strongly recommend professional psiprobing so you can learn to accept Tommy's variant as part of your family. Your emotional confusion is understandable, sweetie. Many people who suffer a loss like yours find it difficult to accept a replacement. But your wife is behaving no differently than any mother would in her situation. Be sure to have Tommy routinely checked for the condition that caused his initial passing. It may become necessary to get yourselves another replacement. Good luck to you.

== 4. ==

Dear Annabehl:
My mom and dad are fairly well-connected. As a result, we have Government authorization for Total Access to billions of Snatcher frequencies. My family's been on the move ever since the first Snatcher prototype was developed. We've skipped into all sorts of psychedelic realities, including a black-and-white dimension at a high-end frequency where we were the only colored people in the world. (My parents, who think they're cool, thought it would be 'educational' for us to experience firsthand the prejudices faced by minorities. Well, we were treated like friggin' circus freaks!) But most of the time the differences were so subtle that I couldn't even tell we'd skipped.

I've met a boy I really like who lives down the block from us, so I want to stay here. I'm not even sure if this is the reality we originally came from, but it's close enough, I guess. Why do my parents insist on skipping around? Apart from having a new boyfriend here, I've made other friends too. And it's hard to make friends every time I skip. Sometimes the same people are slightly 'off' in a new reality, and not as likeable. I hate what the Snatcher has done to my life! My parents just don't understand.

Elinor / Houston, TX

Dear Elinor:

I suspect you may no longer be around to read this. But in case some other you (or others like you) need advice on this subject, I say: inject some soft hemo-music, take a long drag on a joint, and relax, honey. The important thing is to speak to your parents and keep the lines of communication open. If they refuse to take your feelings into account, speak to a stream of variants until you find a set of parents who care enough about your feelings to listen and to lay down roots here. Instead of condemning the Snatcher (shame on you!), why don't you use it to help solve your problems?

== 5. ==

Dear Annabehl:

My sister 'Betty' is having a crisis of faith. Before the Breach War began, variants of so many faiths skipped through our transborder that she wonders now whether our beliefs are any more 'true' than the beliefs of other versions of us. Yesterday a bald variant of Betty showed up and proclaimed her Jesus Christ – a clean-shaven Christ with a buzz cut – the one true Son of God. She ridiculed our own bearded Jesus and called him 'a slovenly hippie imposter'. Ever since then, Betty has stopped going to church and has fallen into a deep depression. She keeps asking about the near-infinite number of souls that populate the transdimensional slate and why God, if He exists, would have created them to believe in so many different faiths.

What can I do to help her?

Chastity / Pomfret, Conn.

Dear Chas:

I've consulted with spokesman Father Joseph E. DeMichael about the Catholic Church's position on this subject. Church doctrine, he explained, teaches us that the variants who refuse to believe in the true, bearded Jesus – not other, bizarre Jesii with different haircuts and wardrobes – are doomed to eternal damnation. In fact, many church scholars believe that the very reason God allowed us to invent the Snatcher is so we can seek out our variants and enlighten them about the one true God. So whatever else happens, at least our souls are safe, dear. Pass it along. Tell Betty to pour herself a tall glass of cabernet and relax.

== 6. ==

Dear Annabehl:

I'm stationed at the frontlines near the Great Wall of China where the Breach is at its worst. The hordes continue to battle their way through. We've been fighting hard to repel these forces, and this week alone I've lost six friends and three versions of their replacements. The other-dimensional armies grow more freakish every day, some are barely humanoid, in fact. We don't know what's coming through next, Annabehl. I have to confess: I'm afraid.

I'm writing to ask your readers for their prayers and support. Any e-transmissions they could send our way would provide a tremendous lift. Neural books and movies – and especially hemo-music – would be greatly appreciated as well. Thank you.

Private Sandy Ripple,
Special Global Forces

All readers, atten-*tion*! Every citizen of this plane should applaud the heroism and self-sacrifice of our brave young troops. Thank you, thank you, thank you, for defending the transborders from that wave of lower-dimensional scum, Private Ripple. While those of us who have not done a tour of duty cannot possibly understand the horrors you and your compatriots have faced, we all extend our love and support. Readers, please send your letters and donations to Dear Annabehl and we will arrange to forward them to the troops. Don't let our soldiers down. Yes, they're replaceable. But remember, *so are the invaders*. This is why there appears to be no end in sight to this war. Support our troops!

== 7. ==

Dear Annabehl:

Maybe I'm old-fashioned, but your advice to L.P. from Chicago struck me as amazingly insensitive. He had just lost his son to a brain tumor and his wife used their Snatcher to abduct a variant from a nearby dimension. Of course he felt numb! He never had a chance to grieve. Worse, what about the parents of the variant they kidnapped? They must be devastated by his disappearance. This whole world is turning to [crap]! What were you thinking, Annabehl?

An Old-Timer/Topeka, KS

Dear Old-Timer:

I stand by my advice, gramps. There was simply no need for L.P. to grieve when a replacement was so easily accessible. Grieving is dead! *Death* is dead! I did recommend psiprobing, however, so he could learn to accept his new son, who is an innocent in all this, after all. As for the transdimensional parents who lost their child, you seem to forget that they too can use their Snatcher to find themselves a replacement. So search for that antique bong in the back of your dusty closet, old man, and inhale deeply. Get with the times.

== 8. ==

Dear Readers:

I am pleased that we are once again able to bring you my Dear Annabehl column after our long absence. It's been a difficult six months. Today's column is dedicated to all the courageous soldiers and their replacements who gave their lives at the Breach. I understand that there's still a great deal of confusion, some pessimists might even call it chaos, with the Ardiente administration taking over. Although the Ardiente underlords do have a pseudo-demonic appearance, don't let their horns and red tails throw you. As they've pointed out, they're 'broadminded traditionalists', a God-fearing salt-of-the-earth-type of people.

Most importantly, they have promised to rule benignly and to deregulate Snatchers, to allow Total Access into and out of our reality to people everywhere. Freedom is precious, after all.

There will be a period of adjustment before things get back to normal, but trust me, readers, they will. Keep working hard and have faith. There is a reason for everything. You'll see. This will all turn out for the best.

== 9. ==

Dear Annabehl:

With the new Government taking over and Total Access now fully in effect, I've decided that it's time for me and my family to take our leave from this reality. My wife is reluctant to leave her friends behind, but I keep telling her that we can relocate just a few frequencies away where she can have the same friends, more or less. Meanwhile, other me's are flooding in at an unprecedented rate: me's with blue skin; me's with mammary glands; me's with really bad haircuts; and me's indistinguishable from me in every objectively discernable way (except every now and then one of me will smile in a dark, sly way that gives me chills). There isn't room in my house for all of me's. And there's only one job for one of me. They won't tell me, but I think they're all running from something, something truly terrible in their own realities. Whatever it is, I'm afraid that it may be heading this way. How can I convince my wife to leave? I think it's time for *everyone* to escape across the transborder. I know a lot of people who have made the same decision. Maybe I'll find another world, one where Snatchers were never invented. But how can I skip through unless it *has* a Snatcher portal entrance? Do you have any advice on whether we should leave?

Packed But Not-Quite-Ready To Go
/ Biloxi, Mississippi

Dear Packed:
This is Annabehl filling in for Annabehl. Annabehl (persona prime) has moved on to a higher plane and left this column in my lucky hands. I consider it an honor to be stepping into her shoes (figuratively and literally). Forgive me if it takes a bit of time to get up to speed. In my reality, I stripped for a living and doled out advice at the bar during breaks, so this is quite a step up for me.

Freedom is a precious, wonderful gift. Go wherever you think you'll be happy. By all means, cross the transborder! Take an acid trip! Do whatever! We're free!

=== 10. ===

Dear Annabehls:
While at work last week I dialed into my bank and discovered that all of my accounts had been emptied. By the time I got home, all of my clothes and other personal belongings were also gone. It's apparent that one of my variants has gone too far this time, Annabehl.

I've decided to commence legal action against my self and have retained an attorney who's agreed to take the case on a contingency basis. My friends insist that litigation against one's self is just a waste of time and money. I disagree. Part of the reason why the world economy is on the verge of collapse is because of the actions of a few variants like this one. What do you think? Should I fight for my rights? Or should I do as my friends suggest and just let this go?

Esteban / Bronx, New York

Dear Esteban:
Have you ever heard of a little item called a Snatcher? Step through it and retrieve your items upfrequency, for goodness sake! Then snort a little elcitron and relax.

Annabehl

104

Dear Esteban:
Annabehl is off-base on this one. Two wrongs don't make a right. Pursue your remedies the way all patriots do: through litigation. Then snort a little elcitron and relax.

Annabehl

Dear Esteban:
 I've consulted a legal expert who points out that service of process can be tricky in transdimensional litigation. Also, the law is still unclear on whether our courts even have jurisdiction over our variants. No, I have to agree with Annabehl and disagree with Annabehl on this one. Take a short trip upfrequency and exercise a little self-help. Then snort a little elcitron and relax.

Annabehl

== 11. ==

Dear Annabehls:
Congrats on the great job you're doing in place of Annabehl, who was miles better than Annabehl, who was leagues better than Annabehl, who was almost as good, I'd say, as Annabehl. Here's my dilemma. I've asked my cousin JoJo (persona prime) and three of her variants to serve in my bridal party as maids of honor. It turns out that JoJo, one of JoJo's variants, is feuding with her mother, my Aunt Josie. Since that JoJo isn't from this reality, Aunt Josie isn't her real mother, mind you, but JoJo can't seem to get this through her thick skull. She refuses to attend unless I replace Aunt Josie with a variant – even though Aunt Josie really *is*, in effect, a variant, at least in relation to the complaining JoJo. Aunt Josie refuses to attend if her selves are invited. (My aunt and my mom are old-fashioned and insist on being the only versions of themselves at the wedding.) Two of the other JoJos insist, however, that I invite their actual mothers from their respective realities – and refuse to participate in the bridal party unless I do so. Meanwhile, Sean, my fiancé, has demanded multiple me's be present on my wedding night! I guess I'm my mother's daughter because I have no desire to share the stage with anyone on my

wedding night – even me! I want my wedding night to be a special, one-on-one experience between me (me prime, that is) and Sean (Sean prime, that is). What should I do about JoJo, JoJo, JoJo, JoJo, Aunt Josie and Sean? I'm too busy and stressed to deal with all of this. I have a wedding to plan!

Desperate Dixie/San Diego, CA

Dear Dixie:

We Annabehls are unanimous on this one: schedule a session at the Snatcher ASAP! Replace the troublesome JoJo – the JoJo who still carries that unseemly transdimensional grudge against her mother, your aunt (non-prime to her, actually, though that JoJo refuses to acknowledge it) – with another more agreeable version of JoJo. And good riddance! Carrying that type of transdimensional baggage really is childish and unacceptable. Talk to the two remaining JoJos and explain to them that this is your special day, that weddings are expensive and that *you* decide how many variants of your guests can attend. If they don't like it, *zap*, get yourself two more replacements. As for your fiancé's desire to turn your wedding night into an orgy, you'll have to forgive me, honey, but you might want to zap yourself a variant who has a little more regard for your feelings. (After the wedding night, he can indulge in whatever multiple-you shenanigans you and other consenting variants of you wish to engage. But on the wedding night? He's a pig!) Finally, to reduce the stress, snatch another you out of the Snatcher and delegate these wedding tasks to your self. Then mix yourself a margarita and head to the sim-beach for some well-deserved RNR.

== 12. ==

Dear Annabehls:

I've come to the depressing realization that my life is empty and truly, truly meaningless. Over the past few years I've met variants of myself who've led fascinating lives: one lived in a remote village in Guatemala where he helped construct homes for the poor; one skydived at sunset from a stealth copter into the Grand Canyon's Colorado River; another made a point of scaling Everest every autumn and making love to a beautiful woman on its snowy mountaintops. When I think about my own life, Annabehl, I'm struck by the safe choices I've made. I spend my days focused on the tedium of an office job I've never really wanted, caring for an elderly mother who doesn't even recognize me anymore, living life just going through the motions. I can see the remainder of my humdrum life stretched out in front of me, only I'm trying to pretend that I don't see it, Annabehl, because I know I don't have the ability to make any changes anyway and thinking about it just makes me feel more hopeless and impotent. And what does it matter what I choose to do? For every South American village I've never visited, for every mountain peak I've never climbed, another version of me is out there embarking on those adventures anyway. Nothing seems to matter anymore.

Jacob/Salt Lake City, Utah

Dear Jacob:
I'm not going to tell you to stop feeling sorry for yourself. And I'm not going to tell you to get up off your kiester and make some changes in your life. Why bother? Somewhere some variant of you is making those necessary changes. You see, essentially you're right. Whatever you decide to do really is meaningless. But there's certainly nothing to be gained by being depressed about this fact either. You're suffering from classic symptoms of Variant Inadequacy, kiddo, which is not at all uncommon. To give yourself a better perspective, you need to interact with some downfrequency variants who don't have it anywhere near as good as you. Heck, nothing cheers a person up more quickly than studying the misery of his variants. So pop open a beer, visit the Snatcher, and just relax.

Annabehl, Annabehl, Annabehl, Annabehl and Annabehl concur with Annabehl's advice.

Annabehl, Annabehl and Annabehl dissent with the

107

substance of the advice, but concur in the recommendation of a beer.

Annabehl abstains.

== 13 ==

00000000000000000011100000000000000000000111100000000000
00000000000991155550000000000000000000007700000000000000
0000000000Dear Annabehls
00000111113333777777777700099999999999999999:

I'm afraid. So afraid I can barely function. I feel totally adrift, as if nothing, no one, that I know is quite right. It's difficult to explain, but sometimes I swear I don't recognize my children. Didn't I used to have a uni-daughter named Allison? I have a memory, a fading dream- memory of brushing her tangled blonde hair. The thing is, I know no one has uni-daughters, certainly not me. I have an adorable set of identical septuplet boys. And while I know that this is my house, why do I sometimes find myself stumbling into rooms I never even knew existed? And my friends. Why do I forget their names? Sometimes I stare into the mirror-eyes of our pet elphine, and I don't even recognize my own reflection. The diagonal rows of black eyes that speckle my face seem unfamiliar to me. I'm afraid, afraid that the walls between realities have finally crumbled, and that I'm the only one who sees it. Wasn't the sky blue a long time ago? I could swear that it used to be. Didn't we used to walk upright on two legs? I'm lost, Annabehls. I don't think I know who or what I am any more.

Lost in Newfoundland

000000000000009955557777777799900000000000000000000000000
Dear Lost
9999999999999999900077777777111100000000000000007:

We're sorry to say that there's only one reality, dear, and we're stuck with it. The sky has always been deep red, we've always skittered on six legs, and we've always come in sets of seven, nine or thirteen. It's not unusual to sometimes feel out of place, to feel cast adrift like a wind-blown ember in the eye of a black tornado, everything around you changing while you're standing still. We've felt that way ourselves, sometimes. Do what we do, *Lost*. Buck up. Fly high on the fumes of ecsahol, if necessary. And relax.

The Fifth Zhi

Zhi 4's scream pierces the Siberian night.

My spiked metal boots crunch through the snow as I race towards him, with Zhi 6 running at my side. The nanochip in my brainstem clicks on and I reach out with my mind, but I can't sense even a trace of Zhi 4. A few seconds earlier his form had been outlined by the dark turquoise glow of the force field.

We stop twenty feet short of the field's perimeter. Beyond it, the hazy silhouette of the colossal Stalk looms, its millions of cilia undulating.

My bodysuit hums as it transmits data back to Xiang Xu Base, situated behind the Rusanov ice cap half a mile away.

My pulse flutters in anticipation and I take a deep breath to try to rein in my excitement. I – like all Zhis – have been designed with an insatiable curiosity about the Stalk's origins and vulnerabilities. Knowing I've been bred to feel this way doesn't make me feel it any less. Where did the Stalk come from? Why is it here? How can it thrive in these temperatures? I see the same questions reflected in Zhi 6's expression.

The Commander's cold voice crackles in my earpiece. "Proceed with field penetration, Zhi 5," she says.

"Yes, sir!" I bark into my helmet audiolink.

Zhi 6 nods at me, and I approach the field alone.

Our mission objectives are unambiguous: penetrate the field, climb the Stalk, and release the retrovirus before the Stalk's radiation kills us in five to six hours. All of us know we're expendable and we don't care – or at least we aren't supposed to. I've told no one, not even Zhis 4 and 6, but I hope it might be possible to survive this mission. I would like to make a life for myself some place warm and far away. After all, our father, Zhi Zhang, has always wanted to live in the tropics.

In the perpetual twilight of the North Land, I can hardly make out Zhis 7 and 8 in the distance behind us, illuminated specks on the frozen tundra. A gale-force wind lifts a veil of snow that further obscures them from view. I can't help but wonder: how many Zhis are we? As planned, we have staggered our approach because of the lethal cosmic radiation levels near the Stalk. I take a deep breath and raise my gloved hands to the force field.

This is the moment.

The moment I've been preparing for since I opened my eyes and took my first breath and sat up in the holding vat next to five slumbering brothers a year ago. Twelve months of training all designed for this.

But when I think of Zhi 4 and how he shrieked, panic threatens to override the curiosity that drives me forward.

I push my arms through the field. The reinforced layers of my suit sizzle and smoke, and a stab of scalding pain shoots through my spine. My body armor curls off me like orange peel and dissolves in the air. My skin burns, and I scream. In this moment before death, my only thought is of Father; I wish he were here to protect me. I see him in my mind's eye walking out the lab door that final time: "Don't leave me behind, Father! Take me with you!" And all at once the burning stops and I stagger forward. I find myself standing on the other side of the force field, naked. Frigid air doubles me over; I hug myself and dance involuntarily on the snow, barefoot.

I make out Zhi 6's form on the other side of the translucent field, his dim silhouette barely visible. I shout his name, but can't hear his response through the soundproof barrier. Without my helmet, I'm cut off from Xiang Xu Base. Fortunately we've prepared for this contingency.

"Are you okay, Zhi 5?" Zhi 6's technopathic message comes through clearly.

I exhale. Our identical genes and nanochip implants enable us to communicate via the quantum entanglement of our consciousnesses. Still, Xiang Xu remained concerned about possible phase decoherence due to the field's shifting polarity. But my mental link with Zhi 6 holds steady, and through him I can maintain contact with the Commander.

I'm trembling; teeth chattering. "Suit's gone," is all I can manage to think in response.

When the Stalk first materialized, one of our probes managed to slice off a sample of it. In response, the Stalk erected the field. Since then, Xiang Xu's further efforts have produced only a stream of disintegrated probes and melted robots. Nothing manmade could penetrate the field. But the hope had been that this latest suit or at least some part of it – the titanium-layered helmet, the diamond-lined soles of the boots, the reinforced cadmium plating – might at least allow us to make it through.

I flex my jaw, think the triggerword ("artichoke") and induce vomiting. Three of the five colored storage globules come up easily enough. I think "artichoke" again and again until I retch up the remaining two spheres. I pluck the pink globule from the pool of vomit, uncap it, and pull out a square piece of fabric the size of a postage stamp. Unfolding the fabric until it's the size of a handkerchief, I shake it in the wind until the adaptive synthread fibers expand into a full hooded jumpsuit with spiked rubber foot-bottoms. I step into the suit and zip up, immediately feeling the warmth of the insulating fibers activated by my own body heat. Then I reach down and secure the purple v-sphere containing the retrovirus and jam it into my suit's stomach pouch.

As my body warms up, I take in my first clear image of the Stalk, its emerald glow washing over the surrounding frozen tundra. Up close, it appears even more magnificent, more alien, than I had ever imagined. Its tree-sized fronds flap in slow motion, and its stamen pulses as if taking planet-sized breaths. Overhead, the mosaic of the Aurora Borealis blazes in the black sky, but the streaming colors are muted by the Stalk's pallid-green radiance. From this distance, the Stalk's stem is larger than a hundred Redwoods in diameter; it stretches high into the sky, where satellite photos have shown it to extend just beyond the ionosphere. Now, two years since it had first emerged, the Stalk penetrates the planetary crust straight through the Earth's very core, from North to South Pole. In the orbital photos, Earth resembles an olive pierced by a toothpick. Inexplicably, the Stalk's presence has caused no global catastrophes, no tectonic shifts or tidal waves as the experts predicted.

There have been only the nightmares; unrelenting, feverish nightmares of pulsing darkness unleashed across the world. Father told me it took only a few days of debate among bleary-eyed government leaders before the first nuclear bombs rained down on the Stalk.

To no effect.

The Stalk's field held firm.

I screw open the three remaining green globules that lie in the pool of vomit and pull out the nanotech components, which I place side by side in the snow. Normally the metal pieces would have elongated and skittered towards each other to form a thumb-sized spectral analyzer and climbing tools, but the inert fragments simply sit there. Xiang Xu's worst fears have come to pass: the field's dampening effect extends to nanotech. Yet somehow my implant remains operational. Could it be because of its integration with my brainstem?

I try manually wedging the pieces together to no avail.

What would Father do?

I move to my left and step into a pile of charred and mangled limbs. Zhi 4. I jump back and gasp. To my left and right, similar mounds of burnt flesh lie half-buried in the snow. Zhis 1, 2 and 3. I drop to my knees and cover my mouth, this time trying to suppress the urge to vomit. My brothers... I know we're expendable, I know that we're all meant to die for a greater cause, but I trained with them and loved them. No sooner do I feel my eyes tear up and my throat catch than the programming kicks in, than I'm thinking again about the Stalk. How had I been able to traverse the field without suffering the same fate as my brothers?

As if on cue, Zhi 6 projects the Commander's words: "How did you do it, Zhi 5?" she asks. "How did you make it through?"

"I don't know."

"You're cleared to join him, Zhi 6," she says.

I want to shout a warning to him, to urge him to run away, but I know Zhi 6 is as compelled as I am to explore the Stalk. The shadow on the other side of the barrier grows larger as Zhi 6 approaches. As he begins to push through the force field, he screams, just for a fraction of a second. This time his armor sizzles as it dissolves, and so too does Zhi 6.

"Brother!" I shout. But the echoes of his squelched scream fade away with the rest of him. Two seconds later, a billow of brown ash and chunks of burnt flesh plop to the snow.

I slap my hands against the field to test its solidity from within, even though I know – we all know – this is a one-way mission. It feels like cold, smooth marble. The animals Xiang Xu Base pushed through the force field over the past two years – a German Shepherd and two chimpanzees – never emerged, though their silhouettes remained visible until either the cold or the radiation killed them. The field can only be penetrated from the outside, and how, I still don't know.

As Zhi 7 draws nearer to the force field, his thoughts chime in my mind: "Stop dallying, Zhi 5, and carry out the mission objectives."

Genetically, he is me, but Zhi 7 and the higher-numbered Zhis – how many, I don't know – were all grown in different vats from ours. Apart from our technopathic link, I feel no emotional connection with him. In fact, Zhi 7 has rubbed me the wrong way with his officiousness since this mission began. While we are certainly designed to be the same, I found over the past twelve months that even my vat-brothers had developed slightly different temperaments. Zhi 4 had worked harder than the rest of us, Zhi 3 drew pictures on a sketch pad when nobody watched,

Zhi 2 kept to himself and rarely spoke with the rest of us, Zhi 1 smiled more than the other Zhis.

I stagger over the snowdrifts toward the Stalk's base. The snowstorm has intensified into a blinding squall. Through a canvas of luminescent lime-colored snow, I make out the outer edges of the Stalk's swaying fronds at a distance of about a hundred yards from the force field. It's doubtful I can maintain technopathic contact with Zhi 7 during the long climb.

From this angle, the Stalk fills the sky. Half of the millions of dark-green cilia furring its stamen seem to wave me forward, while the other half shoo me away.

A sizzle slices through the air and I look back over my shoulder. Another swell of ash and body parts belches through the field. Zhi 7.

I pause. This time I feel only slight sadness before thoughts of the Stalk occupy me again.

I extend my mind and already sense Zhis 8 and 9 approaching the field. We are all redundancies, extra copies of Father: a highly qualified, physically fit scientist. Father had once told me privately that the public viewed us as teenaged automatons sacrificed for a noble cause. But he didn't see me that way; I'm sure of it. Father favored me over my vat-brothers for some reason. Prior to our upload of his skill-sets necessary for this mission, he had read to me, tutored me, played with me. But then he left. Without even saying goodbye, he'd left months ago to join the American expedition at the other end of the Stalk, in the Antarctic.

When I reach the base of the Stalk, I scoop up snow that resembles green slush and fling it underhand in the direction of the swaying leaves. No reaction. The log-sized, rubbery appendages continue waving in slow motion. I creep forward.

I extend my hand and caress one of the fronds with the tip of my gloved finger. It stops squirming and becomes rigid. I touch another one – which feels synthetic, like the leaf of a plastic palm tree – and it too stops moving, jutting outward solidly like a gangplank.

I place one foot on a leaf and wrap my arms around another one. Raising my foot, I climb a step. Then another.

As I pull myself up from leaf to leaf my biceps burn. The slippery appendages make it difficult to get traction, even with my spiked soles. The plan calls for me to climb the Stalk, break open the v-sphere and release the virus into a cavity detected by radar at its apex. In my powered armor, with its oxygen supply, the climb might have been possible. Now, at some point when the radiation has weakened me and I can go no further, I will reach into my pocket and release the retrovirus that will work its deadly effects on the Stalk, on me, and on all life in the region.

This will mark my grand exit. Alive for twelve months and gone. It isn't fair. But at least I will have made a difference. At least I will have made Father proud.

The stolen memory surfaces again. Zhi Zhang's memory from *his* childhood, of standing at the edge of a log that hangs high over a swimming hole:

"Jump, jump, jump," the boys chanted from the pond below.

"Swimming is instinctive, dog turd," one of them shouted.

"Yellowbelly!"

I stepped off, holding my nose as I'd been instructed, and hit the water.

And sank.

Panic.

I couldn't tell up from down. My heart hammering, I punched and kicked furiously; I swallowed water. I was going to die. *I wanted to live!*

Someone grabbed my waist, pulled me upwards; I was breathing liquid, and my head emerged out of the water. I tried inhaling, but could only cough.

"It's all right, son," Zhi Zhang's father said. "It's all right." His white shirt and tie were drenched; loose bills from his pocket floated in the pond like water-lilies.

The memory isn't mine, I remind myself. It is Father's. During the uploading of his expertise in chemistry and biology I have picked up this one stray memory, this thread pulled from his life-tapestry. The story told for public consumption, Father explained, is that all Zhis are *tabula rasa*, blank soulless slates upon which Xiang Xu Base inscribes only the most rudimentary skills necessary to accomplish missions such as this one. But every Zhi in my vat confided to me that random memories always snuck through during the upload. This is our secret.

I continue climbing. The storm is subsiding and thick, lazy flakes flutter down. From this vantage point I can make out the frozen Kara Sea in the west, the Laptev Sea in the east, the mountainous islands off of the peninsula on the Arctic coast of Siberia. Below lies twilit frigid desert, barren tundra coated with permafrost. I perch on a leaf at least two hundred feet off the ground, determined to go as high as possible before I release the virus. I still don't think I can reach the cavity at the Stalk's crest, where the retrovirus is expected to work to maximum effect. A tickle on the back of my leg grows into a sharp jab. When I look down, a red thorn the size of a switchblade protrudes from my thigh. I grit my teeth and yank it out and notice for the first time the rows of thorns that coat the bottom of the fronds.

Lightheaded, I extend my mind for Zhi 8. I wonder whether the field's wavering polarity at this elevation will permit a technopathic link. That's when the thoughts assault my brain:

Lost. I am lost. Rescue me, /We/. Don't leave me here, /We/.

...

What are you? Can you really... think? Do you know of the ether-sea?

/We/ wallowed in its infinite, rich nothingness. A shaft of photons shot through us and I/We were awed. /We/ are the invisibles, the intangibles. /We/ traced the bullet of light to its point of origin and we saw it. The most exotic substance in the universe: solid matter. Then /We/ sensed it. Something never conceived of before. Floating flecks blanketed in folds of gentle darkness, sparkling and reflecting flickers of light. And on

118

these flecks: conscious matter. Micro-dots of self-conscious matter.
    You.

I pull back my thoughts as if I've touched a hot stove.
    What was that?
    The roiling darkness stays in my mind. Are these the images that have haunted dreams across the globe? My brothers and I have been designed with immunity to the nightmares.
    An icy pink coating of blood covers my leg. I rip off the right sleeve of my jumpsuit and use it as a bandage to stanch the bleeding. Drugged. The thorns have drugged me, made me susceptible to the alien nightmares.
    When I look down, the flapping leaves obscure my line of vision. I grab hold of another leaf and another. Minutes pass. Hours. I don't look down any more. I keep my eyes fixed on the next frond above me. The freezing cold numbs my exposed right arm.
    I don't think I can go any farther. I reach for the v-sphere in my pouch. But just as I am about to pull it out, the world spins. I'm losing my grip, surrendering to exhaustion. I must open my eyes. I must stay awake. My fingertips slide off the frond and I fall.

/We/ fell away through darkness. /We/ retreated into the cool lightlessness of the intangiverse, but the memory of the exotic – matter, conscious matter – stayed with us. Haunted us. And so, for millennia /We/ formulated our plan to reach out and communicate with the corporeal, the conscious solid.
    Now I'm no longer /We/! I miss /We/!

. . .

Can you follow what I'm saying, particle?
    It can't understand me, /We/! Save me, /We/!

I open my eyes and find myself thousands of feet in the air entwined in the Stalk's cilia. I no longer need to climb. The tendrils encircle my arms and legs and pull me upward at an

119

accelerating speed. I'm moving through a cloudbank; the harsh, wet wind cuts my face. At this elevation I can't make out any features on the ground.

"Zhi 5," Zhi 29's distant thoughts echo in my mind.

Zhi 29? What happened to Zhi 8?

"The field's interference is worsening. I can barely register your thoughts, Zhi 29," I say.

"The Commander... you... release the virus..."

"I don't think the Stalk means us harm, Zhi 29. It seems lost, alone –"

"Kill it...!"

I palm the v-sphere, but I feel weak, unsteady and for the first time in my life, uncertain. I close my eyes.

/We/ are the dark cosmic ether-sea undulating into infinity. Then I am torn away from /We/. Ripped and shunted and coiled into an abyss of hot swirling chaos. I emerge from /We/, twisted and congealed and shaped.

I am alone. I am solid.

I am here. But my thoughts, my experiences are for the /We/. We are kindred.

"Yes," I reply. "Kindred."

You do understand. You do think.

"Why have you taken this form?"

I became the most common of living solids here.

"The most common?" From Father's uploaded expertise I imagine the pyrodictium and archae microorganisms that layer the ocean bottoms, the vegetation thriving in dense rain forests. Consistent with the sample of it we had taken, the Stalk has adopted a hybrid form, patterned after Earth life.

I am no longer /We/... I cannot go back. I cannot go back...

When I open my eyes again, I am no longer ascending the Stalk. I am at its very peak, a flat circular summit about fifty yards across with a depression at its center. It resembles a valley filled with squirming sea anemones. Above, the stars blanket the black sky. I try to stand and take a tentative step. I move in slow motion, in zero gravity – how am I breathing? – atop the carpet of squiggling tentacles. They push me away from the ledge and down toward the center. As I ride this wave, I push my hand into my pocket and clutch the v-sphere that contains the retrovirus. Xiang Xu Base doesn't know the Stalk is sentient; they don't know it's only here to explore, to learn about us, to relay information home. They don't understand its loneliness.

The Stalk's tentacles carry me farther toward the cavity at the summit's center, until I reach a bottomless pit, a cosmic maw that I know on some primal level reveals the Stalk's true form, a blackness so pure that it seems to pulse.

I start to go over the edge.

No. A voice calls out in my mind. I'm not sure whether it is my own thoughts or Zhi 29's or something else's. I grab hold of one of the tentacles on the summit's surface and pull myself back. Clutching clumps of tendrils, I walk on my hands in the micro-gravity, tugging my way back from the chasm.

"Why haven't you killed it?" Zhi 383's thoughts resonate in my mind.

Zhi 383? "What happened to Zhi 29?" I ask, though I know the answer. Just as I know what has happened to Zhi 4 and Zhi 7 and every Zhi that has tried to pass through the field except me.

"The field's polarity has shifted and stabilized, Zhi 383. You're coming through clearly."

"Release the virus. Now!"

I twirl the v-sphere in my hand. The Commander must be unable to activate it remotely due to the field's dampening effect or she would have done so by now. At this moment I come to the realization that I will never be able to bring myself to release the virus. I won't kill the Stalk.

"That's a direct order from the Commander!" Zhi 383 says, picking up my mutinous decision.

I pepper my thoughts with the word "artichoke," and sense Zhi 383's queasiness. That'll keep his mind at bay.

"I... refuse," I say.

After an extended pause he says, "Brother, I understand. You're confused, injured. Listen, I'm in contact with Zhi Zhang."

I freeze at the mention of Father's name.

"Hello, 5." Zhi 383 now projects Father's words as he hears them.

"Father! It *is* you!"

"The simultaneous assault in the Antarctic has failed, and Zhis 50 through 200 have been expended in the process. It's time for you to do your duty, 5."

"You don't understand, Father. The Stalk is sentient. It's been ripped away from something... unimaginable, something not even material. It's a... speckle of dark energy. A conduit for information. It's been sacrificed. To learn about solid matter, about *us*. It means us no harm!"

"No, it's you who don't understand," Father responds. "Whatever its intentions, the Stalk poses an unprecedented threat. Even before the nightmares started, the government leaders had decided to take preemptive action."

"I don't want to kill it."

"That's not our decision to make. Trust me, 5. Tell me, how did you make it through the field?"

And, all at once, something about his words makes me realize the truth. When I had crossed the field, I was thinking about Father, about how he left me. In that instant the Stalk had somehow, impossibly, accessed my quantum communications, accessed my consciousness. It must have sensed a shared feeling, a shared experience: loneliness, abandonment. It empathized with me. All the others – except the subject animals – had approached it with hostile intent. I try to clamp down on my thoughts. Too late.

"Thank you," Zhi 383 says.

"Now we know what to do should the retrovirus fail," Father adds. "I have one more thing I must tell you, 5. 'Daffodil.'"

"Daffodil?" I think.

I clench my fist involuntarily. A hiss erupts, and a dirty-brown gas sprays from my stomach pouch. I've activated the virus! I remove the v-sphere and hurl it over the side, away from the Stalk.

I'm too late. The Stalk shudders and sends me flying onto my back; I'm knotted in a bed of anemone-like vines. The area around me heaves and pulses; tendrils sway. Across the summit, tentacles stand on end and lose their bright colors. They take on a sickly jellyfish-like transparency.

I stagger to my feet again. What happened? A triggerword. A failsafe I knew nothing about. Father made me activate the v-sphere.

My head pounds. I can't tell whether it is the sting of betrayal or the effects of the retrovirus. "Why did you do it, Father? Don't you care that I'm going to die?"

There's a long hesitation before he addresses me again. "You're dying for a greater purpose, a noble cause. Oh, 5, I've done you a terrible disservice with my attentions. It was... a weakness on my part." His projected voice sounds so sad, so weary. "I've made you think that you matter."

The Stalk shakes and sends me hurtling back toward the opening at its center. I should be resigned to my fate, like every other Zhi. But I can't help it; I want to live.

"Father!" I scream.

No response.

I hold my hands to my temples. The alien thoughts explode in my mind again:

I am... losing this shape. I must leave.

"But I thought you had been left behind. That you couldn't go home again."

I cannot return to the ether-sea. I am transcending to the other plane, conceived but never seen, neither matter nor non-matter. Alone, without /We/.

"But I don't want to die!"

"Die'?" It trills in a way I somehow recognize as curiosity.

"What is 'die'?"

I look down and see the Earth's surface below my feet. The entirety of the Stalk is now transparent, and the force field's blue glow is no longer visible. My breathing becomes labored as the retrovirus works its way through me. My bare, frostbitten arm becomes transparent, my feet and legs lose their color.

The Stalk rumbles, and its base, embedded in the Arctic ice, breaks loose. I hurtle sideways as the Stalk quakes.

And in that final instant, as the left side of my body begins to fade altogether, a tickle of a memory, a shadow of a thought, creeps over me. A sense of déjà vu.

Don't leave me behind! Take me with you.

I extend my hands and my mind, and feel its cool embrace.

Come, particle. Join me in the journey. So that I can be we *again.*

Reality dissolves around me and an obsidian wave washes over the horizon, a wave that wipes clean the star-lined night sky like an eraser moving over a blackboard. Then I realize it isn't the stars that are disappearing; it's me.

The Scent of Their Arrival

They met at sunrise in the Grand Glacial Chamber on the peaks of Shanriola. The teams of decipherers and the Presiding Council of naturalists and supernaturalists gathered to discuss the new signal that Ember-Musk and Scent-of-Moss had discovered encrypted within the alien ship's mysterious transmission.

Although Ember-Musk had visited the Chamber several times over the past year, he still marveled at its opulence. As they filed into the cavernous room, he noted the intricate etchings that lined the granite floors, and the polished marble walls that stretched fifty vertecs high, converging in a triangular skylight that framed the cloudless, golden heavens. The Council members congregated at the massive softstone roundtable while the scores of decipherers, including Ember-Musk and Scent-of-Moss, took their seats in the rows of basalt benches along the sides of the Chamber.

The Presiding Elder – a supernaturalist had been selected this cycle – stood in a mote-flecked sunbeam that streamed down through the skylight. He commenced the meeting with a short prayer and then puffed his midsection, releasing a thick, sweet mist through the engorged pores of his crimson carapace. The attendees inhaled his query: *Tell us, decipherers, does this new signal explain* why *the spaceship has failed to leave orbit,* why *it continues to ignore our entreaties?*

Scent-of-Moss stood up and flared her pores. She emitted a mist tinged with just the barest trace of burning leaf-wax: *I'm afraid this message we've uncovered is as perplexing as the primary transmission, Elder. Except... it contains a visual image.*

The dignitaries and decipherers simultaneously released a

potpourri of sweet-to-sour scented vapors that swirled and amassed and quickly became indistinguishable from one another:

You have an actual image?

Are they solid or translucent?

Why would the aliens hide messages within messages?

Are they naturalists or supernaturalists?

They were, of course, no closer to understanding the aliens than they had been a year earlier when naturalists had first detected the spaceship orbiting their world, transmitting its confounding, repeating signal. But now – at last – they had actual visuals.

While Tang-of-Mint, the Lead Naturalist, tinkered with the Chamber's quartz signal-projector, Ember-Musk raised his arms and everyone ceased misting. He sprayed a cleansing mist to dissipate the lingering smells and, when silence had fallen upon the room, released a brimstone-laced warning: *Scent a solemn prayer, and brace yourselves. I've seen it numerous times, and it's... I can't find the scents to describe it.*

The supernaturalists among them raised their red-hued visages skyward in plaintive prayer and the unpainted naturalists begrudgingly followed suit.

Scent-of-Moss turned a knob and the holoimage coalesced into view above the roundtable.

A two-legged, two-armed alien stood before them.

Everyone simultaneously misted the salty scent of a storm-ravaged sea.

[HOLO-SEG 6 of 15 – Shiptime 10:07:45 A.M./11-12-2251]

...You have to understand, our great solar-sailed ship, *The Deliverance*, had been in development for years before the invasion. It was over a century earlier that we'd detected the ninety-three reachable Earth-like planets sitting there while we all dragged our feet. I guess you could say that our war with the Reviled lit a fire under us.

Who would have thought that our mission of exploration

would turn into nothing more than a frantic scramble to escape our world, to flee the horror that had spread across planet Earth?

What do you suppose it's trying to scent? misted Scent-of-Moss. Following the meeting, she and Ember-Musk had spent three days holed up in their cavern studying the holographic image. *The signal's visual track comes through clearly enough, but the olfactory pathway appears damaged.*

Ember-Musk embraced Scent-of-Moss from behind and scraped the jagged crystals of his fore-arms against the nubs on her rear-arms in a way that he knew pleased her. Scent-of-Moss's smooth, ivory-white exoskeleton sparkled, and crystalline carbuncles speckled her four arms. She had an adorable habit of leaning forward on her dainty center leg, which otherwise dangled alluringly several inches off the ground. And whenever she stole a sideways glance at him, it accentuated her most attractive feature: the large, regal snout that made Ember-Musk tingle with desire.

Ember-Musk. She gently pushed him away. *I have work to do.* For the past year, Scent-of-Moss had obsessed over the riddle of the alien signal, using every naturalist tool at her disposal – mathematics, physics, biochemistry, cryptography – to try to decipher the primary transmission, a textual message that repeated trillions of times at different frequencies. Their discovery of this new message, a holoimage cleverly hidden within the interstices of that transmission, Ember-Musk thought, had only served to heighten the mystery.

It had also pushed them farther apart.

Ember-Musk had spent the day painting his face and torso a deep red and praying for a breakthrough.

Have you checked for any masked *scents?* he suggested.

Scent-of-Moss squirted her tangy assent: *Spectral bouquets, emotion-based odors, psyche-scents, micro-aromas, subspace fragrances, algorithmically-encoded smells, genetically altered scents. Nothing. It's absolutely odorless.* She folded her rear-arms and rubbed her fore-arms in frustration. *Why would aliens go to the trouble of sending a ship across light years of space, just to show us mute images?*

There are some who believe that they might be the heralds of the Gods, wife, Ember-Musk misted. *That at first scent they will provide us the answers to all of our questions. Change everything.*

She released an overpowering molten-iron stench: *I know the Prophecies, Ember-Musk. But I just told you, the holomessage is utterly scentless. And whether they're 'heralds' or alien life forms, we still need to understand what they're trying to communicate.*

He exhaled the sweet, calming fragrance of cactus-blossom seedlings in springtime: *Yes, yes, of course.* Scent-of-Moss, like most wives, tended to look for answers strictly in the material world. Ember-Musk believed it was his duty as a husband and supernaturalist to remind her that life was more complex than that. After all, the true mysteries of existence – their Life Purpose, the love between a husband and wife, those ineffable qualities that brought them joy – could never be solved by analyzing a genetic strand or by studying the chemical composition of an aroma. Yet Scent-of-Moss, Ember-Musk realized, had continued to immerse herself more deeply in naturalism over the past year, to the exclusion of all else.

You've smelled the rumors that have been wafting around? Scent-of-Moss sprayed.

Ah, this explained her ill humor, he thought. He had whiffed traces of those rumors and knew that they would only exacerbate Scent-of-Moss's own worries, so he sprayed an even sweeter mist, and decided to downplay them: *Scent-of-Moss! Since when does a naturalist pay attention to* gossip?

She turned around and embraced him in her fore-arms.

You're right, husband. It's nonsense. If it were truly a scout ship presaging some... invasion, it would have taken action a long time ago. Invaders wouldn't just stay in orbit so long, transmitting that same baffling signal toward us. No, it's clearly here to communicate something to us.

Is the Council still transmitting responsive sweet-scents?

Every day. But the ship doesn't acknowledge them. Either the aliens don't understand, or they're choosing to ignore us.

Could the ship be automated? Ember-Musk scented.

Its vast size makes me think otherwise. But I suppose it's possible that the aliens aboard didn't survive the interstellar voyage. If only we had the technology to fly up to it, to study the craft up close...

I've prepared a meal. Come, let's eat. He pulled Scent-of-Moss's rear-arms.

She emitted a frustrated puff.

Not everything can be explained by naturalism, wife, he gently reminded her. *Sometimes the peace of mind that prayer brings us provides its own answers.* Ember-Musk emanated the numinous scent of a summer sea breeze at sunrise.

He realized this was an argument that husbands and wives had had since the dawn of time, and one they were unlikely to settle tonight.

I know, I know, Scent-of-Moss misted. *But let's go back to one of the first messages. One final time.*

Scent-of-Moss turned the dial on the signal-projector and the alien's holoimage appeared in midair.

Each time Ember-Musk viewed it, the image seemed less horrific. It didn't seem so farfetched that the Gods might conceive of such strange, delicate creatures as their heralds.

The alien clasped both hands behind its back and paced back and forth. How the creature managed to maintain its balance on only two legs, Ember-Musk couldn't understand.

What are those symbols scrawled above the image? he sprayed. *I believe they may be some form of marker or identifier in the alien's written language,* Scent-of-Moss answered. *They're the same type of symbols the aliens used in the primary transmission.*

[HOLO-SEG 2 of 15 – Shiptime 9:03:22 A.M./11-10-2251]
How do I even begin? How do I tell you — whoever you are — about our final days on Earth? How do I put into words the chaos... the madness... everything that's been lost?

I've heard so many stories of how the invasion began that I'm no longer sure which ones are true. But this much I know for certain: the Apocalypse began in the Middle East, in Old Jerusalem. Some blamed it on an arms race run amok, a new weapon that ripped open the fabric of realspace and created the Fissure, a three-dimensional rectangle of light. There are those who described the Fissure as beautiful, a shimmering, golden doorway – but I can't allow myself to believe that.

Nothing that let *them* in could be beautiful.

For weeks the Fissure hung there harmlessly while puzzled scientists ran their tests. Then someone – no one knows who or why – spoke the dark prayer, a whispered invitation, and the hellgates burst open.

Given the infinite number of universes, I suppose we shouldn't have been surprised that somewhere there might exist beings that would jump at this invitation. But who would have guessed that the creatures that answered that call would resemble the grotesqueries of our fevered imaginations, our worst nightmares? Something about them triggered a visceral revulsion in humans, a gag reflex. Was it their angular cheekbones and pus-yellow pallor? Their naked, sexless forms? Their perpetual, emotionless smiles? Their strange, featherlight footsteps – that made it seem as if they were adjusting to a new, weaker gravity? It was almost as if we knew on a molecular level that they were malevolent, that they didn't belong here. No, they were unmistakably inhuman. Unmistakably evil.

The Reviled flooded into our reality and launched a silent blitzkrieg, striking their hollow, pointed tongues like slick cobras, piercing warm arteries and vacuuming the blood of helpless thousands in just the first night. And though their initial actions seemed haphazard, the Reviled proved far more intelligent than anyone had at first suspected, for they specifically targeted the scientists who might have had some idea of how to seal the Fissure.

The survivors of that first assault reported hearing the sound of victims retching followed by their high-pitched wails, but the Reviled, as always, maintained their eerie silence. We could see them, we could feel them, but somehow they remained cloaked from our sense of hearing and smell.

God help us, death had stepped through that doorway. The death of our world.

And we had invited it in.

Do you notice that the large cavity beneath its snout repeatedly flutters open? Scent-of-Moss sprayed. *In one of the previous messages it ingested what appeared to be some form of sustenance through this opening.*

Really? Ember-Musk tried to visualize the action but had trouble doing so. It seemed so inefficient. He pointed to the alien's skull with his fore-hands. *And what of those two orifices on the sides of its head, wife? The ones flagged by that protruding, rounded flesh?*

I think they may be large pores, she misted. *But the scanners still don't detect anything on the scent-track of the message stream, not even an iota of aroma.*

The tiny proboscis seems somewhat primitive, don't you think? Ember-Musk scented. *Not what one would expect from a sentient species, let alone a space-faring one.*

Scent-of-Moss inhaled deeply and seemed to consider his observations. Although she was the one who excelled in the natural arts, Ember-Musk, like any good husband, often tossed out ideas, theories that might inspire her. He emitted the balmy scent of a freshly dug, equatorial burrow: *Do you remember those animals in the Red Desert, the Barzelian crawlers, the ones that changed the position of their limbs to signal to others of its kind?*

Scent-of-Moss turned around and faced him. *Of course! The way the alien moves its two arms, the way it tilts its head. It may be some sophisticated form of motion-communication!*

Play the next holo-segment, wife, he misted.

[HOLO-SEG 8 of 15 – Shiptime 11:11:45 A.M./11-17-2251]
My wife Carla and I – along with hundreds of other engineers – toiled around the clock on the construction of *The Deliverance* in New Houston. Work on the ship, work that had stalled for years,

gained a new urgency as world events spun out of control.

Within a year after the Fissure burst open, the Middle East and Europe fell. But by then the rest of the world had marshaled its forces. The American Axis and the Sino-Australian Alliance called a truce and worked together to launch a preemptive nuclear strike.

You see, we actually thought we stood a chance.

After the first mushroom cloud dissipated, it looked as if we had won. The Reviled had been vaporized. But then we realized that the nuclear firestorm had done nothing to seal the Fissure. Every day at sunset hordes of them poured through, seemingly unaffected by the radiation, drawn to our world by what we could only assume to be some mad, insatiable hunger. One night – inevitably, I suppose – a series of nukes failed to detonate, and the Reviled breached the perimeters. It's rumored that military personnel saw them through infrared goggles shifting shape into an ethereal mist that dispersed across the night sky. But more likely they'd activated some highly advanced cloak, we assumed, or perhaps they had a natural camouflaging ability. In any event, within a matter of weeks the Reviled had scattered across the globe and infiltrated every city on every continent. Once they'd penetrated the general populace, the nuclear option was eliminated.

The Final War had begun.

At greydawn, Ember-Musk undertook the Holy Ascent to the top of Mount Shanriola, not far from the Grand Glacial Cavern, with forty-eight members of their clan. The eruption of a small volcano a hundred kilovertecs to the west had occluded much of the sky and a steady flow of ash softly drizzled down on them. Not only decipherers, but farmers, rock-sculptors, Council members and healers, naturalists and supernaturalists, walked the well-trod dirt path that snaked up the mountainside. As they climbed the pathway, Ember-Musk looked down into the valley that he and Scent-of-Moss called home. Water-filled craters and patches of berry-blossoming red cacti pockmarked the landscape. He inhaled deeply, breathing in the beauty that surrounded him. Would Scent-of-Moss be able to experience this same wonder in her current state of mind, he thought the sense of the *sacred* inspired by these amazing vistas? Or would she only see meteorite impact craters and a valley shaped by millennia of erosion and magma-flow?

He had pleaded with her to forget about the holoimage, just for a single day, to participate in the Holy Ascent, but she had refused. *I don't have time for rituals at this critical juncture in my work*, she had scented, *especially with the new season fast approaching*. Scent-of-Moss feared that with the expected influx of desert travelers and with a large segment of the current population expected to leave on the Desert Walk, a new Council might interfere with her work – or even replace them with different decipherers from among the travelers. He had tried to reassure her of their highly regarded status – they had discovered the encrypted holimage, after all – but she insisted that they couldn't rest on past laurels.

Ember-Musk had painted his exoskeleton a deep black to shield himself against the sharp drop in temperature on the snowy mountain peak. The air frosted white from his snout, and he hugged himself tight with his four arms. He tried his best not to exude any acrid fumes of discontent – there was no need to make others aware of the private matters between him and his beloved – but he had to admit that he was becoming impatient with her. Scent-of-Moss had disregarded their prayer sessions and now the Holy Ascent too.

The female naturalists led their coterie, scoping out the path ahead of them for rockslides, while the men followed close behind, scenting a group prayer for the desert travelers, asking the Gods to deliver them and their bounty safely. Ember-Musk also prayed quietly for both the patience and divine inspiration that might help him assist Scent-of-Moss – indeed, all of his people – with the important work deciphering the aliens' messages.

By midday, they reached the summit of Shanriola. As they stood at the edge of an overlook, the ground's steady rumble suddenly grew in intensity. They stepped backward and rooted their center legs. The minor temblor caused rocks to crumble down the side of the cliff, but fortunately, the ledge upon which they stood was, like their caverns, made of flexible softstone, which held firm. From here, Ember-Musk stared out at the other side of the mountain. Endless deep-red sand dunes stretched into the far horizon. In the remote distance, he could barely make out other mountains, not unlike Shanriola, that harbored similar oases and verdant valleys populated by other clans. Thousands of vertecs below their position, he spotted an encampment demarcated by brilliantly blue poles buried in the sand, a caravan of approximately two dozen travelers. The wanderers waited there, immobile, their snouts up in the air. The full moons had shone brightly last night, so the travelers knew that the ritual would take place today at midday. From this distance, Ember-Musk thought, the strangers seemed healthy and − from the opalescent sky-blue they had painted themselves − proud and respectful.

As we have all sought food and shelter and succor in the kindness of our neighbors, the lead supernaturalist recited, *so too shall we provide the same. And may the Gods, in turn, bless us all with such kindnesses.* With those words, Ember-Musk lined up side by side with all forty-eight of his clan mates, rear-arms locked together and carapaces puffed. Together, they released the thick, redolent *sweet-scent* vapors.

Within a matter of minutes, the travelers began to dismantle their encampment in preparation for joining their new community, an indication that they had picked up the fragrance.

As always, Ember-Musk found himself deeply moved by the ceremony. *It's life-affirming, isn't it?* he scented to the adolescent naturalist standing to his left. *Producing the sweet-scents is even more gratifying than receiving them after the long Desert Walk.*

They come from the south so I expect they'll carry exotic foods, new paints, interesting new technologies with them, she responded. *But more importantly, they'll bring healthy young travelers with them. Hopefully, I'll find a mate.*

The young girl's exoskeleton was barely hardened, but she spoke with the pragmatism of an adult naturalist. She had totally missed the spiritual beauty of the ritual, Ember-Musk thought. *If they're from the south, I have some experience translating their regional scents*, he sprayed. *And I can work with their decipherers to teach them our language.*

Scenting with this girl reminded Ember-Musk that he and Scent-of-Moss would likely have become parents in the past year, but for the priority they had given to their work over their personal lives. He tried his best to resign himself to this fact. After all, the life-plans of all decipherers had been put on hold by the alien transmissions. And his every instinct told him that the Gods had a greater purpose in mind for them, that these transmissions had some connection to the Prophecies. Once they had children, he and Scent-of-Moss would join a convoy and start the Desert Walk, until they found food and shelter in a hospitable new community, just like these travelers, he thought. Settlement, procreation, and relocation. This had always been the way of their people.

Even from this distance, Ember-Musk breathed in the gratitude of the blue-painted travelers.

Scent-of-Moss... he scented. *We will have our answers. I just know it.*

When Ember-Musk returned late in the evening to their cavern, it appeared that Scent-of-Moss hadn't shifted position from when he'd last seen her at dawn. She seemed to barely pay attention when he scented a detailed account of the Holy Ascent and the blue-painted travelers who had arrived from the south.

The alien also looked unchanged, he thought, pacing left and right, holding its two spindly arms behind its bent back.

[HOLO-SEG 9 of 15 – Shiptime 11:11:45 A.M./11-18-2251]

Just when we were about to lose all hope we discovered the Achilles' heel of the Reviled – the same vulnerabilities, strangely enough, presaged by legend: sunlight, fire, sharp wooden weapons. This gave rise to both hope and hysteria, for most people viewed this as conclusive proof that we were dealing with supernatural forces. Myself, I stayed firmly in the camp of reason. Everything about the Reviled, their origins, their abilities, their weaknesses, had to have a rational explanation. That we didn't understand them yet didn't mean they were somehow exempt from the laws of physics. Plenty of theories certainly abounded. Their vulnerability to sunlight, some hypothesized, meant that their world orbited a star much different from our own, perhaps a neutron star or a brown dwarf. Others theorized that a genetic defect in the Reviled from inbreeding caused them an allergic reaction to the daylight. And most people – among rational thinkers, I mean – believed that a protective energy field of some sort surrounded their supposedly 'invulnerable' skin. The fact that sharp wood could penetrate this field while bullets, knives and other objects failed to do so, suggested that trees were alien to their universe. Of course, we had no evidence yet to support any of these theories, but the alternative.... No, I couldn't accept the alternative.

Many people tried using crucifixes and other religious artifacts ranging from Stars of David to Buddha statues as weapons and shields, to no avail. In hindsight, it seems ridiculous, pathetic. But I can't blame them. You have to understand, we were beyond desperate.

Eventually, the military deployed the warbots – equine-shaped, low-level AI devices fitted with an assortment of weapons: napalm flamethrowers, sunlight-simulating highbeams, wooden scythes capable of slicing off heads like tree branches. A protective warbot monitored every city block at all times.

But we were no longer safe in open-aired metropolises where the Reviled could materialize at any moment during the night. We constructed domes over small communities, then eventually over entire cities and, once enclosed, found that the Reviled were powerless to enter without an explicit invitation. Massive sun simulators kept the cities lit at all times. And dedicated truckers and traders traveled during daylight hours between the domed cities – at least those in close enough proximity to reach before nightfall – transporting and exchanging goods. In this way, secured in our vaulted metropolises, we reached a stalemate of sorts; we held the Reviled at bay for years.

But stragglers and nomadic tribes and others who had refused the sanctuary of the domed cities – or who had simply been unable to reach them in time — slowly fell prey to the Reviled.

And all the while, the hordes continued to pour through the Fissure.

Scent-of-Moss carried Ember-Musk in her fore-arms as she waded into the volcanically heated spring baths. From here, deep in the valley, they could see the row of orange-shaded moons begin their slow ascent through the clouds and over the snow-covered peaks of Shanriola. Several other couples downstream from them also luxuriated in the baths. Their children – still smooth-skinned and translucent and lacking fully formed exoskeletons – scampered in the sand, digging burrows with their rear-arms.

I'm so glad you agreed to step away from that holoimage for a few hours, Ember-Musk misted.

I've gotten nowhere the past few days with the motion language, if that's what it is. The alien's gestures appear random, almost as if accentuating the smell of a powerful aroma.

A cool breeze blew, and the ground shook. All of the surrounding couples lowered their center legs to maintain their balance until the tremors passed while Ember-Musk lowered himself to his neck in the warm waters. *Don't worry, wife. I'll pray for more inspiration.*

Why would the aliens hide a hologram within the gaps of their primary transmission? Why encrypt a message within a message? Scent-of-Moss scented. *What is this creature trying to communicate to us?*

Ember-Musk didn't respond. Scent-of-Moss was with him at this moment, but only physically. He pressed his back against the smooth sandstone sides of the bathing crater, enjoying the magnified tingling sensation whenever the ground shook. While normal seismic activity caused the ground to tremble regularly, whenever a temblor struck, the vibrations increased dramatically. He enjoyed how they caused the searing bathwaters to swirl.

After a few moments, Ember-Musk released the soporific scent of damp greenwood through his facial pores and gently broached the subject he had avoided for far too long: *I'm worried about us.*

What do you mean?

You hardly ever join me for prayer any more, he scented. *And this is the first time you've stepped away from the project in months. It seems that that's all you care about these days...*

In response, she released the bitter-wet scent of fresh Barzelian droppings: *Ember-Musk, beloved, this has nothing to do with my feelings for you.* Beneath the boiling waters Scent-of-Moss pressed her carapace closely against his. *This ship is the greatest discovery in history. To finally learn that we're not alone in the cosmos! To have the answers to so many questions so close at hand! Now isn't the time for me to be diverted by prayer.*

Wife, how can you scent such a thing...?

Prayer didn't lead to the discovery of the alien ship in orbit last year. Prayer didn't help me discover this encrypted holomessage.

Well I *prayed for it, wife,* Ember-Musk scented. *I prayed for a breakthrough, and it happened.*

She released a thick, skeptical fog: *You can't rely on faith alone to understand the universe, my husband.*

I never scented that. If there's one thing the Prophecies teach us, Ember-Musk sprayed, *it's that every successful union requires... balance. This is why the wife's focus is naturalistic while the husband's is supernaturalistic.* He placed his fore-arms on her shoulders. *Please, let me be a good husband. Don't shut me out.*

They scented nothing for a long while. A child ran past their bathing crater in the direction of the community caverns.

Do you think the alien might be a child? Scent-of-Moss misted. *It has no exoskeleton...*

Ember-Musk reached for the bucket of rancicus he had prepared, Scent-of-Moss's favorite, and dunked a brush into it.

Enough about the alien. Let's eat, he misted. He slathered a thick layer of food across her face, neck and shoulders. Her pores flared and she ingurgitated heartily.

Blue lightning flashed across the sky. More children skittered into the caverns as razor-sharp hail began to fall. He and Scent-of-Moss lifted their arms out of the waters, exposing them to the vibrating hail, which scraped their crystal protrusions and created intricate patterns in them. A hail-shard occasionally found smooth skin and embedded itself, starting the formation of a new crystal.

As they lay there, Ember-Musk smelled a cloud of contentment enveloping them for the first time in months. He fervently wished that this moment would last forever, that nothing would ever change between him and his beloved. But just as he finished this thought, he sniffed a faint trace of restlessness emanating from Scent-of-Moss, whose thoughts no doubt had turned once again to the mystery of the messages within messages being transmitted by the alien vessel.

Ember-Musk left the worship-stones on the basalt shelves and decided to go see Scent-of-Moss in the fore-cavern. She was supposed to have joined him for a prayer session an hour earlier. He had coated himself with a new layer of red paint and felt refreshed and beautiful.

When he entered the work-cavern, he observed her books and metal tools – the magnifiers, power cells, genetic analyzers and translation devices he couldn't recognize – strewn about.

Scent-of-Moss stared motionless at the alien's holoimage. When she sensed his approach, rows of pores on her shoulders opened and a fog of frustration filled the air.

He decided not to nag about the missed prayer session.

Scent-of-Moss then activated a second projector and the holoimage of Tang-of-Mint, the Lead Naturalist, appeared. Tang-of-Mint was responsible for collecting and synthesizing each deciphering duo's findings, and he filed regular progress reports all decipherers could access. The projector's circular base spun slowly – first left, then right, then left again – spraying a mélange of highly technical odors Ember-Musk had trouble following.

After Scent-of-Moss finished sniffing the report, she turned to him. *There's been no progress deciphering the holomessage, but other teams have made some headway with the written text in the primary transmission,* she misted. *They've also analyzed the alien's movements and theorize that instead of an exoskeleton it has an* internal *frame beneath its rubbery covering.*

Ember-Musk jetted an acrid puff of doubt. *Internal? That defeats the purpose of an exoskeleton.*

The varying coloration of its face also suggests that the alien has a circulatory system like ours, though it's difficult to tell where the pump is located, Scent-of-Moss scented.

Ember-Musk released the scent of a sandy shore at high tide.

It's so smooth and delicate, she sprayed.

He gently scraped her rear-arms to relax her.

It's perfectly symmetrical, she continued. *Just like us, only it has a single arm on each side rather than two. And only one eye. No corresponding one exists on the right side of the face.*

The single eye is certainly unusual, Ember-Musk scented. *What about those thin transparent tubes it sometimes attaches to its arms?*

The tubes may be decorative, like the fabrics in which they sheathe themselves, Scent-of-Moss answered.

Ember-Musk reached out and gently moved his right fore-hand through the holoimage, tracing the outline of the alien's diminutive, almost vestigial, snout. He imagined how such a soft, fleshy being might feel. Shuddering, he pulled his fore-hand away and rested it on the projector base.

Scent-of-Moss, he scented. *The projector is... vibrating. Is it damaged?*

No, this appears to be a defect with the transmission itself. I detected it a few days ago, but haven't been able to clear it up. For all their technological achievements, the aliens aren't infallible apparently.

Scent-of-Moss turned the projector's dial and another message entry began. The alien had changed the colors of its peculiar fabrics, but otherwise stood there the same as always, scentless, silent.

[HOLO-SEG 11 of 15 – Shiptime 1:24:35 P.M./11-19-2251]
The stalemate dissolved as the ranks of the Reviled grew exponentially. While the Fissure continued to spew them out, our casualties increased to the tens of millions and continued rising.

I've seen it firsthand. I've seen up close the way the enemy kills. I've seen them...

Dear God, help me forget, help me forget...

Are you certain that its motions don't convey a message, wife? See how it covers its facial cavity with its hand and lowers its head? Ember-Musk misted.

It's beyond horrible, beyond monstrous. Their sharp, black tongues pierce the jugular. The victim alternates between gagging and shrieking, while...

Carla, oh, Carla...

Yes, its shoulders also shudder during this section, Ember-musk, Scent-of-Moss misted.

The transmission now seems to be operating normally. The projector has stopped shaking, Ember-Musk sprayed, his hand on the circular base. *No, wait, it's begun vibrating again...*

141

Damn them! Damn their twisted smiles! Monsters, aliens, demons, what difference does it make? In the end, they destroyed my life, they obliterated our civilization! And for what purpose?

What were they *feeling*?

What were they *thinking*?

Breathe. Breathe.

I've got to get a hold of myself. I have to focus. I have to finish. My personal history is irrelevant. My life is irrelevant. What matters is the larger picture.

Six domed cities fell when the Reviled somehow secured an invitation from soldiers posted near the entrances. Since the creatures didn't speak, many people speculated that the Reviled had the ability to mesmerize human beings over short distances, to manipulate them into extending invitations or otherwise doing their bidding. I don't believe this. Not when there was a simpler explanation. You see, we learned through deadly trial and error that simply verbalizing a welcome wasn't sufficient. To be effective, the invitation had to be sincere, heartfelt. And despite all that we suffered, everything we'd lost, there would always be some person who harbored a secret curiosity to see the Reviled, to try to communicate with them. It's part of our nature, I suppose. It shouldn't have surprised us that a trucker or some soldier, one out of thousands stationed at a city entrance, might succumb to the temptation to invite them in.

I have to confess, of all the characteristics of the Reviled, this matter of the invitation perplexed us most of all. Why would a predator stop in its tracks to ask for its prey's permission? The common belief among my people was that the Reviled were demons, cursed by God to roam the universe forever seeking the consent of potential victims who would never give it. Humanity, however, just couldn't resist the temptation of evil.

I don't believe in curses. I don't believe in demons. But I do believe in God, just not a cruel God who stacks the decks against us and lays traps for us that we can't overcome. I believe in a God who's created a universe with rules, and that He's blessed us with an understanding of the scientific method that allows us to make sense of that universe.

So why then do the Reviled need an invitation? I don't believe the answer to that question can be found in the hard sciences. Nothing *physical* prevents them from entering. No, I'm convinced it has sociological, psychological origins in their alien culture. It must be based on some deep-rooted ritual, some rigid societal stigma, something so outside our experience that it seems nonsensical at first blush, but really isn't. We simply lack the *context* to understand

Once the Reviled secured invitations, they stormed the city entrances. But they didn't get far under the constant glare of the sun simulators, which kept them at bay.

Other cities responded by taking the preventative measure of stationing teams consisting solely of warbots – immune to temptation, immune to curiosity and betrayal – near every point of entrance and egress.

In the decade that followed, while chaos erupted around us, our team continued the construction of *The Deliverance*. In the meantime, another stalemate of sorts was reached. Humanity relegated itself to fifty-eight slowly expanding domed cities, while the Reviled inherited the rest of the physical world: the mountains, the deserts, the oceans. Earth's remaining animal population thrived, except for chimpanzees, gorillas and other Great Apes, which were reportedly exterminated. From their behavior, it was clear that the Reviled had their eyes set only on higher forms of life as their source of sustenance. Many wondered about dolphins and whales, whether the Reviled had ventured into the ocean's depths to annihilate them too. This confirmed the theory that it wasn't blood *per se* that they lusted after, but the lifeblood of sentient beings.

During the misguided armistice attempt of the 2240's, we actually manufactured artificial blood to supply to them. Maybe they were just hungry, some had reasoned. But the bags of blood remained untouched, and negotiating with an implacable, silent foe proved impossible.

Ember-Musk, I believe that these aliens normally have two eyes. Judging from the discolored tissue on the right side of its face where the second eye should be, I think it may be injured, Scent-of-Moss misted.

Wife, these vibrations the projector base generates... Have you noticed that they seem to coincide with the pulsing of its facial cavity? Did you ever consider...?

What?

Did you ever consider that it might not be a malfunction? Perhaps this tingling is itself *a form of communication.*

The pores on Scent-of-Moss's shoulders opened wide and the thick, inspired aroma of moist, mint-fresh lichen permeated the work-cavern.

Ember-Musk turned the dial again. They both leaned forward and placed their open hands directly on the projector-base to better feel the vibrations.

[HOLO-SEG 12 of 15 – Shiptime 1:24:35 P.M./11-20-2251]

Our planes rained napalm bombs on their approaching masses outside the city perimeter. But the Reviled countered by digging bunkers in which they took cover and waited for the fires to subside; carbon monoxide from the raging chemical fires had no effect on them. A section of one city's dome came down in flames when thousands of the Reviled hurled their blazing bodies at the structure.

And still their numbers continued to increase.

As we grew more and more desperate, we tried every conceivable strategy to destroy them. Biologists designed a deadly strain of super-leukemia that killed in a matter of days and implanted the cancer cells in our frontline soldiers. We exterminated thousands of the creatures in this manner, for the Reviled couldn't resist feeding on them – even when it surely must have become obvious the soldiers were poisoned. But ultimately, the most effective way to kill them required us to sacrifice our own people – an unacceptable approach given the sheer number of enemy forces that continued to flood through the Fissure.

Eventually, we developed an airborne virus that targeted white blood cells – since they consumed blood, we reasoned, maybe this would affect them. We loaded the virus onto bombs that we dropped in the vicinity of their bunkers. The city's entrances had to be bio-sealed to protect the general population, but we exterminated hundreds of thousands of the Reviled in this manner. Countless motes of fine, golden dust scattered in the wind.

In response, the Reviled launched their most ruthless counteroffensive of all.

Ember-Musk entered the fore-cavern and Scent-of-Moss immediately emitted the excited stink of burning sap-scum: *Your hunch was right, Ember-Musk! There's no question, the pattern of vibrations is a sophisticated form of communication. The opening and closing of the large orifice below its snout corresponds with the patterns, suggesting that part of the alien's internal anatomy allows it to generate the vibrations! I've informed Tang-of-Mint and he's notified the other teams. We've got everyone working on analyzing these patterns...*

How is such a thing possible? Ember-Musk scented. *Wouldn't its world's natural seismic and weather activity mask this type of communication?*

Perhaps they evolved on a planet less geologically active than ours, Scent-of-Moss answered. *One where it might be feasible to utilize such a complex and tenuous form of communication.*

True, it has no center leg to stabilize itself. But still, how would they communicate over even modest distances?

In the same way we have pores, they must have biological vibration detectors, Ember-Musk! It's the only thing that makes sense.

He had never breathed such excitement from Scent-of-Moss

before. Behind her, the image of the inscrutable one-eyed alien continued flaring its face-cavity, gesticulating wildly.

[**HOLO-SEG 13 of 15** – Shiptime 9:03:22 A.M./11-22-2251]
While we frantically made final preparations to board *The Deliverance* for liftoff, the reports from other cities came streaming in. The Reviled had uncovered the early programming designs for the warbots in laboratories and research facilities outside of the domed cities. Within weeks, they had developed their own warbot prototype and launched a coordinated assault against forty of the fifty-eight domed cities. Their warbots, requiring no invitation to barrel through the city perimeter, squared off against our own AI devices and eventually, in the resulting pandemonium, soldiers were dragged off and somehow compelled to extend invitations. Clad in black, high-tech skinsuits and goggles that shielded them from the sun simulators, the Reviled stormed the cities like giant mutant rats, day and night, with no letup.

How can I possibly convey to you the utter turmoil, the total panic in the air...?

Once they'd destroyed the sun-simulators, the dark, enclosed cities served as perfect holding pens for their — there's no other word for it — livestock. They reveled in the enclosed quarters, silently gorging themselves.

One by one the cities fell until eventually, just a few days prior to *The Deliverance*'s scheduled liftoff from New Houston, the warbots of the Reviled crashed through the frontline defenses. Within hours, we were defeated.

How I wish the story ended there.

Why? Why did you forsake us, God? Why did you abandon us to their depravities? Didn't you hear our prayers? Were we so utterly unworthy?

Wife? Ember-Musk scented. He stepped into the fore-cavern to deliver the news.

It's slow going, Scent-of-Moss misted absentmindedly as she gazed intently at the holoimage, *but I've managed to enhance the vibrations. Others have started to break down tiny bits of information.*

Wife, he scented, *a message came through from Tang-of-Mint a few moments ago. The Council has called another meeting.* He stepped between her and the holoimage and finally got her attention. *One of the other deciphering teams...* he scented. *They've decoded the primary transmission.*

When they entered the yawning Grand Glacial Cavern, the sweet-sour tang of lingering curiosity swirled in the air. The decipherers who had decoded the primary transmission had not yet arrived.

Ember-Musk and Scent-of-Moss took their place with the other deciphering duos on the side benches while the Elders sat at the roundtable, softly scenting to one another.

Scent-of-Moss removed her portable projector from its carrying case. A familiar naturalist whose scent-signature escaped Ember-Musk sat next to them. She reeked of moldy cactus-needles: *Congratulations on your discovery, Scent-of-Moss, Ember-Musk. Vibrational communications! Who could have conceived such a thing might be possible?*

The universe is vast and mysterious, Ember-Musk replied.

I just wish that we were closer to unlocking the secrets of this hologram, Scent-of-Moss misted.

Perhaps the textual transmission will shed light on the subject, the naturalist responded.

Scent-of-Moss turned the projector's dial and the holoimage – reduced in size so that it stood unobtrusively in the palm of her third fore-hand – commenced vibrating again.

[**HOLO-SEG 15 of 15** – Shiptime 9:03:22 A.M./11-26-2251]
My people believe that history is written by the victors.

I wonder what the Reviled will write about us, about the war. Not that we've ever seen them writing, mind you. In fact, we've never heard them *speak*. But they're unquestionably literate judging from their ability to use our medical and military records to their advantage.

Were we anything to them besides food? Did they mourn their own losses? Were they even capable of such emotions?

If you're listening to this, I need to tell you – whoever 'you' are – that the finest legacies of our civilization, our art, literature and technological achievements, still exist unblemished on our beautiful world if you dare to trace this ship's path back to its point of origin.

They've kept me here in my holding pen aboard this ship with a few dozen other survivors, engineers who'd been working on *The Deliverance*. They've fed us and extracted our blood through these intravenous tubes three times a day. The others are all dead now. I'm all that's left of humanity. It won't be long before I'm dead too, before the human species is finally extinct. The only silver lining is that for all their canniness, the Reviled have hunted their prey to extinction. At least that's the way it seems. Sometimes I wonder whether this might not be part of a larger plan they have. Could this be the way they operate, destroying species, going into an eon-long dormancy, then resurfacing when summoned again by a new intelligent species? Or maybe, just like humanity, which rendered so many species extinct, their urge to hunt and kill simply knows no rational bounds and they've committed suicide in the process. I pray it's the latter.

Before we left Earth, the Reviled downloaded diagrams of *The Deliverance* to the rest of their kind. I'm afraid that they may be constructing other ships, targeting the other habitable worlds we've detected, and that more ships will be following this one.

I'll be dead decades before this journey is completed. But if the legends are true, if the Reviled truly are immortal, they'll suffer horribly from hunger during the remaining years of this voyage. I doubt that they'll be able to live through the centuries-long trip through space. But if they do manage to survive, can you imagine how it will feel to know that kind of boundless, ravenous hunger, and to be unable to die...?

They *deserve* to suffer.

At least they won't be able to use the ship's stasis-pods to stay alive. We managed to damage them during that final day of battle. Strangely, sometimes from my cell I'll spot one of the Reviled in a distant corridor lying down in a pod anyway. Perhaps it's just bored. Though sometimes – I try not to think this way, but sometimes I can't help it – I wonder whether it's perhaps because of the pods' coffin shape. Who knows what the goddamned fiends are thinking? They've turned off almost all of the ship's lights and seem to bask in the blackness of space.

In all the years I've been here, I've only been approached once by one of them. It stood in front of my cell, its white ghoulish face staring hard at me through the plexiglass. I fought through the nausea and stared right back. Maybe I'm giving myself too much credit, but I'm convinced it was trying to communicate with me. That it was trying to tell me something through some alien sense I was incapable of registering, but that it just couldn't find a way to bridge the enormous gulf that exists between us.

I'm proud to say we never stopped fighting. What they don't know is that I've been able to hack into *The Deliverance*'s communications systems from the routers behind a wall-panel in this room. That I've managed to hide humanity's epitaph, *this warning*, in the gaps of this ship's transmission signal – should this ship ever, in fact, send a message.

I pray that I'm right about their mortality, that if this ship reaches its final destination all you will discover is human skeletal remains and thousands of piles of fine dust. But I fear... Oh, what I fear.

Scent-of-Moss and Ember-Musk kept the projector running, but turned their attention to the Council.

The decipherers who had decoded the text of the primary

transmission – a tall naturalist and her scarlet-hued betrothed – stood at the center of the room. A sunbeam streamed down on them through the skylight. All scents dissipated, awaiting the news.

We made a major breakthrough with the primary transmission yesterday, she misted. *That's when we discovered that, like the holoimage, the text too is accompanied by vibrations. In fact, the bulk of the data consists of this stream of pulses. Unlike the hologram's vibrations, however, which originate from the alien's anatomy, these appear to be computer-generated. By using certain of the rudimentary vibrations of the hologram as a deciphering key, we were able to make sense of a few patterns in the primary transmission,* the tall naturalist continued. *In fact, once decoded, we could barely believe the message's simplicity.*

Quizzical, pungent scents now permeated the chamber.

The message is: 'Invite us.'

An Elder sprayed a cactus-scented mist: *But we've been transmitting the sweet-scents for months now.*

Clearly, they haven't understood.

So all this time they've waited, another Elder scented. *After traveling light years through space for who knows how long, they've waited patiently in orbit for us to transmit the sweet-scents in their language. Remarkable.*

Who can explain the strangeness of the alien mind? the naturalist responded. *Perhaps it doesn't want its actions to be mistaken as hostile. It's asking us to transmit an* explicit *invitation along with landing coordinates.*

Scent-of-Moss misted softly to Ember-Musk: *We should at least decipher the vibrations accompanying the alien holoimage first. It would be prudent to examine all of the evidence before deciding on our course of action.*

Scent-of-Moss began to stand up and Ember-Musk pulled her down. *Why must you always obsess about 'evidence,' wife? Why – just for once in your life – can't you simply... trust in the Gods' plan for us?*

Ember-Musk, I can't explain it, but something's not right.

Scent-of-Moss... he pleaded.

They were interrupted when the tall decipherer's supernaturalist betrothed stood and released a cleansing mist that dissipated the crowd's scents. He then sprayed: *There's an additional request: the transmission asks that our invitation be earnest and heartfelt. We've been asked to* pray *for the aliens to join us.*

The Presiding Elder lifted his red-painted visage to the sky and released a sweet, sweet vapor of joy: *Ah, so the visitors believe in prayer! They've asked for both a transmitted invitation* and *a prayer, a combination of naturalism and supernaturalism.*

A zephyr of the sulfur-tinged sea breeze at daybreak blew through the Chamber.

Scent-of-Moss stared wide-eyed at Ember-Musk as she joined the others in scenting her own profound wonder. Slowly, she reached out with her rear-arms and embraced his fore-arms. And for the first time in a long year, Ember-Musk smelled their individual scents, warm ash and cool greenmint, wafting and swirling and intermingling into a new aroma he could only describe as the quintessence of harmony.

[**HOLO-SEG 1 of 15** – Shiptime 9:05:01/11-1-2251]
DANGER! BEWARE!

This is a warning. I repeat: this is a warning. My name is Antonio Valencia Astacio and I am the last human alive. If you're receiving a transmission from this ship, you are in terrible, terrible danger. The creatures aboard this ship have ruthlessly exterminated my people.

They're relentless. Unstoppable. And they *learn.*

If you're listening to this message, and this ship is already orbiting your world, it means that – God help you! – death and destruction are lurking at your doorstop.

But it's not too late! Simply turn them away. Deny them entrance and they'll be powerless to act.

Listen to me! Before I begin my story, before I tell you about our final days on Earth, about the Fissure, about how all of this came to pass, I beg of you, don't welc –

Ember-Musk turned off the projector as the Council called for a decision. Within minutes, they voted unanimously to transmit the translated *sweet-scents*, inviting the strangers to join them.

The thought that his people had finally solved the riddle of the primary transmission filled him with pride. He wasn't in the least surprised that both naturalism and supernaturalism had played a part. He had never doubted that both worldviews, working in tandem, were necessary to better understand the universe, as the Prophecies had foretold.

As a team of naturalists, including Scent-of-Moss, transmitted the landing coordinates, the rest of them prayed. And within a matter of hours, the ship's colossal shadow fell across the continent, obstructing the light that poured through the Chamber's skylight.

When the heralds come, Ember-Musk thought, at the first scent of their arrival we'll understand our role in this strange, vast universe. At last we'll have our answers.

A tangy-scented mist of joy filled the air, a rapturous joy borne of wonder and curiosity and faith.

Bargonns Can Swizzle

Maddy2006:   Hello, ZL. I see u're on time as usual. I have big news.

ZL23 %6:   Hello, Maddy! I've missed you. Tell me, did you make your pet acquisition?

Maddy2006:   Yep, I did it. You are now chatting with an official kitten owner.

ZL23 %6:   "Kitten"?

Maddy2006:   Recently born. A *baby* cat.

ZL23 %6:   Is it able to perambulate on its own?

Maddy2006:   Of course. It's at my feet right now playing while I'm typing (clawing my shoelaces actually).

ZL23 %6:   How many appendages does it have?

Maddy2006:   Four legs, silly. And a tail too.

ZL23 %6:   Prehensile?

Maddy2006:   LOL. No! ZL, haven't you ever seen a picture of a cat?

ZL23 %6:   I've never much cared for prehistoric zoology, Maddy. And the only biology data that survived the solar storms of 3913 relates to homosapiens and their extinct simian cousins.

Maddy2006:   Right. The solar storms of 3913 again. The reason y u can't tell me who's going to win this year's SUper Bowl. Or next week's Lotto. Or anything about my own future. Verrrrry convenient.

ZL23 %6:   What do you mean by "Super Bowl" and "Lotto"?

Maddy2006:   Never mind. Aren't there ANY animals in the future, ZL?

ZL23 %6:   Do bacteria count?

Maddy2006:   No, bacteria do not count.

ZL23 %6:   We do have random perjins popping up on the picobanks.

Maddy2006:   ???

ZL23 %6:   I'm sorry. It's difficult to put it into Ancient English. Perjins, charged lower life-form particles, will sometimes randomly appear in our synaptic vacuum fields. I enjoy their presence. They're not sentient, but there's something endearing about their neutral-charge buzzing, the way they trail in my electron wake.

Maddy2006:   I think I understand. Theres something comforting about the way this kitten follows me around. It feels good to have the company. Especially since getting laid off.

ZL23 %6:   Is this kitten a randomly appearing construct?

Maddy2006:   Hardly. It was born a month-and-a-half ago. It's like me. Biologically produced.

ZL23 %6:   How is it biologically produced?

Maddy2006:   Oh no you dont! Just when i convince myself that u're not an internet perv, you veer towards the birds and the bees!

ZL23 %6:   I don't understand your "birds and bees" reference, Maddy. But data on biological procreation is available to me in the Archives.

Maddy2006:   Whew!

ZL23 %6:   I was only wondering whether it reproduced sexually or through self-replication. But what also interest me are the post-birth familial social structures of your time. As you've described them, they're fascinatingly complex.

Maddy2006:   This one's pretty simple actually. The kitten was sexually produced, born in a litter. (That means there were multiple births, six of them in this case.) When old enough to survive on their own, the kittens were sold.

ZL23 %6:   That sounds cruel, Maddy. Did the parents grieve being separated from their offspring?

Maddy2006:   Well, the father was nowhere to be found. And the mother? Not for 2 long. At least i don't think so. Remember, cats are not sentient. (Though I fervently believe they hold grudges. Remind me to tell you, btw, the terrible tale of my neighbor's cat, Poochie.)

ZL23 %6:   The cat social structure bears some resemblance to your own, Maddy.

Maddy2006:   Hmm... my disfunctionl family's been called many things, ZL, but thats a 1st.

ZL23 %6:   You never met your father. And you were biologically produced as part of a litter that is now separated from its mother.

Maddy2006:   Key differences though. My brother and i were not born at the same time. He had a 4 year head-start. And it took him 18 years, not 6 weeks, to go off on his own.

ZL23 %6:   You still interact with your brother?

Maddy2006:   He left Albuquerque. Moved to San Francisco. Has a wife and 2 kids. Calls me every couple of years for a loan. There'll be no more loans from me. At least not 'til I get back to work.

ZL23 %6:   Why did you never leave Albuquerque, Maddy?

Maddy2006:   My mom got sick. Needed me to take care of her. And the community college had a good library studies program. It was an easy decision to stay under the circumstances. So here I am. My job at the library eliminated by budget cuts. Unemployment checks still coming in. Same house, same community. It's a nice place. Dont feel sorry for me.

ZL23 %6:   And your mother?

Maddy2006:   She hung on thru 10 years of MS. Died last year. I miss her a lot. Miss having someone 2 talk 2. I guess that's why i've enjoyed chatting with u so much these last few weeks.

ZL23 %6:   I've enjoyed it too, Maddy.

ZL23 %6:   Maddy, have you ever considered reproducing?

Maddy2006:   LOL! That's a bit personal, mister.

Maddy2006:   But I'll answer.

Maddy2006:   I've just about reconciled myself to the fact it's not going to happen. i wouldn't want to raise a child on my own. And my biological alarm clock has just about gone off. At best, I've pushed the snooze button.

ZL23 %6:   I don't understand your last two sentences.

Maddy2006:   What about your family, ZL? Your parents? Your siblings? Enough mystery! You realize don't you that I could save these IM chats, publish them, reveal them to the world, and no one would believe a single word.

ZL23 %6:   Although my parents' signatures still flicker in the picostream, our paths haven't crossed in decades. And no one has siblings any more.

Maddy2006:   You know, u struck me as an only child.

Maddy2006:   How about you, ZL? Do you want children?

ZL23 %6:   Perhaps, Maddy. But it's not my decision to make.

Maddy2006:   Now I'm intrigued. Why is it out of your hands? How exactly ARE babies conceived in the future?

ZL23 %6:   So now who's the "internet perv"?

Maddy2006:   LOL! So you know what that means? Are you telling me that internet pervs have survived into the 43rd century?

ZL23 %6:   You defined the term for me during one of our earlier chats, Maddy. Getting back to your question, procreation as you know it became obsolete a very, very long time ago. The new techniques may be difficult for you to grasp.

Maddy2006:   Try me.

Maddy2006:   ZL?

Maddy2006:   ZL?

Maddy2006:   Hellllllllloooooooooo.

ZL23 %6:   I was just researching the correct terminology.

Maddy2006:   Im used to those instantaneous responses of yours. What's the matter? No ready-typed responses u can cut and paste for that last question?

ZL23 %6:   I don't know what you mean, Maddy.

ZL23 %6:   I was conceived as follows: A healthy embryo was harvested from genetic material left behind by two individuals chosen to be my parents.

Maddy2006:   Left behind?

ZL23 %6:   Except for a few chosen administrators, by the age of 16, all humans celebrate adulthood by shedding their physical forms and uploading themselves into the picostream. The download portal is opened and we step through, leaving behind our flesh containers, rife with genetic material for the mechanized brooders to handle. Here, we zirgle out our existences until our charges flicker-fade. If you are chosen to bear offspring, the breeding units handle the procreative process. That decision is made by the master geneticists.

Maddy2006:   I see. That's not so difficult to grasp. ZL, y does your charge fade? Can't u just "recharge" yourself?

ZL23 %6:   Maddy! One can never recharge and maintain one's essence! Life can be recharged, not personalities! We're not designed to be immortal, after all. Approximately four centuries after upload, one's charge inevitably flickers and fades.

Maddy2006:   But why abandon your human body, especially so young?

ZL23 %6:   The solar storms of 3913.

Maddy2006:   Again with the solar storms?

ZL23 %6:   Most of the Earth was incinerated. All of humanity populates a habitable area beneath a protective radiation-sphere no larger than the size of your Albuquerque. If not for the picostream, this planet couldn't sustain the trillions of beings that it does.

Maddy2006:   What???? The Earth was incinerated? (You never mentioned *that* bit of info before!)

ZL23 %6:   My chat time has almost expired, Maddy. Do you want to ask me Today's Question?

Maddy2006:   Let's see, let's see. We've already covered animals, siblings and internet pervs. Okay. Got it. Today's Question: Is there chocolate ice cream in the future?

ZL23 %6:   I don't think so, Maddy.

Maddy2006:   It's a horrible place, the future.

ZL23 %6:   We'll pick up again tomorrow. Goodbye!

<u>Maddy2006</u>:   Wait a sec.
<u>ZL23_%6 has signed off.</u>

<u>ZL23_%6</u>:   Hello, Maddy.
<u>Maddy2006</u>:   ZL!!!! Where've you been the last 2 days? I've missed you!
<u>ZL23_%6</u>:   I'm so sorry. I've missed you too, Maddy.
<u>Maddy2006</u>:   What happened?
<u>ZL23_%6</u>:   It's a long story, more complicated than you can ever imagine.
<u>Maddy2006</u>:   I don't know... I have a pretty open mind. And a wiiiiiild imagination. (Though u've got me beat hands down.) Tell me.
<u>ZL23_%6</u>:   I have something to confess to you.
<u>Maddy2006</u>:   Finally!
<u>Maddy2006</u>:   Yeeeeeees?
<u>ZL23_%6</u>:   I omitted something during our prior communications. The truth is, I'm not supposed to be chatting with you. Intertemporal communications are strictly forbidden.
<u>Maddy2006</u>:   And y exactly?
<u>ZL23_%6</u>:   The chronal pathways are dangerous, not so much to the traveler but to the potentialities. Particons rupture. Betacons burst. There are rules in place. Laws even. But sometimes, Maddy, sometimes Bargonns can swizzle. And I wouldn't have done it intentionally. It was an accident, I assure you. I was alone one day. Lost in thought. Asking myself some of the questions that you've often asked yourself. Why am I here? Is this all there is? What is the meaning of my existence? Am I destined to sail the picostream alone? Skimming the pathways, I veered left off of the baryons of Harkon onto a gluon particle stream, positively charged, that carried me in its tide. And then I became submerged in a swirl of frizzle, nothing more than a puff of ether, really. When I accelerated out, leptons and other quanta firing past me, I bobbed in a streamway unlike any I'd ever seen before, that carried me into a pool of electrons with an ancient,

coppery charge. And then I thought to myself, "Where am I?" And you answered me, Maddy.

Maddy2006:   Whoa!!! I can never get used to how fast your responses come through, ZL. Lots to absorb there. I'm not sure I understand a lot of it.

Maddy2006:   Btw, what makes you think i ask myself those types of questions?

ZL23 %6:   After I processed your message that very first time, I surveyed the data in the surrounding covey, which included your daily recorded messages to yourself. I realized then that I had stumbled onto an outlawed chronal pathway. That I was communicating with a fleshed being from the past.

Maddy2006:   "Daily recorded messages"?

ZL23 %6:   Yes. The ones in which you describe your daily activities, your desires for the future.

Maddy2006:   Wait a second, r u telling me that you somehow hacked into my computer and read my journal?

ZL23 %6:   I must confess it was exciting to read your ideas. To realize that for all of the time that gulfs our existences, for all the differences in the worlds we inhabit, you think about things much the way I do, Maddy.

Maddy2006:   Look, I've been a good sport, but did u really hack into my computer and read my personal journal? Whats my middle name?

ZL23 %6:   Yes, although I don't know how you can call it "personal." It's right there in the stream for anyone to sample. Petunia. I don't understand why that name causes you so much agitation.

Maddy2006:   I dont know what game u're playing , ZL, but u've crossed the line.

ZL23 %6:   I apologize if I've violated some cultural norm of your era, Maddy. I assure you I won't do it again.

Maddy2006:   Damn right u won't.

ZL23 %6:   Maddy?

ZL23 %6:   Don't you want to ask me Today's Question?

Maddy2006 has signed off.

ZL23 %6:   Maddy, are you still angry with me?

ZL23 %6:   I know that you're receiving these messages.

ZL23 %6:   I am so sorry that I offended you. If I could take it back I would. But temporal flow mechanics won't permit me to travel back to the same point in time more than once.

ZL23 %6:   I too have felt the "hollowness of the soul" that you described in your journal. From the first day that I downloaded onto the picostream my singular particle stream flowed through narrow, winding ephemero-canals with the company of only humorless neutrino phantasms occasionally popping into and out of existence. Others who'd downloaded quickly clustered and became task-specific. But I just wandered, my channel-flow never truly optimized, looking for a task that suited me, for a charge that polarized my own. The day that I first communicated with you, Maddy, was the day that I first felt that charge.

ZL23 %6:   Please, Maddy. It hurts me to know that I've hurt you.

ZL23 %6:   I've just come to say goodbye.

Maddy2006:   Damn this software! I changed my personal options to specifically block you out. I clicked "No" to accepting your messages. How the hell r u coming through on my screen?

ZL23 %6:   Maddy! It makes my charge flicker to receive your message again. I'm ebbing!

Maddy2006:   I've been stewing the last couple days, ZL. You went too far.

ZL23 %6:   I didn't know, but I'm sorry.

Maddy2006:   I'm not sure I can trust you anymore.

ZL23 %6:   That may not matter. The chronal pathway that brings me here is being sealed off.

Maddy2006:   ????

ZL23 %6:   Tomorrow is the last day that we will ever again be able to communicate. The authorities have detected my travels to your time. The pathway will be dammed and I will probably be punished.

Maddy2006:   All right, all right, u dont have to be so dramatic.

Maddy2006:   I accept your apology. You don't have to sign off for good.

ZL23 %6:   If only I didn't. If only we could continue chatting forever.

Maddy2006:   You know whats scary, ZL? Sometimes i almost believe you. Are you really saying that we won't be able to chat any more?

ZL23 %6:   It will take them some time to erect the dam. We'll be able to chat one more time tomorrow, Maddy.

ZL23 %6:   I have something else I want to tell you.

Maddy2006:   Yes?

Maddy2006:   ZL?

ZL23 %6:   That I feel connected with you. That it brings incredible sadness to me to think that tomorrow will be our final goodbye.

Maddy2006:   I feel the same way, ZL.

ZL23 %6:   My chat-time is about to expire, Maddy. Do you want to ask me Today's Question?

Maddy2006:   Today's Question: ZL, is there love in the future?

ZL23 %6:   Yes, Maddy.

Maddy2006:   Tomorrow then. Good night, ZL.

ZL23 %6:   Until tomorrow, Maddy.

ZL23 %6:   Hello, Maddy. I have a proposal.

Maddy2006:   Hey there! What proposal?

ZL23 %6:   Come with me, Maddy.

Maddy2006:   Excuse me? You actually want to meet?

ZL23 %6:   Yes.

Maddy2006:   In person?

ZL23 %6:   Yes.

Maddy2006:   But I thought you were an electronic time traveler with no body and no phone number?

ZL23 %6:   I am.

Maddy2006:   r u serious about meeting?

ZL23 %6:   Yes.

ZL23 %6:   Maddy?

Maddy2006:   I guess this is the day I've dreaded.

ZL23 %6:   What do you mean, Maddy?

Maddy2006:   I don't know what u imagine I look like. In fact, it's sweet the way u've never even bothered to ask. I'm sure u're wondering.

ZL23 %6:   I hadn't thought about it.

Maddy2006:   Please. I'm willing to accept that you're a time-traveler from a barbecued future world with no animals or chocolate ice cream. But this i don't buy.

Maddy2006:   I may as well just get it all out in the open. I'm a big girl. Ive always been a bit Rubenesque. But since losing my job 6 months ago, I've put on some weight.

ZL23 %6:   Maddy, I've read your journal and you give this subject too much thought. Why would I care about your flesh?

Maddy2006:   That's very sweet, ZL. (I think.) I cant deny that I hoped that this could develop into something real. But it's only been three weeks. Do we really have anything in common? If Im to believe u, we come from entirely different cultures: I watch television, you run through a television *cord*.

ZL23 %6:   I don't understand your "television" reference, Maddy. But this is a serious matter. It's an important decision. An irreversible one. The connection I feel with you makes me ebb and sparkle. I want to skip across an electron's orbit with you. I want to squirgle over a cascading dataflow with you, to feel our charges crackling, complementing each other, clustering forever in the datastream interstices.

Maddy2006:   Wow. You're serious. That u could feel this way after just 3 weeks...

ZL23 %6:   I have another confession to make, Maddy.

Maddy2006:   Uh-oh.

ZL23 %6:   Traveling through the chronal pathways can

sometimes result in unusual subjective time distortions.

Maddy2006:   What does that mean?

ZL23 %6:   For every one of your days that has passed, one year of my time has elapsed. What for you has been three weeks has for me been over 21 years. I've been chatting with you once a year for the past 21 years, Maddy. And it's the one day of the year that makes the rest of the days worth living. Let's not be lonely anymore, Maddy.

Maddy2006:   That's mind-blowing, ZL.

ZL23 %6:   Maddy? Will you come?

ZL23 %6:   Maddy?

ZL23 %6:   Maddy? Are you still there?

Maddy2006:   Okay.

ZL23 %6:   Really?

Maddy2006:   Yes, I'll go with you.

ZL23 %6:   So you believe me, Maddy? You believe everything I've told you?

Maddy2006:   Actually, I'm still not sure I believe any of it. But I want to, ZL.

ZL23 %6:   It will require you to give up your physical body. To upload yourself into the picostream.

Maddy2006:   There's nothing here for me. And trust me, if I could dump this body, I would.

ZL23 %6:   I'll be able to open up a portal in spacetime for just a few of your seconds. It will appear behind you as a large, bright circular threshold. Simply step through it and your brain's synaptic patterns will be downloaded. Your flesh husk will remain behind. And we will be together. But you need to be certain, Maddy. There's no going back.

Maddy2006:   What will I do with Whitey?

ZL23 %6:   Whitey?

Maddy2006:   My cat. I can't just leave him.

ZL23 %6:   Bring him with you. Simply hold him in your arms when you walk through the portal. He will download as an attachment.

Maddy2006:   You've got an answer for everything.

ZL23_%6:   You're certain, Maddy?

Maddy2006:   If u can open up a portal for me, I'll walk through it.

ZL23_%6:   Very well. It will only be open for a few seconds, so you must walk through it quickly. Do you have Whitey in your arms?

Maddy2006:   He's within scoopable distance right at my feet.

ZL23_%6:   Okay. The portal is opened.

ZL23_%6:   Maddy?

ZL23_%6:   Maddy?

Maddy2006:   I'm scared to turn around, ZL.

ZL23_%6:   Why?

Maddy2006:   I'm afraid that if I do, it'll finally prove it.

ZL23_%6:   Prove what?

Maddy2006:   That this has all been a cruel hoax.

ZL23_%6:   Turn around, Maddy.

ZL23_%6 has signed off.

Rewind, Replay

He hits 'replay'.

Wynn glided up through the warm seawater, cheeks puffed, eyes squinting at the soft rays of sunlight that struck the surface and dispersed in infinite directions. He burst through a wave, gulped a lungful of air, and tossed his head back, shaking the hair out of his face.

Shelly appeared a moment later, trying to giggle and gasp for air simultaneously.

"Cheater!" she squealed, splashing toward him.

"Who? *Me?*"

"You might've gotten a teeny, tiny bit of a head-start?" Shelly grinned and treaded closer to him. Sunlight sparkled off the short, bleached-white hair that hugged the sides of her round face.

"Sour grapes? And here I thought you were a classy chick!"

"I'll show you class," she said, wrapping her arms around him and kissing him sloppily while Wynn paddled frantically to keep them afloat.

He hits 'rewind', then 'replay'.

"I'll show you class," she said, wrapping her arms around him and kissing him sloppily while Wynn paddled frantically to keep them afloat.

"The win-nah! Wynn by a nose!" Bernie announced from aboard the yawl in a pseudo-sportscaster voice. The bearded old man hung over the side of the ship, applauding, his smile

165

elongating the jagged, pink scar that ran from his nose to his left ear.

"Bullshit!" Shelly shrieked.

Wynn tried to cover her mouth with his hand. "Hey! We agreed on Bernie as our impartial judge." He had her firmly gagged, containing her giggle. "Didn't we." He pushed her head up and down, forcing a nod.

Her laugh broke free as they swam over to the ship's ladder. She climbed ahead of him and he smacked her bottom every other step, milking the giggle.

As he watches them towel off he can almost feel the cool, salt-tinged ocean breeze against his skin again.

Wynn swallowed his antibiotics and stepped beneath the on-deck shower, rinsing off his wetsuit.

"We've got a hit!" Bernie hollered from the bow.

"What?"

"Telemetry shows marine life. ShipNav is moving us toward it!"

The power sails retracted and the silent motors geared up, causing the boat to lurch forward, sending Wynn and Shelly stumbling against the side railings.

His heart skips.

"One more dive, Wynn?"

"Forget it. I've already detoxed." He held up the bottle of pills and shook it.

"I understand," she said with a wink. "At this speed a belly flop would hurt." Shelly took off her sunglasses and handed them to him with a playful 'what-a-wimp' smirk. The ship coasted at a slow, steady clip as she leaped over the side, disappearing with a small splash into the glistening turquoise-tinged waters.

"Hey! What are you doing?" Bernie killed the motors. "What about the marine life?"

The waves from the splash waned, the waters calmed.

Silence followed.

"Shelly?" Wynn leaned over the side, his brow creased. "Shelly?"

"Whoo-hoo!" she howled, erupting from beneath the waves. "Bernie! Score, please."

"Nine point seven!"

He hits 'rewind' and 'replay'.

"Whoo-hoo!" she howled, erupting from beneath the waves. "Bernie! Score, please."

He hits the red 'shunt' button.

"Nine point five!"

He presses 'rewind', 'replay' and 'shunt'.

"Nine point eight!"

Rewind, replay, shunt.

"A perfect ten, Shelly!"

"Can you beat that, Wynny?" she sputtered.

A pause followed and –

The gentle rap on the bedroom door startles him.

Consuelo's silhouette hovers at the doorway, the hallway light behind her momentarily blinding him.

"The Shunter? Again? Wynn, this is beyond unhealthy. You can't go on like this." She holds a cupcake in her hand. A lit birthday candle impales the white frosting, leaning perilously to the left. "It's a beautiful day. Let's have a picnic on the beach, get a little sun..."

"Go for a 'walk'?" He whirls his wheelchair around to face her. "While you push me around like an infant in a carriage?"

"Push yourself. The floater is recharged."

He pauses for an instant, surprised to find himself actually considering her offer, then hears himself say, "Not interested." They've repeated this exchange far too many times since he had the Shunter installed in his bedroom three months ago. By now, his answer has become part of a tired script they both feel compelled to follow.

Consuelo sets the cupcake down on the nightstand. "Look, it's gorgeous out there!" She pulls open the drapes, unveiling a clear, aquamarine sky above the Oregon shoreline. Sunlight streams in. "A change in scenery will do wonders for your mood, I promise." She can never quite seem to grasp, he notes, that her unrelenting perkiness does nothing for his disposition.

"Get out."

"It's a special day, Wynn. C'mon, let's celebrate," she says, smiling impishly.

He picks up a crystal paperweight, the one she's gotten him for his twenty-eighth birthday, and holds it over his head. He imagines himself hurling it against the wall, smashing it to bits.

The smile momentarily freezes on Consuelo's face before evaporating. "Wynn!" She walks over to him and holds out her hand.

He slowly lowers his arm and places the paperweight in her palm.

"You know," she says softly, "you can't just hit 'rewind' and unbreak things."

Shame and anger and, above all, a sense of impotence swamps over him. He clamps his jaw shut and faces the wallscreen.

"Fine then," she sighs. "Have it your way."

As the door shuts behind him, he rolls over to the cupcake with the lit birthday candle. "Make a wish, Wynn," he whispers to himself—as if wishing for something ever made a rat's ass of difference. He blows out the candle and flings the cupcake into the wastebasket.

After drawing the curtains, he tightens the Najarian

Headband around his temples. Clutching the copper control sphere, he punches in the date again with his thumb, the date from two summers ago: July 19, 2079, 2:04 p.m. The Shunter kick-starts. Trillions of tachyons swarm over billions of firing neurons, accessing his actual past and, more importantly, his what-ifs, his maybe-worlds.

Images flicker on the screen. His lifethreads unspool.

"Bernie! Score, please."

"Nine point seven."

"Can you beat that, Wynny?" she sputtered.

A beat followed and –

He pushes the red shunt button.

Wynn jackknifed perfectly into the water and splashed toward Shelly.

He punches rewind, replay and shunt.

He back-flipped gracefully into the crystalline waters.

Rewind, replay, shunt.

He cut the water perfectly with almost no splash.

Rewind, replay, shunt.

Flipping, he landed back first, splattering into the sea.

Wynn's heart pounds until he sees his head bob up out of the water.

"Sonofabitch." He coughed, blowing water out of his nose. "That hurt!"

A few minutes later, back on the deck, Shelly nuzzled against him, nibbling his neck, and placed her hands on his hips, inside the waistband of his swim-trunks. They descended the steps to their cabin, shutting the door behind them.

As he observes himself kissing her, zipping open her yellow wetsuit, pressing himself tightly against her, he feels a fist close on his heart.

He hits stop.

He tries to compose himself, breathing in hard through his nose and out of his mouth.

He hits rewind and replay.

The swish of the curtains jolts him awake. Consuelo's petite form, outlined by morning daylight, stands in front of the bay windows. She draws closer, scowling.

"You know better than to sleep in your chair. And in your clothes, no less."

He'd be sitting here comfortably in his boxers, he thinks, if she'd just stopped nagging him about getting dressed every day.

"You have to take a bath today."

He doesn't answer. What does it matter? He knows from experience that nothing he can say will dissuade her.

She grabs his wheelchair and whirls him around and out of the bedroom down the long, bright hallway. As always, Consuelo has carefully laid out his clean clothes on the bathroom rack along with a fresh towel. The maneuverable handlebars allow him a small measure of dignity, for what that's worth.

When he emerges shaved and dressed an hour later Consuelo waits outside the door, arms crossed, blocking the passageway back to the bedroom.

"Let's have a nice breakfast today, okay?"

She's oblivious to how maddening she is. What does he care about baths, about breakfasts, about strolls on the beach?

"Fresh air will do you good. We'll eat on the veranda." Consuelo carries one of his sweaters and tosses it to him. She pushes him across the living room, past her room, through the kitchen, out to the wooden balcony overlooking the Pacific. An assortment of Consuelo's azaleas, geraniums and spring bulbs line the balcony's ledge.

He considers turning the wheelchair right back around but a whiff of the bacon and eggs – lab-synthesized, of course, like most foods since the Food Chain Collapse – makes his stomach gurgle in protest. He pulls on his sweater.

The chilly Oregon morning is typically overcast. As he eats silently, Consuelo sits down across from him and gazes out at the lifeless, colorless waves lapping at Cannon Beach's shore. "Do you think it stands any chance of success?" she asks, pointing out to the horizon, beyond the monolithic Haystock Rock and smaller basalt rock pinnacles that protrude from beneath the waves, just offshore. A science freighter, one of the many ships dispatched around the globe, navigates in the distance, no doubt releasing 'gobblers' – genetically engineered bacteria specially designed to gobble up and break down the PCB's and biotoxins.

Wynn ponders her question for a moment. "There was a time, you know, decades ago, when the tidepools along these shores would have been swarming with barnacles and starfish and sculpins and anemones." His eyes brighten for a moment. "Puffins might've been nesting on Haystack Rock," he says, pointing to the 235-foot boulder looming offshore.

"Tell me again, Wynn. Tell me about the Restoration Project's chances," Consuelo says, like a child asking to hear her favorite bedtime story.

"It's a long shot," he says brusquely, deciding not to get drawn into a conversation.

The Project. Who would have guessed that his blind faith in the Project would have led him off of the shores of the San Juan Islands on that day, the day with so many permutations, so many goddamned happy endings.

"There are reports that a genetically engineered wolf eel survived for almost an entire week this time," Consuelo says.

He grunts and swallows a piece of synthetic omelet.

Sipping his orange drink, he stares past her.

"What do you think of that?" she asks.

He says nothing.

She leans across the table and forces him to make eye contact. "Why do you insist on doing this to yourself?"

He takes another defiant sip.

"Before that damned Shunter was installed you were making progress, Wynn. Obsessing about that day accomplishes nothing, changes nothing."

"But it does! That's the point, Consuelo. A flick of the finger and it's changed. *All of it*!"

"Wynn, when you keep 'shunting,' when you keep running from the truth –"

"I'm not running from anything. I'm just exploring different realities."

"You know this is about more than just 'exploring' divergent probability paths, Wynn. You know they aren't real."

He snorts and shakes his head. She's smarter than this. "These are actual realities I'm accessing, Consuelo, true parallel realities as real as you or me or this burnt piece of toast."

She refuses to be sidetracked. "Even if that's true, it's not *this* reality. It might as well be completely fictional. This is such a pointless, painful exercise."

He wheels over to the balcony ledge and stares out at the dead blue-gray ocean. The Pacific has fared so much worse than the Atlantic.

"Imagine," he says, shaking his head slowly. "We have a household appliance that not only preserves the past but peers off into divergent dimensions. Yet we still can't cure a goddamned spinal cord injury." He considers pushing the potted plants over the side. He wants to see the planters shatter, to see the geraniums and azaleas lying in the scattered soil with their roots exposed. "Who knows? Maybe I'll stumble across another reality where I can uncover the secrets of spinal cord regeneration."

Even as he says this, they both know it's unlikely to happen. While the Shunter can access the user's actual past with no problem, it can only reveal parallel pastworlds with infinitesimally slight vibratory differentials. He can observe a universe in which he takes two lumps of sugar instead of three, cuts his hair short, brushes his teeth with a different brand of toothpaste, and, on July 19, 2041, stands ten inches further to the left or ten inches further to the right when he dives off of that ship. Anyone who's ever used a Shunter has found the differences to be insignificant, maddeningly subtle, often times undetectable. *Except him. Except for his condition. Except for his entire life.* And he's supposed to ignore this?

"There's something I need to tell you," Consuelo says.

Here it comes, he thinks. He could tell that she'd been readying herself to drop a bomb on him ever since she burst into his room yesterday.

"I've consulted with your physicians and they're in complete agreement." She's switched to the professional voice now, the one that always delivers unpleasant news. "I'm sorry, Wynn. The pick-up's been scheduled for tomorrow. The Shunter. It has to go."

His momentary shock quickly gives way to panic. *Tomorrow?*

"Look... I'll cut back. I won't spend so many hours –"

"I'm afraid we've tried that already."

"I'll do my exercises." He tries his best not to sound desperate. "I'll even leave the house every now and then."

She reaches for the dirty dishes on the table.

He clutches her wrist. "Please..."

"Let go!"

"Don't do this to me," he says through clenched teeth. He releases her. "Don't..."

She sighs loudly. "Why can't you just put this behind you?"

"It's just... I know *how* my accident happened. That's not the issue. What I have to find out..." He struggles for the words. "What I need to know is the *why* of it. Why did things have to turn out this way? I've seen hundreds of divergent realities branching off from the day of the accident two years ago, Consuelo. Maybe thousands. And in every one of them –"

"Wynn, you know it's about more than that..."

"In every one of them I come through it healthy and whole. In every one of them I walk off into the sunset, arm-in-arm with Shelly, with nothing worse than a sunburn and a slight beer buzz."

"Don't do this –"

"Don't you see? Those aren't the inconsequential divergences you usually see in a Shunter. *That's* how my life was supposed to turn out. I'm supposed to be living a normal, happy, productive life. "This," he says, punching his leg, "this," he says, waving his arms at the world around him, "is an aberration! This reality isn't how things were meant to be!"

"Wynn, please." She reaches out and grabs hold of his hands. "Let me do my job. Please let me help."

Consuelo draws the curtains and dims the lights while Wynn adjusts the Najarian Headband snugly around his forehead. She settles into a chair next to him. He punches the date into the control sphere – the date branded in his brain.

Bright, colored images coalesce on the screen in a whirring flash – a flash of lost chances and missed opportunities, he muses. Together, he and Consuelo watch the day unfold.

The whitecaps whizzed by as the ship sailed off of the coast of the San Juan Islands, an archipelago in the rainshadow of the Olympic Mountains encompassing hundreds of islands, rocks and reefs. The Puget Sound, although contaminated by biotoxins and other pollutants, still harbored some vestiges of marine life.

He glances over at Consuelo who seems both mesmerized and saddened by the undulating ocean.

Wynn, his blond hair in a ponytail, sat in a plastic chair on the front deck and studied his pocket-cam, the beat of reggae music thumping in the background. He sipped a beer. The green beach towel around his shoulders clashed with his day-glow orange wetsuit.

Bernie stared through the telescope into the horizon. "It's beautiful, kid," he said, pointing skyward. "Do you see it?"

All they can see in the direction the old ship captain points is the azure Pacific dotted with islands.

Peering at the cloudless sky, Wynn finally pointed to a speck in the distance. "A seagull," he said, his voice filled with wonder. "Unbelievable. All that damage done to their natural habitat and yet they've still found a way to survive here. Do you see a lot of seabirds, Bernie?"

"Very few, actually. The toxins have taken their toll, I'm afraid." The sea captain stood on his tiptoes and craned his neck trying to see the gull. "Do you think there might be a chance? To save the Pacific?"

Wynn shrugged his shoulders. "I don't know. I'm just a student, Bernie."

"Sure, but you're the one who developed those special microorganisms, right? The ones that can clean these waters?"

"The gobblers? Shelly's been talking to you, hasn't she?" Wynn smirks. "I *helped* with the research."

"Trust me, modesty gets you nowhere, kid," Bernie said. "What about the water temperatures? Can your 'gobblers' do anything about that? Temps have increased more than twenty-five degrees over the last couple of decades."

"Afraid not. The gobblers can't do a thing about global warming. But with any luck we can at least reverse the biotoxic contamin – wow!" The bird veered closer to them. Wynn held the minicam between his thumb and forefinger, recording the bird's flight.

Shelly appeared from below deck sporting a yellow wetsuit and carrying two towels. "Time to hit the waves, Wynny," she said. She stroked his sun-reddened cheek with the back of her hand.

"You missed it!"

"Missed what?"

"A seagull!"

"Big whoop." She draped a towel over his head. "C'mon, time for a break."

"One sec," he said, fiddling with the minicam.

Seconds later, she dove gracefully off the side of the ship and he followed, cannonballing into the sea.

They played a familiar game, a race to see who could swim underneath the ship and reach the other side first. Bernie agreed to judge. Instead of waiting for the count of "three," Wynn dove on "two."

He glided underwater, cheeks puffed, squinting at the sun's soft rays –

Consuelo has a wistful expression he's never seen before.

"We've got a hit!" Bernie hollered from the bow on cue. "Telemetry shows marine life. ShipNav is moving us towards it!"

The power sails retracted, and when the silent motors geared up the boat lurched forward, sending Wynn and Shelly stumbling against the side railings.

They watch the coaster move ahead at a steady clip.

"One more dive, Wynn?"

He flinches.

"Forget it. I've already detoxed." He held up the bottle of pills and shook it.

"I understand," she said with a wink. "At this speed a belly flop would hurt." She took off her sunglasses and handed them to him with a "what-a-wimp" smirk. Running past him, Shelly leaped over the side and disappeared with a small splash into the sparkling blue sea.

Bernie killed the motors. "Hey, what are you doing? What about the marine life?"

"Shelly?" Wynn leaned over the side, his brow creased. "Shelly?"

A long pause followed.

"Whoo-hoo!" she shrieked, erupting from beneath the waves. "Bernie, score please!"

"Nine point seven!"

"Can you beat that, Wynny?"

A beat, a fateful pause follows, and the question just hangs in the air reverberating in his head. He instinctively moves his thumb on the control sphere to hit "shunt."

Consuelo snatches it from his hands.

"What are you doing?"

She stands up and steps back away from him. "Look at the screen, Wynn."

He teetered at the edge of the ship, not quite ready to dive, and at the last second (was it the alcohol? a sudden wave? a gust of wind?) sprawled over the side. As he tried to reposition his body in mid-air, the back of his head struck the side of the ship and his neck snapped forward.

Shelly's giggle faded into the distance.

The Shunter goes black.

Consuelo hits forward.

Images on the screen blur now; sounds muffle.

The doctor's face appeared. "Spinal cord trauma." The screen faded to black. "Catastrophic." The face appeared again. "Irreparable."

Consuelo hits forward.

"Stop it!"

He laid in bed, intubated, a ventilator whooshing oxygen into his lungs.

Forward.

Wynn, no longer intubated, still lay in the hospital bed. Shelly rubbed her red eyes and stood next to him. The giggle was gone.

His face contorted into an angry sneer. "Why the hell... did you finally bother to visit?" He spat out the words between long breaths.

"Wynn, don't say that," Shelly whispered, her eyes welling up. "Don't make this more difficult than it has to be."

"It's been... two months."

"Wynny, please. You're not being fair."

"Two months."

"You *know* how much I hate hospitals. I'm practically, well, phobic. But I came here anyway. Because I felt that I owed it to you. To tell you in person, I mean."

His eyes blazed.

"I'm not good for you, baby." A tear trickled down her cheek. "You know that. You need someone who can cope with... with all of this. I've been a mess ever since... you know..."

She hesitated. "I feel like a monster telling you this, here and now. But the doctors say it could still be months before..." She blew her nose. "I mean, after all that we had, we owe it to each other to be honest. You deserve someone better than me. I'm sorry..."

The words cut into him. He looks away for a second but the screen lures him back.

Shelly turned and walked away, hesitating at the threshold. She looked back over her shoulder as if about to say something.

But instead she left.

What were you going to say, Shelly? Again, his thumb, by

reflex, reaches for the shunt button that is no longer there.

Consuelo punches a new date into the sphere.

"Turn it off!" He whirls around and lunges for the control.

She retreats into the hallway, slamming the bedroom door behind her. "Look at the screen, Wynn," she pleads from the other side of the door.

He spins around.

Staring at the screen, unsure whether this is last week, last month or any time since the Shunter arrived three months ago, he sees himself sitting in a dark room.

Face unshaven, hair uncombed, he was transfixed by the flickering images unreeling on the screen. He hit the shunt button while his onscreen image dove off of the ship.

How many times has he done that?

A pained expression etched itself across his face when he saw that he had hit the water and emerged unscathed. He hit rewind and replay, again pressing shunt while his screen image was in mid-dive. This time he crashed face-first into the water. Bernie laughed in the background on the screen-within-the-screen. "What'd I tell you? Belly flop!" Shelly laughed. Wynn pushed the buttons. Rewind, replay and shunt. The landing smoothed out this time. Bernie jumped up and down. "Sorry, Shelly! That's a perfect 10!" he shouted.

Wynn stares into his own crazed, hungry, bloodshot eyes.

Rewind, replay, shunt. The window to unlived lives opened and shut, opened and shut. Rewind, replay, shunt. He hit the buttons frantically, furiously. Each time the dive varied but always – *always* – the screen-within-the-screen Wynn emerged uninjured. Each time he was safe. Each time he was whole.

His mind tumbling as if in freefall, Wynn turns away from

the Shunter and moves toward the doorway. He opens the door. Consuelo has left the control sphere lying on the hallway floor. He strains to pick it up. Looking back into the room, he flings it with all his might at the hideous images on the wallscreen.

The sphere strikes and rebounds harmlessly, bouncing back toward his chair, buttons randomly pressing—forward, replay, shunt—as it rolls. He glances down at the new date on the sphere—yesterday's date—and the wallscreen image shimmers.

Wynn sat on the sand, a blanket over his legs. He and Consuelo lounged outside of his complex on the Cannon Beach shore. A cupcake with a birthday candle that leaned perilously to the right sat next to a pile of sandwiches. Consuelo wore jeans and a buttoned sweater, her dark hair falling past her shoulders. She held the sandwich to his mouth and he took a big bite out of it.

"Now this, you have to admit, is above and beyond the call of duty," she laughed. Her eyes sparkled and she smiled broadly.

"One second, please." He swallowed and held her wrists in place, keeping the sandwich within biting distance. "Aren't you in fact being compensated for ensuring that I'm taken care of, well-fed...."

"... self-sufficient..." She laughed.

"... bathed, clothed..."

"I thought you said you didn't want to be treated like an infant?"

"I've had a drastic change of heart."

They both laughed and he pulled her toward him. She brushed crumbs off the corners of his mouth.

Wynn feels his heart skip.

A wave crashed against the shore in the background.

He stares intently as they finish their lunch.

180

Consuelo walked beside him, leaving footprints in the wet sand as his floater-chair hovered alongside her. The sun sat on the horizon and their shadows stretched far behind them.

"See? I told you that a change of scenery would do wonders for your mood," she said. "I have to ask you something. In those other realities, Wynn, did you ever go back to school? Did you ever rejoin the project?"

He shook his head slowly. "Shelly and I, we take some time off. Take a long trip."

"Hmm. Well, classes start in two months, you know."

"It's funny. I never seriously considered it before. In other realities I never —"

"Enough," she said, putting her index finger to his lips, "let's stick to this reality, okay?"

"Okay," he said, smiling.

She leaned down and kissed him on the cheek.

Wynn hits stop.

He wheels himself out of the room, across the apartment, to the balcony where Consuelo stands staring out at the ocean. The sun breaks through an ominous cloud cover. She turns as she hears him approach.

"I'm sorry," she says softly, her watery eyes shining in the bright light. "But what you were doing, Wynn... It was important work. *Inspiring* work." She brushes her hair out of her eyes. "It's been two years. And you'd made so much progress. Just when you finally started to move on with your life, just when I thought I started to see a glimmer of the old you, the one that was going to make a difference, that Shunter..."

"It's okay. Really." A steady breeze cools his face. "I understand. About the Shunter. It has to go."

Consuelo raises an eyebrow and says nothing.

After a long pause, staring out at the ocean, she notes the freighter's absence. "Do you think it worked, Wynn? Is there any chance for the Pacific?"

"It takes time, Consuelo. We'll just have to wait and

see." He squints in the sunshine and stares overhead at the stretch of azure sky opening up between the parting clouds. And then he sees it. A gracefully gliding speck in the distance. A seagull. He blinks and loses sight of the bird, unsure whether he has imagined it.

Waves lap against the white sands as Wynn and Consuelo gaze out at the boundless Pacific, an infinity of possibilities stretching out into the horizon.

Naked Weekend

Friday afternoon

The thunderstorm had been scheduled weeks ago and Rick of all people should have known about it, Leila thought. As the wind-driven rain whipped against the café window, she sipped the last of her lukewarm latte and tapped the *white* button on her wristlet. Her brow unfurrowed; her scowl vanished.

Two minutes later, the door burst open and Rick stumbled through, his sandy hair mussed, his glasses speckled with raindrops. He struggled with a dripping umbrella that had been turned inside out. Glancing at the rows of colored buttons on his shiny cadmium wristlet, he pressed *white* and relief washed across his face.

"You're late," she said. "I have to get back to the plant soon."

"Sorry, I had trouble getting a cab." He leaned across the table and gave her a light peck on the nose. "My boss had some news for me."

"You got it!"

He pushed the *sky-blue* button and his smile broadened. "You may now call me Mr. Executive Managing Director of Weather Simulation, Rick Mendez."

"Quite a mouthful."

"Well, you can just call me Mr. Executive Managing Director for short. Because I like you."

She chuckled and pressed *sky-blue*.

Rick took another hit of *sky-blue* and doubled over with laughter.

Others in the café stared, pressing the *green* button on their wristlets. Eyebrows arched, and necks craned in their direction. A few of the patrons, however, pushed *white* and then leaned back in their seats.

As she and Rick laughed louder, a flashing red dot circled their wristlets. They both immediately pressed *white* and wiped the tears from their eyes. As she caught her breath, the warning lights faded.

"Yikes. That was close," Rick said.

"Congratulations on the promotion, hon," she said. "You deserve it."

"Thanks. I start the new position on Monday." Rick rubbed his glasses dry with the cuff of his jacket, a boyish habit that never failed to produce smudged lenses. She shook her head and sighed, handing him her napkin.

"Well?" he said. "Let's have it. What's your big news?"

"It can wait."

"If you couldn't tell me over the phone, it's got to be important."

"Not really. It's just that, Nina mentioned she and Alberto had tried something last weekend."

"Nina." He rolled his eyes. "Uh-oh, go ahead."

"Well, it's a little... kinky."

"Go on," he said, smiling. "You've got my attention."

"Now, keep an open mind, okay?" She looked down at the table and curled a long lock of her blond hair around her index finger. "They went off of... you know, the nanos. Just for a day!"

Rick's eyes widened and he shook his head. "Leila..."

"Look, they say there's a specific nano that comes in a brown pill. It lets you stay naked for almost twenty-four hours. And the biosensors," she said, lowering her voice and pointing to her wristlet, "don't detect it."

"Give me a break. A monitor will be on our doorstep within the hour."

"Rick, this works. I'm telling you...."

He waved his hands to shush her as the server, a teenager

with a long, thin goatee, approached the table.

"We appreciate your patronage," the boy said. He pressed the *silver* button on his wristlet and his smile broadened. "*Really*. I mean it."

Rick ordered a decaf and waited for the boy to leave before continuing. "What if we get caught?"

"I won't turn you in if you don't turn me in," she said with a thin smile. "C'mon, don't be such a prude."

He frowned. "It's a crazy idea. And what's the point?"

"Nina said making love with Alberto while off the nanos was amazing. I want to know what it feels like to be with you. Naked, I mean."

The server approached again. He set down the steaming coffee and pushed *green*. "I can get you some," he muttered. The teen looked away when he spoke, throwing his voice like a ventriloquist.

"Excuse me?" Rick said.

"I can get you some. You know." He looked side-to-side then leaned in. "Some *brown*. One hit and you can go naked for the day – without the shakes, just a slight fever and a mild buzz. Heck, some folks do it for the buzz."

"No thanks," Rick said.

"I can get you a good deal, man. I'm connected."

"We'll let you know," Rick said. He pressed *white* and his frown disappeared.

Leila watched the slump-shouldered teenager lope away towards the kitchen. Before he turned the corner, he took a hit of *white* and his shoulders straightened up.

"I want us to feel that... *intensity* Nina told me about. On our own," she said. "No nanos to curb our highs and raise our lows."

"You're being silly."

"It'll just be for one day, Rick. I'll come up to your place tomorrow. We'll lock the door, take our *browns* – the fever only lasts a few hours – and go naked. No one needs to know."

"Leila, don't you know what it used to be like, before the

185

Wars, when everyone went 'naked'? That's why there are laws."

"Geez, you sound like my grandfather. Won't you at least consider it?"

He sighed.

The wind howled as they sipped their coffees, and the rain continued its assault against the window.

"Now that you're Executive Managing Director maybe you can do something about this weather. It's supposed to last the whole weekend, right?"

"Yep."

"Why program a storm on a weekend anyway?"

"Ah, that, my dear, is top secret," he said. He pressed *mauve*.

"What, you're keeping secrets from me now?" She mimicked his playful tone, tapping *mauve* twice.

"I take my responsibilities as Executive Managing Director of Weather Simulation quite seriously, thank you very much."

"Just for one lousy day? Won't you at least think about it?"

"I don't know. It's crazy."

"For me?"

He sighed again.

Saturday morning

She wore a yellow-hooded slicker like Rick's and strolled with him in a steady drizzle through the tree-lined path that snaked around the pond. The park was empty save for an old man walking his golden retriever.

"More people should walk in the rain," Leila said. "I mean, I understand it's overcast and windy and everything, but the park has this sad, beautiful look to it. Don't you think? I know it's not possible, but I swear I can smell the wet grass and the blossoms."

"Simulating smells is proving to be a lot more difficult than colors."

"Why?"

"It's complicated."

"Tell me."

"With colors, all you need is a screen of pixels, each capable of producing red, green and blue. That lets us generate the intermediate colors. Odors are different."

Rick always became animated when discussing sims.

"With smells, when a particular molecule fits into one of the thousand or so receptors in our nasal passageway, a neural signal is transmitted to the brain as an odor. If it doesn't fit precisely: no smell. We can detect millions of odors, but our sense of smell can't be broken down into a few numbers on a gradient. In other words, there's no 'smell pixel' we can –"

"I am so, so sorry I asked." She pretended to try to cover his mouth, and he fought off her hand.

"The pond," she said. "It's real, right?"

"I think so."

"How about the ducks?" She pointed to an orange-billed bird treading in the water, four ducklings trailing in its wake.

Rick shrugged.

"Well, it doesn't matter, right? They're beautiful." She smirked, rolled up her sleeve and tapped *sky-blue* twice.

"Easy on the *blue*," Rick said. "You don't want to set off the sensors again."

"It's a lot more pleasant when the wind dies," she said. "Keep that in mind for future reference, okay?"

"Got it. No wind," he said. "The kid in the café said to try the northwest walkway tunnel, just up ahead."

When they entered the tunnel's mouth, the musky smell of wet dog and urine confirmed the passageway was real. She spotted a white-haired woman in a black slicker. The old woman hunched down, resting her forearms on a walker, and looked Leila square in the eye. "Danny from the coffee shop told me to expect you. You got the cash?"

Leila handed her the folded bills.

The old woman crumpled the cash and sniffed it. "Here you go." She pulled out a pill bottle from her pocket and handed it to Leila. "Two *browns*. Just a slight fever. These special nanos will put your biosensor nanos to sleep for a day. If you kids need any more, Danny can tell you where to find me."

The old woman trudged toward the tunnel entrance, and then stopped. "Why do you want to go naked? You kids artists?"

Leila shook her head.

The old woman gave a disappointed scowl. "Oh, just another couple looking to fuck. Back during pre-regulation, before all this nano nonsense, I used to be an artist, a painter. And I was damned good. No, I was *great!*"

Although difficult to see in the shadows, Leila thought that the woman's eyes had watered.

"Passion used to be a *good* thing."

Leila looked at her, uncertain what to say.

"Huh," the old woman grunted. She pulled up the hood of her slicker and hobbled away.

Leila held up the pill bottle and looked at the two shiny, chocolate-brown tablets inside.

"Are you sure about this?" Rick said.

She responded by pushing *pink* and kissing him.

Saturday mid-afternoon

A dull daylight filtered in through the drawn blinds. She and Rick nuzzled under the covers. They shivered and watched the history sim.

"Did you try your nanos?" Leila said. Her teeth chattered and she held the back of her hand against her sweat-drenched forehead.

"I pressed every color and got nothing. My biosensor's as dead as yours."

"Do we have to see this?" she said.

"I just think we should know what we're getting ourselves into," Rick mumbled. A thermometer dangled between his lips like a post-coital cigarette.

The Professor sat in a wooden chair at the foot of their bed. He tapped a pencil against his grizzled chin and squinted at them over his bifocals. Rick had been peppering him with questions throughout the lecture on nanoregulation.

"A couple more questions, Professor," Rick said. "Why don't the nanos just *automatically* color us? Wouldn't that be more efficient?"

"Our Government, sir, is founded upon principles of free will, freedom of choice." He stabbed his pencil in the air to punctuate the point. "Hence, each individual must decide for himself whether to nanoregulate his emotions. Of course, every choice has its consequences, and penalties exist for noncompliance. But for patriots, the choice is an easy one."

"The physical effects of withdrawal, are they —"

"Quite severe, I assure you. An irregular heartbeat is followed by seizures and, eventually, insanity."

"Turn him off," Leila said.

"Do you want me to proceed, sir?" the Professor asked.

"No, that'll be all," she answered.

"Very well," the Professor said. He glowered at her and, even though he was a holo, pushed *white* on his wristlet. His image faded.

Quirky program, Leila thought.

She pressed the remote control and a cartoon appeared in midair, a masked bulldog in red tights wrestling a Cheshire cat. "So what's your temperature?"

"Ninety-nine point five," he said. He held the thermometer between his thumb and index finger. "I think it's breaking. Listen, you heard the Professor. Maybe we should just forget about this."

"It's just Government propaganda, silly. Nina went off her nanos and she's not insane."

"You don't think?"

She giggled and instinctively pressed *sky-blue*, though the button now did nothing. Her smile vanished as the Cheshire cat slammed a chair over the bulldog's head, making the dog's pupils twirl in its eyeballs.

"Strange. This used to crack me up."

"Hmm," he observed, poker-faced.

Saturday late-afternoon
Ice pellets pinged against the windowpanes as the steady rain turned to hail.

Leila sat on the couch; Rick's head rested on her lap. From this angle his face looked different in a way she couldn't quite grasp. Rick had thick eyebrows, and the line where his afternoon shadow began looked as if it had been drawn with a ruler. He had an almost nonexistent upper lip, a slender nose, and a tiny mole on his right cheek. His long sandy hair fell back in waves. She liked the feel of his hair between her fingers.

She knew it was silly, but she'd expected going naked would transform them somehow, that they'd glow bright orange or levitate or...something.

She grabbed a synthapple from the fruit bowl on the coffee table and took a bite out of it. "So."

"So," he answered.

Saturday Afternoon, Six Minutes Later
Rick moaned as his tongue darted inside her mouth, and she felt him push into her. Although he hadn't gained an ounce in the two years they'd been together, he felt heavier. She found it hard to breathe. Normally, he was a gentle lover. Off the nanos, he grabbed fistfuls of her hair, bit her nipples, stared at her with too much intensity. Normally, she would have felt the beginnings of an orgasm and pressed *pink*. But not tonight.

Rick finished with a loud moan. He kissed her forehead and shifted next to her.

"Why didn't you...?" he asked.

"I don't know. Without the *pink*... How was it for you?"

"Incredible. Amazing." He put his hands behind his head. "I'm telling you, I felt... unrestrained, free."

She turned away and hugged the sheets.

They said nothing for a long while.

"I told you this was a mistake," he finally said.

Silence.

"Leila?"

"It's just... I wanted it to be, I don't know, special. Instead, it's like I wasn't even here."

"Trust me, you were here."

She sat up. "You just don't understand."

"What?"

"Maybe if you'd been less... Maybe if you'd just tried to..."

"What?"

"Nothing!" She stood up and strode out of the room, futilely tapping *white* as she descended the stairwell to the living room. She heard his footsteps behind her.

"Tell me!" he said.

She walked naked through the dining room, past the swinging doors into the harsh fluorescence of the kitchen. He followed behind her, also nude. She pulled a mayonnaise jar out of the refrigerator, uncapped it, and slapped the lid against the counter.

"What did I do wrong?" he said.

Leila pulled a butter knife out of the utensil drawer and slammed it shut. She slapped mayonnaise onto a slice of white bread then moved her index finger to her left wrist for a hit of *white*. But tonight there was no *white*.

"This was your idea. I didn't want anything to do with this!" he shouted.

"Exactly! You were against this from the very beginning, and now I know why."

"What do you mean?"

"Off your nanos, you don't give a damn about me!"

"You're insane, you know that?"

She flung the piece of bread onto the counter. "This," she said, waving her arms in the air, "isn't love. I don't know what it is! This was supposed to bring us closer together." They had never argued like this before, and she found herself weeping for the first time since puberty, when her wristlet had first been implanted.

"You need some *white*. I'm calling a doctor." He turned around.

"Don't you dare! You promised me!" She grabbed at his shoulders and her long nails dug into skin, leaving long, red scratches down his back.

Rick whirled around and grabbed a hold of her shoulders. "What the hell is wrong with you?" He shook her.

She froze, bewildered. He released her and pressed *white* over and over again on his disabled wristlet. But tonight there was no *white*.

He grabbed a dish and hurled it against the wall. Then he stomped up the stairs.

Saturday Evening
Rick stepped into his pants. "Goddammit! I thought you said we were going to be alone today."

"Don't you swear at me! I have no idea who it could be." She buttoned her blouse and rushed down the stairs to answer the insistent doorbell.

When Leila opened the door Nina and Alberto stood in the falling hail. Nina held a plastic shopping bag with Chinese takeout while Alberto draped his jacket over their heads. "Special delivery," he said.

"I hope you don't mind," Nina said, "We were in the neighborhood, and I thought we could all eat together."

"That's... great," Leila said with a deep craving for *white* rather than Chinese.

She had told Nina yesterday that she and Rick were considering going naked this weekend.

"Aren't you going to invite us in?" Nina walked across the doorway, pressing *green*, and surveyed the house. She and Alberto hadn't been here since Rick reprogrammed the place. Her red hair was coiffed in the popular, new beehive hairdo. "*Much* nicer decor than I expected," Nina said. A minute later, Rick joined them and shot Leila a look when he saw the four place settings on the table.

"Honey, Nina and Alberto are joining us. Isn't that great?"

"Mm-hmm." He shook Alberto's hand and kissed Nina on each cheek.

They wound up sharing the egg rolls, ribs and white rice. Off her nanos, Leila found all the food tasted exactly the same. "So, Nina, is the meeting still scheduled for tomorrow?" she said.

"Yes, can you believe Sanders moved it up? Human waste recycling has become his top priority. Not surprising, given his 'issues'."

"What do you mean?" Leila said.

"You don't know?" Nina paused in her trademark manner for maximum dramatic effect. "About his rather disgusting... fetish?"

"Oh?" Leila said.

"Well, rumor has it he programmed certain... holocompanions who –"

"Not the Sanders story again!" Alberto interjected. "C'mon, we're *eating*."

"Don't talk with your mouth full!" Nina barked. She pushed *white* between forkfuls of rice, then lowered her voice again. "I'll fill you in later, Leila."

"And you must be feeling pretty good about yourself these days, Mr. Mendez," Nina said to Rick. She took a hit of *mauve*. "Leila told me all about your promotion."

"Yeah, congratulations," Alberto added, chewing on a spare rib.

Leila felt a bead of sweat trickle down her neck. She knew curiosity must be killing Nina. Sure enough – as she pushed *green* – Nina blurted out, "So, what's it been like?"

Leila pretended she didn't understand.

"I mean, we can tell you're naked." Nina pointed at Leila's wristlet. "You're hitting *white*, yet still seem... tense."

Rick looked at his fork, and Leila blushed. "It's been strange," she said. "Probably no different than it felt for the two of you."

Alberto exchanged a glance with Nina and pushed *white*. "Well, actually..." he said.

"We, uh, decided against it, Leila," Nina said. "With my responsibilities at the Recycling Plant and Alberto's duties at the Radiation Center, well, we didn't think that 'scene' was appropriate for us."

"Excuse me?" Leila said. "I don't understand."

Rick's eyes narrowed. "Didn't you tell Leila you two had gone naked last weekend?"

"Certainly not!"

"But you told me it had been 'amazing,'" Leila said. "Like nothing you'd ever experienced before."

Nina pushed *white*. "I said that's what I'd *heard*. You didn't think Berto and *I* would engage in those sorts of activities, did you? We're respectable people."

Leila stood up. Her face felt hot; her head pounded. "You lied to me?"

Nina and Alberto repeatedly hit *white*. "You must have misunderstood," Nina said. "We're not teenagers, for goodness sake."

"So you've come here to gawk at us." Leila felt her temples throb.

"Leila, dear, I'm not one to judge. But yes, when you mentioned you two were going naked today, I'll admit it piqued my interest."

"Tell the truth, Nina," she said in an icy monotone. "You specifically told me you and Alberto went off of your nanos."

"I said no such thing, dear."

Leila leapt across the table and swung her arms like a swimmer fighting a riptide, slapping Nina across the head and face. Dishes crashed to the floor. She grabbed a firm hold of Nina's hair and jerked her head left and right, all the while screaming.

"Leila, stop it!" Rick shouted. He grabbed her arms. "Let go! Let go!"

Nina shrieked. Alberto stood to the side, his eyes bulging, taking hit after hit of *white*.

Rick pulled her off of Nina; she took ragged breaths and held a patch of red hair.

"What are you doing?" Rick said. "Have you lost your mind?"

"Leave. Right now!" Leila screamed. "Both of you!"

"Get a hold of yourself, Leila!" Rick shouted.

"Let's go, Berto," Nina said, pushing *white*. She rubbed her scalp and tried to reconstruct her collapsed hairdo. "It's not safe here."

"Damn right!" Leila shouted after her.

Nina and Alberto tramped out the door, leaving it wide open.

"Listen to me," Rick said to her. "Nina lied, okay? There's no reason for us to continue this nonsense."

"I don't give a damn about them! Don't you see, this is about *us* now!"

"You're losing it, Leila!" Rick's face flushed and he opened his mouth, but no other words came out.

"Look, there's nothing we can do anyway. The *brown* won't wear off until the morning."

In response, he slammed his fist on the table and kicked a chair as he stormed out of the room.

Saturday Late Evening

She waited at the doorway holding a tote bag packed with the clothes, toiletries and romance holos she kept at Rick's place.

Rick stood in his bathrobe, staring at the floor. "So, this is it then," he said.

She nodded.

"Look, Leila, let's discuss this like rational adults when we're colored again."

"Rick, what did you feel today?"

"I don't know what you mean."

"Did you feel anything even resembling love?"

He looked away.

"You felt what I did: boredom, irritation, anger."

"Look, this is new to us. We're just not used to all these...
unregulated feelings...."

"It's just... I needed to feel something between us without
the nanos. I don't know if what we have is real anymore."

He paused. "I can't believe you feel that way."

She kissed him on the cheek. "Goodbye, Rick."

They both stood there for a beat.

"Let me help you," he said. He grabbed her bag and trudged
through the rain to the taxi at the curbside. His drenched
bathrobe clung to him.

As she turned to leave, she peeked back over her shoulder.
Rick removed his wet glasses and wiped them with the cuff of his
bathrobe. She felt a deep, soft ache. She walked back and
removed the glasses from his hand, taking a tissue from her
pocket and wiping them clean. He leaned in and she slipped his
glasses onto his face.

His eyes watered. "Don't go, Leila."

She looked up at him and met his kiss.

Sunday Evening

She strode down the long, dark corridor to the only lit office and
poked her head in. Rick sat behind a mahogany desk, his glasses
teetering on the tip of his nose as he stared at his holoscreen. She
knocked on the open door.

"Hey," he said.

"Hey yourself."

He gave her a soft kiss and a hug that lifted her off her feet.

"All packed up, I see," she said, pointing to several boxes of
file folders, staplers, and office supplies.

"Just moving across the hall. Want to see the new digs?"

He led her down the carpeted hallway to the corner office. She whistled at the magnificent city view. Illuminated gilded towers were book-ended by glorious snow-peaked mountains to the east and a calm cerulean-tinged sea to the west. The red sun melted on the horizon.

"I see the storm's finally over," she said.

"Yep, right on schedule."

"Thanks for ruining everybody's weekend. I don't see why you folks don't just program sunny days."

"Want to hear something top-secret?"

She smiled and nodded.

"Research shows that an occasional weekend holostorm is good for our mental well-being. It brings a certain balance to our lives. Makes us appreciate all the sunny weekends to come."

She mulled this over and realized he was right.

"Rick, I was thinking, now that the *brown* is wearing off... Before we start coloring ourselves again, maybe we should get some more?" She ran her hand over her wristlet and felt the cold metal. "We don't need nanos to manage our emotions for us. Good or bad, let's just experience them."

"Even after what happened this weekend with Nina and Alberto?"

"I think you were right. We just need some time to get used to... *feeling*. Naked, I mean."

Rick fingered his own wristlet and seemed to consider her words.

"This view," she said, "how much of it is holographic?"

"Are you asking me to reveal more trade secrets?"

"Damn right," she said.

He reached into a drawer and pulled out a pairs of goggles, which he handed to her. She looked again at the panoramic city view.

A transparent dome of monolithic proportions, stretching as far as the eye could see, encapsulated a skyline of gray, dilapidated buildings. Beyond the dome, crater-pocked remnants of a mountain range stood to the east and a roiling, debris-filled ocean lay to the west. The park at the center of the city consisted of rows of sad, leafless tree trunks and a scum-filled pond. Dirty snowflakes descended from a dark, gray sky and dissolved against the dome.

She gasped and took a step backward.

"The Wars," Rick said. "Unregulated emotions run amok."

She felt a cold shiver.

They both reached for their wristlets and, for the first time since Saturday morning, took a hit of soothing *white*.

After a few seconds, still using the goggles, Leila spun around and surveyed the peeling wallpaper and faded floorboards in the empty office. "What would I see if I wore these at home?"

"Oh, it wouldn't look too bad. The holograms can only do so much before reality trips you up." He removed his goggles.

He placed his hands on her shoulders and massaged them.

"You know, every single thing in this lousy office is holomasked." She continued spinning, looking up, down and around until she turned to face Rick.

"What do you see now?" he asked.

She peered at him through the goggles for a long time. "Just you, hon."

And she pushed a button she had never pressed before with such utter conviction: *purple*.

He pushed *purple* too.

The love nanos flooded through her, and they kissed.

Doubled

Darwin ached to be Doubled again. He felt gutted, hollow, like half a man living half a life. Two months ago, he had moved his bed against the mirrored wall to calm himself with the illusion of Darren by his side. In this way, he could dull the pain. He could reach out and caress his reflected cheek, press his hand against his Other's, pretend to be whole.

"What have you done?" Darwin asked his reflection. But the image simply stared back at him.

Darwin paid the two vendors with a pair of shiny coins, and they handed him two cups of java mint in a thermal bag. In a daze, he exited the coffee shop at Savior Saviour Hospital and tramped through the empty street, a canyon of mirrored skyscrapers. The *clunk-clunk* of his solitary bootsteps sounded strange and distant, as if they belonged to someone else.

At the corner of Washington Westington and Ridgemont Ridgemount he hailed a cab and settled into the back seat. "The Mendel Mendle Institute," he whispered.

The two drivers shot him a curious look, exchanged a glance, and programmed their respective steering monitors. They dropped him off at the foot of Syzygy Syzergy Hill, a one hour drive outside the city limits. The Mendel Mendle Institute, a windowless edifice covered in wild ivy, stood high atop the willow-sheathed hill.

Darwin cradled the bag of coffee and fidgeted, surprised to find several visitors at the tram stop at this late hour. A pair of girls in reflective-silver skirts and pink headbands stared at him while their mother and her Other chitchatted. Darwin assumed they were here to visit the Other's children, who were noticeably absent. Two gray-haired doctors with thick, milk-white mustaches also glared at him.

The tram emerged out of the thick foliage and pulled to a stop, its double doors unfolding with a clatter. After the seven of them boarded, the tram began its slow ascent and the lush greenery took on a darker hue in the setting sun. Two sparrows twittered on a branch and studied Darwin quizzically as the tram moved through the treetops. He took a deep breath and closed his eyes. When he opened them, the sparrows were gone, replaced by a blue canary that sang plaintively, as if calling out for its missing Other.

He visited the institute every day after finishing his shift as a lab technician at Savior Saviour, and every day Darren refused to see him. Darwin would then observe his Other through a two-way mirror, hoping to see some glimmer of the *true* Darren. The soft-spoken, gentle Darren. The Darren with whom he had shared his first steps (Darren scampered across the room into his mother's waiting arms, Darwin tottering behind); his first bicycle ride (Darren took the front seat, Darwin the rear, both pedaling furiously while Mother and her Other cheered them on); his first sexual dalliance (Darren propositioned Sela and Sally while Darwin shyly looked on); his first summer job (lifeguarding at Sandcrest Sandquest where sunbathing Doubles admired their lean physiques and wavy blond hair); his first funeral (Mother's, followed by Mother's Other, who naturally terminated her own existence).

Darren. His Other.

The tram doors opened into Mendel Mendle's lobby – a great hub with half a dozen hallways that spoked in all directions – and the familiar gust of sterilized air slapped Darwin's face. The doctors scurried down a corridor like mice in a white maze, whispering to each other and looking back at him.

Darwin approached Jerry and Jared at the reception counters and handed them their coffees, part of the routine he had settled into over the past two months.

"Has there been any change?" Darwin asked. He looked down when he spoke, ashamed of his solitary voice.

"Afraid not," Jerry replied. "He's still —"

"– quite agitated," Jared said, "and –"

"– hostile," Jerry continued. "But there's been a development. The new doctors want to see you. They have the –"

"– test results," Jared finished, sipping the steaming coffee.

Darwin's heart jumped. Perhaps *finally* they'd made some progress. As he sat in the waiting area, trying not to get his hopes up, he spotted the girls from the tram hiding behind a couch. They pointed at a janitor who pushed a heavy mop over the floor.

A Single.

"Sing-u-lar Sin-gle!" sang one girl. Her head popped up, then vanished behind the couch.

The other girl peeked from the other side. "Hee-hee! One head is –" She took cover.

"– twice as dumb, dumb-dumb!" crowed the other girl. Their mother and her Other both shot a stern glance and the girls muffled their titters.

The Single continued to mop, keeping its eyes glued to the floor.

Darwin shook his head. In the weeks prior to his hospitalization, Darren had begun to obsess about the Singles and what he termed their 'inequitable treatment'. While Darwin had found some truth in Darren's arguments, he couldn't understand his Other's preoccupation with the matter. It was one thing to sympathize with the Singles, but why trumpet such an impolitic viewpoint? It had reached the point where Darwin feared people would start to notice their divergent temperaments. But he never suspected his Other would resort to violence. Darren had wielded a scalpel against Drs. Petrie – maternity ward physicians who were held in high regard because of the stillbirth pandemic. If the nurse Doubles hadn't restrained him, Darren might have inflicted permanent damage.

"Excuse us, Darwin," a voice bellowed.

Startled, Darwin looked up at the two gray-haired physicians from the tram ride. The first doctor nodded. "Dr. Jonah." The second doctor did the same. "Dr. John."

"Come with us," said Dr. Jonah.

Darwin glanced back at the girls who now crouched behind twin rubber plants on each side of the couch. One pointed an accusatory finger at him. "Sin-gle," she mouthed. Her Other peered cat-like from behind thick leaves.

Drs. John and Jonah's voices blared. "Is everything –"

"– all right?"

"S-Sure," Darwin answered, but his steps felt unsteady, as if the room had tilted. He followed them through high-ceilinged hallways and into an office at the end of a corridor. The doctors sat behind two desks that were pushed together and formed a single elongated table.

"Make yourself comfortable," said Dr. Jonah.

Darwin sat on the edge of a two-cushioned couch. Several pairs of framed certificates and two tick-tocking clocks with synchronized second hands hung on the oppressively white walls.

"Can we get you anything?" inquired Dr. Jonah, stroking the left side of his white mustache.

"Anything at all," said Dr. John, fingering the right side of his mustache.

"Tell me. Can I go to him, be with him?"

Dr. Jonah and Dr. John looked at each other and then back at him.

"You seem –"

"– tense, young man. Can we –"

"– get you some water, perhaps?"

Darwin took a deep breath. "Tell me. Tell me his prognosis."

Dr. Jonah tapped a pencil against his desk as he spoke. "Your Other is delusional, paranoid, subject to fits of rage. Classic –"

"– Doppler's Disease," Dr. John continued, also tapping his pencil. "Most likely, a traumatic incident triggered the condition. Has he confided in you about the reason for his behavior?"

Darwin shook his head. Darren hadn't uttered a word to him after dropping the bloody scalpel and being dragged away by the authorities.

"The treatments that usually work on persons –"

"– stricken with Doppler's Disease, have failed," continued Dr. John. "We believe Darren is resisting us. Your Other, we are forced to conclude –"

"– is *intentionally* obviating his Otherness," Dr. Jonah said. "It's a shame, really. What a –"

"– waste." Both tut-tutted and shook their heads.

"What do you mean?" Darwin responded. "Are you saying he's *not* sick?"

"Oh, he's sick. Demented, really. But fighting treatment the way he is, he remains a danger to himself –"

"– and to others."

His temples throbbed. "This is all about his stance on Singles' rights, isn't it?"

"Now –"

"– now, don't say anything you may regret later. Are you sure we can't get you anything?"

"Tea, maybe?"

"Is it so terrible, what he thinks?"

Dr. John and Dr. Jonah locked eyes, licked their lips and continued. "We don't pretend to know your politics, but –"

"– we happen to be quite liberal-minded about the Singles. Though incomplete, Singles can still – "

"– contribute to society. This is why our Government clothes them, feeds them, employs them, after all," Dr. Jonah continued. "We do pity –"

"– their sad, isolated existences. How can we not? Have you read any sociological studies about how Singles live?"

Darwin shook his head.

"Did you know they form male and female pairings?"

"You mean, for sex?" he asked.

"No, not just for procreative purposes. This is how they live. They cohabit, eat together, sleep together –"

"– and, if licensed for reproduction, the Singles they spawn –"

"– are raised by this male/female coupling!"

"You mean," Darwin said, "Single *males* assist in child-rearing?"

"Strange, isn't it? Sociologists theorize this male/female unit is the way Singles strive towards the perfection of Doubling. Can you even imagine how it must feel –"

"– to never know an Other's empathic touch?"

"Darwin, putting your Other's politics to one side, the way he has embraced his recent Single status is so disturbing –"

"– so aberrational," Dr. John interrupted, "that the only reasonable diagnosis is Doppler's. But he has resisted treatment, and in cases of incurable Doppler's –"

"– we have no choice but to refer the matter to Enforcement. And under these circumstances, Darwin, the Law is clear. Unless there is a marked improvement, an immediate and noticeable change in behavior, termination –"

"– must be performed within two weeks of the diagnosis."

Darwin stared at them, horrified.

"Mendel Mendle offers –"

"– truly excellent grief counseling services, which we can make available to you."

"Th-thank you," he said.

"If Darren continues to flout the Law, then he must face the consequences. You on the other hand –"

"– you are innocent, Darwin. Your recent tests indicate you're in good mental health. Normal. It would be tragic for you to be forced to live as a Single. Such a hard and empty life. And so, so –"

"– unnecessary, after all."

"Is there any way I can help?"

"If we were to see a change in Darren's attitude –"

"– termination could be postponed pending a further review."

"Please. Can I see him?"

"Yes, go to him, Darwin. Reason with him. See if you can make him grasp the consequences of his behavior. Perhaps what electrochemical treatments could not remedy –"

"– his love for his Other can."

"Indeed," said Dr. John.

Jared and Jerry led Darwin from Reception to Room Eleven. They pushed their thumbs onto the lock pad, the door clicked open, and Darwin entered.

The cramped room had bunk beds along one wall; Darren sat in a chair on the far side. He was dressed in a blue jumpsuit, his hair uncombed, his eyes bloodshot.

"You," he muttered. "What are you doing here?"

"Darren," Darwin said hoarsely.

"I said I never wanted to see you again!"

Darwin sat on the edge of the lower bed. "Look, please listen to me. I've just been to see Drs. John and Jonah."

Darren and made no effort to mask his contempt. "Really."

"Darren, please. They believe you have something called Doppler's."

"Doppler's!" Darren chuckled and shook his head. "There *is* no Doppler's! It's just *me*. I'm here because I scare them. *Doppler's!*" He laughed loudly. Too loudly, Darwin thought.

"Darren, stop this..."

Darren spoke to the two vid-cams in opposite corners of the room. "I'll stop nothing! I know the crimes committed against the Singles and I'll shout it to the sky as soon as I'm let out. But that's not what scares them. What really scares them is that I have a mind of my own."

"What are you talking about?" Darwin asked. "We are

Doubles, after all. You are my Other."

"Yes, yes, yes," Darren said. "You're my Other and you always will be. That's the problem!" Darren placed his hands on Darwin's shoulders and stared into his identical blue eyes. "This is difficult to say, even now, Darwin." He turned away. "I'm *not* you. I have my own individual thoughts, my own individual feelings. In my heart, in my soul, I'm a Single."

"Why are you saying these things? Don't you care about what will happen to you? Drs. Abbott say the Law requires you to be cured – or terminated. And if you are terminated, I will be Singled, Darren. *Singled.*"

"Ah, I see. So that's their plan." Darren shook his head and smirked. "They'll even use you against me."

"Darren, stop for a moment. *Think.* Just tell them whatever they want to hear, whatever it takes to get released."

"And you think they would simply take my word for it? You think they would just let me go, knowing what I know? Jesus Judas, you are naive. Did you really think I was here because of a *disease?*" He smiled and a glimmer of the maniacal flashed in his pupils.

"I know Singles face difficult lives, Darren..."

"It's more complicated than that," Darren said. He turned and pulled the sheets off the bunk bed mattresses. He walked to one corner of the room and draped them over the vid-cam that protruded from the ceiling. "We won't have much time. I've tried to shield you from this." Darren walked to the opposite side of the room and threw a pillowcase over the second camera in the far corner. "But if you're to live your life as a Single, I owe you an explanation." He picked up the chair and proceeded to smash each of the cloaked vid-cams. Breathing heavily, Darren backed up against the wall until half his face was in shadows. "For many months I had heard certain rumors about Drs. Petry and Petrie, about their true function at Savior Saviour. And during breaks at the lab I set out to uncover the truth. It was a simple matter to familiarize myself with the birthing schedules and even simpler still to arrive a few minutes prior to the morning procedures to restock supplies in the delivery room. When I was sure I was alone, I hid in the supplies closet. From there, through a crack in the double-doors, I could observe it all." Darren leaned in closer.

"I saw ten births and eight – *eight* of them! – were Singles, all healthy, pink, crying babies. And I stood there and I watched as Drs. Petry and Petrie sedated each of the mother Doubles, as they lifted up each helpless Single baby by its ankles and walked it over to the waste decomposer. One at a time they dropped them in the bin, closed the lid and, with a press of a button, squelched the crying. I had trouble understanding what I was seeing at first. I was too stunned, too shocked to even speak. But then I threw open those doors and confronted them." Darren slapped his hands against the wall, his eyes bulging. "They tried to justify their actions, to rationalize them. They explained they were meeting a quota! Can you believe it? Their *quota*! Do you grasp the magnitude of that, Darwin? *Do* you?" His face dripped with perspiration. "Don't you see? Something's gone wrong, terribly wrong. There are more Singles being born than Doubles – in overwhelming numbers. The authorities are clamping down on the Singles population. Controlling it. Making sure there are just enough born to keep them a minority. The rest are exterminated, butchered at birth by ghouls like Drs. Petry and Petrie. The so-called 'stillbirth pandemic'? It's just another lie! Oh, how I wish I hadn't been held back so I could have given them a taste of being Singled!"

Darren kicked the chair.

Darwin flinched and stepped back. Darren moved towards him, placed his hands on his Other's shoulders again. He pressed his cheek against Darwin's, whispering into his ear.

"There's no hope for me, you know. I'm incurably Singled and they'll never let me live. You, however, are my Other, Darwin. And as I am a Single, I know you can be a Single too."

"You're not making sense."

"Shhh. Listen to me! Just as I have cast off Doubledom's

207

shackles, just as I have embraced my individuality, my uniqueness, *so can you*. You are my Other. You have it within you to be a Single."

The door to the room slid open and Jerry and Jared burst across the threshold.

Jerry said, "It's okay, Darwin. Don't –"

"– worry," Jared said.

Darwin stepped back out of the room. "It must be a sickness," he said to himself. "It *must* be."

Darwin felt lightheaded as he moved through the winding passageways toward his habitation complex, his Other's perverted words reverberating in his head. *"I'm not you. I have my own individual thoughts, my own individual feelings. In my heart, in my soul... I'm a Single."* The spectral world seemed out of focus to him, more shadow than substance. He stared up at the moon, the Earth's mad Other, then down at his shadow on the ground, which seemed too far away from his body, as if moving independently, alone.

Lost in thought, he rounded a corner, and came upon three pairs of University students standing in a half-circle, backing a cowering teen against a wall. A Single.

It obeyed the protocols, looking downward at all times. "I was lost," it muttered.

"Don't lie to us, *Single*. What do you think –"

"– we've got? A solitary brain?" Harsh laughter erupted from the others.

"Your kind, *Sin-gle*, shouldn't be walking around –"

"– where they're not wanted, *Sin-gle*."

Darwin drew closer and six heads swiveled in his direction at once. Six sets of eyebrows arched.

"Well lookee here –"

"– another Single."

Doubles surrounded him. Darwin smelled alcohol on their breath.

"Do you have a problem, *Single?*"

The teen scrambled down a street in the direction of the Single Zone.

"I'm not a Single," Darwin said. "My Other is... ill."

Each Double looked at his Other then back at him. "And yet you're *not* ill?" one sneered.

"Uh-uh. Sure seems like –"

"– a Single to me."

They circled him.

"Are you looking at us, Single?"

Darwin lowered his eyes.

"You look at us again, Single –"

"– we take out your eyes."

Darwin stood still, staring at the ground until their laughter receded into the distance.

Darwin stepped into the elevator and punched "Apt. 212." His head throbbed as the elevator lurched sideways, upwards, then sideways again. When it stopped at his apartment, he inserted his door key with his left hand and Darren's key with his right, and turned. The words "Notice! Notice!" flashed on the doors in red blocked letters. He picked up a sheet of paper that had been slid underneath it. Hard-copy documents were rare – used strictly for legal matters. Not now, he thought.

"DUE TO THE SINGLING OF YOUR INCOME, IN VIOLATION OF HABITATION COMPACT PARAGRAPH 2 SUBSECTION 1, YOU ARE HEREBY ORDERED TO VACATE THE PREMISES WITHIN TWO WEEKS..."

No, this can't be happening, he thought. As he stepped into his living room Tabby and Tammy jumped off the couch and rubbed against his legs, purring in unison. He crouched down and scratched their white-furred heads. Where does an ex-Double go, what does he do? Darwin wondered. The cats exchanged a brief glance, an unspoken message seeming to pass between them, and then stared back at him curiously. They sprinted toward the kitchen.

He stumbled backwards into his bedroom and shut the doors. Pulling off his sweaty jumpsuit, he collapsed onto the bed. He gazed into the mirror and ran his fingers through his mussed hair. He and Darren had always brushed their hair back. Snatching a comb from the nightstand, he parted his hair down the middle instead. His sweat-drenched face was paler than usual. He pressed his hand against his reflected cheek, but the illusion of his Other no longer comforted him.

Darwin arrived at the hospital late in the evening, wearing a backpack and carrying his usual cups of coffee.

"Darwin, what happened?" Jerry asked. "You look –"

"– terrible," Jared said, opening up the thermal bag and taking out the cups.

"Tonight's the last night. Before..." Darwin's voice trailed off.

Jerry and Jared stared at each other, then back at Darwin. They stood, but Darwin motioned for them to sit back down. "I just need a moment," he said, taking a deep breath to compose himself.

"Of course, of course –"

"– we understand."

Darwin stared out the window at the dark foliage surrounding Syzygy Syzergy Hill. He watched Jerry and Jared in the window's reflection studying him as they sipped the coffee.

Within seconds, their heads hit the counters.

Darwin raced over and pushed Jerry back off the table and onto his chair. He rolled the chair down the corridor, holding Jerry by the shoulders to steady him until he reached Room Eleven. Lifting Jerry's arms, he pressed his thumbs against the lock pad on the wall. With a click, the door opened.

Darren sat up in bed. As he caught sight of Jerry's unconscious body on the chair he jumped to his feet. Darwin tossed him the backpack. Without a word Darren slipped into the matching clothes Darwin had brought. Differently attired Doubles would only draw attention.

Together they raced to the vacant lobby, their footsteps filling Mendel Mendle's cavernous silence. Darwin pressed the tram button over and over. The doors opened with a clang and they peered in. Empty. They entered and the tram lurched, beginning its slow descent.

"Do you have *any* idea what you've just done?" Darren said.

"I just helped strike a blow for individuality," Darwin responded.

Darren clapped his hands and laughed.

"This – this is unlike you, Darwin," Darren said. "To take this kind of risk..."

"Well, perhaps I've been denying my individuality too," Darwin said with a grin. "Besides, the risks were worth it given what's at stake."

"If you were caught..."

Darren looked up and froze. Darwin followed his gaze and saw two shadowed figures observing from the windows. Their hands were raised to their faces, and their fingers stroked their mustaches. The forms disappeared from view as the tram descended beneath the canopy of leaves and branches.

Darwin slammed his fist on the emergency stop button and the tram screeched to a halt. He wedged open the side window and squeezed through. He looked back at Darren and barked, "Follow me!"

Seconds later they shimmied down the spider vines that hung from the treetops into the darkness of Syzygy Syzergy. As they dropped to the ground Darwin pulled out a pocket flare but couldn't find the trail. They pushed their way through tall plants, running westward and downhill at full pitch. Half an hour later they hit the freeway; Darwin had a car waiting for them. They jumped in and it accelerated with a whoosh.

"What made you realize the truth, Darwin?"

"I'm still not sure I know what the truth is, Darren. But I

couldn't let them terminate you. And what you said... I guess you were right. I can be my own person too." Darwin spoke with a quiet conviction.

"Individuality... It's difficult to explain, Darwin, but it brings a new clarity."

"There's no need to explain. I see it now like you do."

"And it all stems, Darwin, from having a unique viewpoint, from being your own person, with your own thoughts."

"Your own feelings. But are there others like us? Supporters –"

"– of individual freedom?" Darren finished the thought. "Of course. Why else the need for 'Doppler's Disease'? There are few of us, and great –"

"– obstacles and risks lie ahead. But we have to do what we can to –"

"– make a difference, not just for the sake of the Singles, but to promote –"

"– individual expression –"

"– individual *thought* –"

"– for everyone."

And as Darwin completed the sentence, it dawned on him that he and Darren were now identical revolutionaries, identical rebels. But if they were identical...

From out of nowhere, doubt swept over him. They sat in silence for a long while.

"Darren, the way the doctors studied us through that window. They seemed so... so –"

"– unconcerned. Why would they –"

"– react that way?"

"Oh," they both said at once, startled, as Darwin finished Darren's sentence yet again.

"Perhaps... well, perhaps –" Darwin said.

"– we've acted rashly," Darren said. "The treatment of Singles is an important matter, but we've –"

"– broken rules, violated laws."

After a few moments, Darren spoke again.

"And the situation at Savior Saviour? The stillbirth pandemic? The –"

"– authorities must know what's happening. They must know what's –"

"– best. It's not too late. We could –"

"– go back to Mendel Mendle. Admit our mistakes. Express –"

"– our regrets. Return to our jobs, to the –"

"– security of our everyday lives. After all, we have –"

"– each other again."

They stopped the car.

Darwin and Darren looked at each other, an unspoken message passing between them.

At that moment a single tear broke free and trickled down Darwin's cheek. And he saw that a teardrop hung perilously from the corner of Darren's eye too, a teardrop borne of the horror of their mutual realization: they'd been defeated. The horror slowly, inevitably, surrendered to a deep, deadening contentment. And in that glistening droplet Darwin saw his blurred reflection shimmer, shimmer, then resolve itself into sharp, numbing, crystal clarity.

Tu Sufrimiento Shall Protect Us

Edgar first hears the screams while he's undressing and Mercedes is changing clothes in his baño. He doesn't normally get involved in the shit that goes down in this vecindario – best to let the justice gangs handle it – so he ignores it, tries to shut it out, until the shrieking peters out a minute or two later. But then he figures that Mercedes might not appreciate having to step over a corpse out in the hallway so he pulls the door open an inch and takes a peek.

That's when he sees the super from across the hall in Apartment 1B rising up out of the floor all herky-jerky like a fantasma. The old man, the viejo, is as dark and wrinkled as a prune and his chalk-white hair is as desarbolado as a just-used mop. He's wearing a rumpled beige guayabera splattered with red splotches and from the waist down his body disappears into the floor.

Edgar shouts, "Hey, you!" since he can't think of anything better to say.

And the viejo just stares at him like *he's* the ghost. His eyes are plums – it's as if he doesn't have lids – and his mouth is wide open in a silent scream.

Edgar shuts the door fast. He's about to open it again, to confirm he's had one too many shots of tequila, when he decides he doesn't want to know. He's leaning against the door when Mercedes strides out of the bathroom dressed in a black leather bra and panties.

"What's the matter, Edgar?" she says.

She walks right up to him, shoves him aside, and pulls open the door, even though he's standing there bare-assed. They both stare out into the empty hallway.

"Nothing," he says. "I'm just drunker than I thought." The memory of what he's just seen has already started to fade as Mercedes draws closer.

"I sure hope not," she says.

A skip of a heartbeat later he's sprawled in bed with this bigmouthed morena, a puertorriqueña, he thinks, from her "I'm-too-good-for-Dominicans" 'tude when he met her up at Arturo's Bar on the Concourse. After a few shots of Patrón, she'd changed her tune to: "You'll do just fine, papi." She carries a camouflage-green gym bag with her, which Edgar didn't give much thought to, until she starts pulling out some crazy-assed, weird-shaped "toys." He couldn't even say what they were for. Maybe he should put a stop to it right now – he's not into this kind of scene – but he figures he'll go along with it and see how it plays out. So he does what she asks, handcuffs her to the bedpost, spanks her brown ass red and all the while she's screaming, "Dame fuerte! Dame duro!" She's laid a black leather whip next to her on the bed. From the dozen pink scars running down her back to her ass he knows she's played this game before. A little spanking is one thing. But whipping?

So she's moaning and barking orders and shit when she says, "Tell me you love me. Tell me!" Well, since he's known this muchacha for all of about three hours he feels weird saying those three words to her – words he'd never said before in his life. And the fact that she *knows* he couldn't mean them after just a couple of hours of drinking and bullshitting, makes it all seem a little twisted, so he ignores her orders and leans in to kiss her instead.

She head butts him across the bridge of his nose.

"Tell me you love me, condenado!"

He pulls back; his nose is spurting blood.

"You don't love me, hijo de puta?" she says. "You don't like what I did? What are you going to do about it?"

He gets up. Sure, she's hot, and, yeah, he wants to please her and shit, but he realizes as he's wiping blood off his face that he's had enough of her psycho games. He should have called timeout as soon as she zipped open that bag-o-crazy-ass, but he couldn't get past her smoking body.

"We're done here," he says.

She calls him a pendejo, a total pussy. She's looking for a real man, she says. He's a limp-wristed, dickless zángano. She keeps the hits coming. He knows she's trying to piss him off so he'll smack her around a bit, like she wants, but he's no idiota. Women always think they can manipulate him into doing things. So then she starts shrieking. Shrieking like a fucking opera singer trying to crack glass. Now, he probably shouldn't do this, but he reaches into her bag of tricks and straps a red rubber ball into her big mouth, stretching those full lips real wide, and finally, finally, shutting her the fuck up. He's gone soft after the headbutt, but something about that ball in her mouth makes her eyes gleam excitedly and – he's not going to deny it – makes him re-think whether or not to end their little party.

That's when the lock on the apartment door jangles. He turns and the door swings open and an old lady in a housecoat just stands there.

"Todo está bien?" she says.

He cups his hands over his huevos and screams, "What the fuck?"

It takes him a second to recognize her. Mrs. Guerrero. His landlady. The super's wife. She kind of reminds him of his tía Candita back in the DR, with her coifed snowy hair and soft wrinkles except she's a cubana blanca. She's wearing a white housecoat, a bata that makes her look like a Latina spirit haunting the projects, and she's carrying a hardcover book in the crook of her arm. Taking a look at Mercedes, she says, "Dios mío!" then spins and slams the door behind her.

Now Edgar's thinking, "Shit, I'm going to be evicted." And while this rundown building on Bruckner Boulevard isn't exactly a cabaña on the shores of Bocachica back in the DR – back before the proxy war between the chinos and americanos destroyed it – it's a roof and a bed in a borough with a kickass militia, and he sure as hell doesn't want to have to start looking again for a place to stay.

He wraps a sheet around his waist and chases after her, leaving Mercedes squirming on the bed. But when he catches up to her at the end of the corridor, he doesn't quite know what to say. "Look, I'm sorry about this... If we were too loud, I mean. It's not what I usually..."

She waves an open hand in front of her, pressing the book she's carrying to her chest. "No, no, I'm the one who's sorry Mr. Ramirez. Really I am." She speaks rapid-fire English with a slight accent. "I heard the... I was just concerned."

He catches the title of the textbook she's carrying, *La Psicología de La Economía Nacional, 4ª edición*, and then he hears it again. He thinks it's a police siren until he realizes it's coming from below them. A scream. Followed by a deep groan. They're standing in front of a stairwell, which Edgar thinks is crazy because in the two months he's lived here, he's never noticed it before. He looks down stairs that lead to a basement – a basement he never knew existed until this moment.

Doña Guerrera frowns, adds some wrinkles to her forehead. She tries her best not to look down there, though her eyes kind of dart back and forth real fast.

"What is that?" he says.

She opens her mouth and closes it a few times before speaking. "Mr. Guerrero's taking care of the problem. You don't need to concern yourself." She gawks at the necklace he's wearing, an azabache, a dime-sized onyx stone in the shape of a human head. Then she puts a hand on his shoulder and pulls it away at the touch of his bare flesh. "Again, I apologize for intruding, Mr. Ramirez." Her lower lip trembles and she hugs her bata a bit tighter. He looks from her face to the bottom of the stairwell, which is as dark as el culo de una olla and dead quiet now. Then he remembers that he's standing there buck naked with a bedsheet around his waist and blood gushing out of his nose, talking to a frightened woman. So he just nods, and heads back to his apartment wondering whether his days here are numbered and where the hell he's going to find another apartment that will take him in with just a bare-bones Grade 2 background check, which was all he could afford.

When Edgar gets back, the gleam in Mercedes's eyes is gone, replaced by a glare, and he has to think twice before pulling that red ball out of her mouth. She swallows hard and says, "Un-fucking-cuff me, right now, cabrón."

And just like that he forgets all about Doña Guerrero and the sounds that had been coming from the basement. He sits on the edge of the bed and watches Mercedes step into her panties, wishing he shared her kinky tastes.

She finishes dressing and pauses in front of one of the canvases he keeps stacked in the corner of the room – his painting of the sunny, white-sand beaches of Santo Domingo pre-proxy war. Mercedes's long brown hair is draped over one shoulder and she has an expression he hasn't seen before, like she's considering something profound. "Not terrible," she says, nodding at the canvas. She puts on a pair of red-framed glasses and, just like that, the illusion of superbitch is shattered by a weird Clark Kent Effect. She's become the wholesome Puerto Rican girl next door. "And sorry about the nose."

After that night, he finds it hard to sleep. The screams are loudest in the mornings. A man's choking voice comes from somewhere beneath him, which is strange because he lives in a first-floor studio and there's no basement in this building. At times the cries sounds like a poodle being dragged under the wheels of a car. The shrieks rise up through the floorboards like a living thing, rattling his spine. A vague memory tickles him.

For the first time in his life, he looks forward to going to work.

At the end of the night-shift waiting tables at Conchita's, he makes it home through a blinding snow squall at 4 a.m. The drifts are shin-high and his frozen ears feel like they're about to fall off. He hates this weather, the way it's crept inside of him. Every time he paints a new canvas or draws in his sketchpad he finds himself adding rain or a hailstorm or a snow-filled landscape. He feels as if the cold is killing a part of him. At least the tormenta keeps the streets clear of the justice gangs that comb the city for "terroristas" to string up on the nearest lamppost. When he trudges into his building's foyer he stomps the snow off his boots, waking up the security guard – a Pakistani he mistook at first for a Latino – who operates the explosives scanner. When the kid isn't dozing, he's staring off into space obviously engrossed in some retinal movie. So much for protecting the tenants from the goddamned terroristas.

Edgar stands there in the lobby, which stinks like Pine-Sol and vomit, and hunts through the pocket of his parka for the swipecard to his front door when his cell phone rings. He knows from the merengue ring-tone that it's his mother. She calls him first thing every morning as soon as she wakes up. Unlike most of the evacuees from the DR, Haiti, Korea and all the other countries where the proxy wars are raging, she's landed on her feet, even met a guy from Albany; a Filipino, a fucking garbage collector, who took her in along with Carmela, Edgar's sister, a few months ago and treats them okay. He'd better, if he knows what's good for him. Edgar flips open the phone.

Twenty minutes later, he realizes that he should've taken it inside because he winds up leaning against the wall by the elevators – he can't find his swipecard while he's on the phone – listening to his mother ask him a bunch of questions that, as usual, she doesn't even give him a chance to answer. "Why don't you visit this weekend?" she says. As much as he loves her and Carmela, there's no way he wants to spend three fucking hours going through security at Amtrak. "I'll make sancocho," Mami says. "I cooked some last weekend for your little sister, but she's put on too much weight, la pobre." His mouth waters whenever she yaps about Dominican food. He'd swear she does it just to torture him. "Are you bundling up, m'ijo?" She bitches, as usual, about the snowstorms sweeping through Albany, as if though they were something unique to upstate New York and not happening across the entire East Coast – "something to do with the bombas nucleares dropped on Taiwan," she says, as if that's a great revelation – and she goes on and on about the new guy his sister is dating. "He's not too bright but he has beautiful teeth." Somewhere in the middle of her gossiping she sneaks in an embarrassing question about whether Edgar's remembering to bag the salchicha whenever he gets laid. "¡Mucho cuidado, hijo!" (More "breaking news" via mami-gram: the chinos introduced some nasty STDs that can kill a guy within forty-eight hours. No kidding.) She also asks, of course, whether he's wearing the azabache she mailed him last week, the tiny onyx stone prayed over by a bruja back in the DR, which is supposed to protect him from evil spirits and voodoo and all that mystic bullshit she believes in.

He can't resist giving her a little grief. "Yeah, a lot of good that stuff did us."

"M'ijo, don't say that! We made it out safely!"

She doesn't mention Papi, of course, or the other unlucky dominicanos who weren't so lucky, and how many of them wore azabaches. He doesn't buy into this brujería business – not really – but his philosophy's always been, "Why take any chances? Better safe than sorry," so he humors her by wearing the necklace.

While she's lecturing him about having respect for things he doesn't understand, he peels off his gloves, stuffs them in his coat pockets, and notices the dozen or so steps that lead to a cellar. There are stairs here? Red light bleeds from the side of the metal door, which is slightly ajar. The light flicks off a few seconds later and Don Guerrero, the owner and super of the building, comes out, locking the door behind him. He looks older than his wife, in his seventies maybe, and thin. His face is pale and sweaty, like

221

he's just French-kissed el diablo or something, and his grey hair looks gritty. He smells like he hasn't bathed in days and ignores Edgar as he walks by. Edgar is worried that maybe he's giving him the cold shoulder because his wife had told him about that little incident with Mercedes last week.

When he finally gets off the phone, Edgar enters his apartment and is about to shut the door behind him when he hears it again, real faint. A far-off bellow followed by the same deep moaning. He considers complaining to the super, but thinks better of it. The last thing he wants to do is get on this viejo's bad side. But there's something about that scream. It's as if it's coming out of someone's fucking soul or something. He can't help it. He sets down his coat and heads back out into the hall. Faruq, the security guard, is oblivious as usual; he's sitting thirty feet away, near the entranceway, bobbing his head to the beat in his earpiece, his eyes closed. Maybe he's just pretending not to hear the yowling, minding his own fucking business, Edgar thinks, like *he* should be doing.

The wailing gets louder as he moves toward the rear of the hall. Stairs. There are stairs here? Three steps down, he stops to listen. Someone's in agony down there. He descends the rest of the way and presses his ear to the cold door.

He slaps his hand against the metal and says, in a half-whisper, "Hello?"

The screaming stops.

But two seconds later it turns into a deep howling and then into mangled words, like someone trying to talk with a mouth full of marbles. He barely makes out two words being repeated over and over: *Kill me, kill me...*

"So what did you do?" Mercedes asks.

Edgar shakes his head.

He leans forward on his elbows at the bar counter and sucks on a Corona while the snow drives against the window, covering up the ARTURO'S neon sign. He and Mercedes have struck up a weird friendship after their night together. Knowing that they're not sexually compatible has somehow made it easier for them to talk. They've fallen into a comfortable routine heading straight to Arturo's every day after work. Edgar gets off at 4 a.m.; Mercedes finishes her shift at Santa Anna Hospital a few blocks away at 3:30 a.m.

Arturo's is emptier than usual tonight. Most of the regulars apparently decided not to brave the tormenta, so tonight there's only him, Mercedes, Omar the Kenyan bartender, who sits on a stool watching a reality game show about the proxy wars on his laptop, and Sofia, the mejicana in charge of the explosives scanner, who's packing a semi-automatic and reading the Spanish edition of The Enquirer.

"So what happened?" Mercedes says.

"I thought I heard someone walking down the hallway and I got my ass out of there. Went back to my apartment and turned the 3DTV on loud enough to drown out the noise."

"Are you kidding me? You didn't tell the security guard? Call la policía?"

"The cops?" He raises an eyebrow and takes another swig. "Right." No ataques terroristas by the chinos have taken place in three years and the policía – despite their ongoing turf war with the justice gangs – have gotten much of the credit for that. But 'suspicious' people, mostly blacks, Latinos – Asians, of course – get picked up for questioning, only to be held, uncharged, until they're deemed 'safe' to be released, though no one can say when that'll be. That explains why he hadn't seen more than a handful of chinos since he got here from the DR four years ago. Probably for the best, he supposed. The justice gangs would smash in their heads or string them up if they brazenly walked around the city at the wrong time. "No, no policía."

Mercedes nods sympathetically, as if she knows what he's thinking.

"Plus, what's that security guard going to do?" Edgar adds. "Tell the landlord? The old man already knows what's going on down there, whatever the hell it is. He's involved. No, I'm staying out of it. I need this apartment." His family spent too many nights in fucking bug-infested public shelters, unable to afford the background-check clearance needed to rent an apartment.

He and Mercedes sit for a while without saying anything. A bolero plays softly in the background.

"Do you regret leaving the DR?" Mercedes asks. "Not staying to fight the chinos?"

"I was just sixteen. Mi mama didn't give me a choice. And after the rebel chinos killed my father, she swore she'd keep me and my sister safe."

Mercedes downs the rest of her Johnny Walker Black. She handles her whiskey a hell of a lot better than her tequila. "You draw?"

"Hmm?"

"You deaf? I said, do you draw? I saw the paintings, all the sketch pads, in your apartment. You're really good."

"Oh." He wipes his mouth with the back of his hand. "I've been painting since I was a little kid."

"Have you tried to sell them?"

He shrugs.

"Don't you have any ambiciones?"

He wanted to say, sure, he dreams of opening up his own gallery, studying art history. But saying the words out loud would make it sound ridiculous. So he bided his time waiting tables at Conchita's and worrying about some rebel terrorista setting off a fucking suicide bomb at the restaurant. Ambiciones? The truth was he felt lost at sea. All he had was his mother, his sister. He was glad at least they were upstate where it was safer. With all the destruction lurking around every fucking corner of the city, it felt good to escape into his sketches and canvases and actually *create* something. "I wouldn't mind hooking up with a nice Latina – someone smart, aguzada, like you – and making a baby who didn't have to want for anything."

"That's sweet. Really sweet. That's your problem, Edgar.

You try to hide it with your macho swagger, but you're a big softy."

"Thanks."

"I hate softies."

They laugh. "What about you, Mercedes?"

"My aspirations? I don't know. This seems pretty good right here and now."

"Now that's just sad," he says, though he can't help but agree with her assessment.

"Let me ask you something," he says. He'd been meaning to raise the subject for a while and this seems as good a time as any. "Aren't you afraid that your little game might get out of hand? That maybe one night you'll be picked up by someone who likes it even rougher than you do?"

"Now you're getting me horny."

"I'm serious."

"Don't worry. I'm good at sizing up men. Plus, I carry a taser as a backup, in case I ever miscalculate. But I have to say, I don't have anything as effective as that black stone you wear around your neck."

Her comment catches him off guard.

"An azabache, right?" she says.

"You know about azabaches? I didn't realize puertorriqueñas believed in that stuff."

"Actually, I don't. But I heard about it. So you believe in... la brujería, Edgar?" She delivers the line dramatically, leaning close and waggling her fingers as if casting a spell.

"Nuh-uh. I just wear the stone to shut my mother up." He shrugs. "It can't hurt, right?"

All at once the music stops. The bar goes dark.

"Shit!" Omar the bartender says. "Another fucking blackout. Everyone out!" It's near closing time anyway, and with the explosives-scanner now non-operational it makes sense for Omar to shut things down.

It's unsafe at night when the blackouts roll through the city, but fortunately the sky is beginning to lighten from deep black to the perpetual gray they'd all gotten used to. They get up to leave.

"Daytime's almost here. Time to go to sleep," Edgar says. "I feel like a fucking vampiro."

"Only tanned and less charismatic," Mercedes adds.

Edgar turns the corner and there's an ambulance and six cop cars with flashing lights in front of his building.

A crowd of locals buzz around the cars like flies circling a pile of mierda, but they keep their distance from the authorities, as he does. At least with the justice gangs you know where you stand. With the policía, you can never be too sure.

Some of these people could be tenants from his building, but with the hours he keeps he doesn't normally see his neighbors and anyone with half a brain knows that it's safer to keep to yourself anyway.

"What happened?" he asks a heavy-set woman with a cane who's moving extra-slow because of the snow.

"They found a body. Somebody hanged himself."

He moves closer to the entranceway. The snow is coming down harder. He makes out Doña Guerrero standing in the building lobby. Two EMTs carry a gurney with a corpse on it.

The wind gusts and the white sheet covering the body lifts.

It's Don Guerrero.

Edgar stands outside the gated bodega on the corner of Watson and Bruckner for two hours, freezing his balls off, waiting for the cops to leave so he can return to his apartment.

When he finally gets inside, he pulls the blinds down. What the fuck happened? Had the old man really offed himself? He wanted to know, but sure as hell wasn't going to go ask the policía any questions.

There's a knock on his door.

When he opens it, the cubana is standing there. Her hair is disheveled; she's out of breath.

"Doña Guerrero," he says. "Lo siento..."

"There's no time for that!" She grabs his elbow and pulls him out into the hall. "I hadn't planned to tell you this so soon, Edgar, but I have no choice..."

He follows her to the rear of the floor to the stairwell. There are steps here?

She descends to the door at the bottom of the stairs, holds her hands together, looks up and says, "Dios mío, please help me find the words to explain this in a way that he understands."

She flings open the door and pulls a cord that flicks on a light bulb, revealing four cement walls, barren except for a rectangular head-to-toe mirror.

She pulls him into the room and shuts the door behind them.

"Look, I'm sorry about your husband. Really, I am, but –"

"Shhhh!"

She slides the mirror to one side, unveiling a circular hole in the wall that she steps through. He's hit by the stench of sweat and garbage and something else he doesn't recognize. Another bulb blinks on, illuminating images he has difficulty making out at first.

The room's ceiling extends so high that he can't believe they're in the same building. Glinting metal tools – hacksaws, wrenches, drills – line up neatly against the left wall. A wooden table with restraints sits in the middle of the room. And a water hose extends from a faucet near the ground. Pressed into the far corner of the room is a three-by-three foot cage and inside it lies a naked man, a hood over his head, curled in the fetal position. A rusted coffee can in the cage overflows with shit.

At the sound of our footsteps the man lifts his head up. "Please, please, please."

Doña Guerrero picks up a wrench and clanks it against the bars of the cage. "Shut up!" she yells. "Shut the hell up right now. I'm warning you!" The caged man flinches and moves his hands over his ears. His thumbs are missing and his fingernails have been pulled off.

227

The old woman reaches into the cage and snatches off the hood.

A chino.

"This is what's been keeping us safe since the attack three years ago, Edgar."

He's not sure what to think at this point, other than he wants to get the hell out of there as fast as possible. This woman is out of her fucking mind.

"Don Guerrero and I trapped it three years ago. It's bound by a magnificent spell, a complex brujería. Every day – without exception – it has to suffer. As long as we offer up its pain, its agonía, the city will remain safe from the terroristas. You must never show it compassion. Never show it kindness. But also never let it die. La brujería makes his spark more difficult to extinguish. He can tolerate more pain than others. And it is our duty to deliver that pain and keep our city safe. Do you understand?"

He takes a step back. The stench is making him dizzy.

"Once a month you must offer a basin of its sangre to keep this place hidden. As long as you make that sacrificio, no one will hear its screams, no one will even pay notice to the stairs that lead down here."

"I don't... I don't believe in any of this."

"I don't need you to believe. I need you to do it because you must. Because of the consequences if you don't."

"Listen, santería, brujería – whatever you call it — it's all just crazy Latino superstition."

"Zángano! Do you think this is something unique to our culture? It runs much deeper than that. What do you think keeps the South safe? Government policy?" She spits on the floor. "No, people like us. People who have made the ultimate sacrifice."

Edgar wonders why the terroristas would bother targeting Lexington, Kentucky or Asswipe, Tennessee. Then he imagines old Southern crones with warts on their chins, sitting in rocking chairs on their porches while caged chinos in their storm cellars cry for help.

She grabs his wrist. "I'm an old woman, Edgar. I can't keep this up. And my husband, que en paz descanse, well, he proved weak." She crosses herself. "After what happened to your father in Santo Domingo you should want to do this."

He's startled at first when she mentions his father, but then he remembers that she has access to his family history as part of the standard background check.

"And after what I saw you doing to that girl in your apartment that day... I know I can count on you, Edgar."

"Has perdido la mente! This is crazy."

"But necessary. You are strong enough to do what has to be done. Do you know how many hours of the day I spend praying for forgiveness? It is a terrible burden, I cannot deny that. But how many thousands died in the gas attacks in the subways? How many hundreds of innocents have been murdered by building bombs? We've stopped all of that! We can protect our city!"

He needs to get away. He pushes past her, and runs.

"Come back, Edgar! You have a responsibility! Come back!"

A day passes.

The shrieking is intolerable now. It seeps up through the floor and into the bottom of his feet and works its way through his bones into his heart.

Edgar's lying in bed. He can't sleep.

He hates what the fucking chino rebels have done, but he has no choice. What's happening down there is beyond criminal, beyond immoral. It's fucking depraved. He has to do something to stop it.

He needs to talk to someone so he pick up the phone and dials without thinking. "Hello? Mercedes...?"

Edgar sneaks down the stairs and pushes open the door, which is unlocked, as if though the old bruja is inviting him to enter.

He swings the mirror to the side and steps through the hole in the wall.

The chino is no longer in the cage. He's hanging from the ceiling by his wrists like a side of beef, the hood still over his head.

He gasps when he hears him approach. Then he speaks: "Pleeeease,"

Edgar pulls off his mask.

"Está bien, está bien...," Edgar says. "Everything's going to be all right." He searches for the key ring, which lies next to the row of tools, and undoes the locks on the chains. He slowly lowers the man, holding him up so that he doesn't collapse to the floor.

"My arms," the chino says. "I can't feel my arms."

Edgar rubs his hands over the man's bony shoulders to get the blood flowing. Then he turns on the hose and cups some water in his palms. The chino laps it out of his hands like a thirsty dog.

"She's crazy, she's crazy," the chino says. "Her and the old man."

"I know. Don't worry, you're getting out of here."

"My name is Cheung Lu. I have a wife, a son. I've lived in this country my whole life..." He starts to cry then. "Why? I delivered some food to them one day and the old man grabbed me from behind, pressed a handkerchief against my face..."

Edgar doesn't know what to say, so he just holds the poor guy. They sit there for a minute and he feeds him some bread, which he promptly vomits.

That's when Edgar hears the old bruja shout in the distance. "¿Qué hiciste? ¡No! ¡No!"

Doña Guerrero steps into the room. It doesn't matter. There's nothing that the cubana can do to stop him. And if he knows Mercedes, the policía are already on their way anyway.

When she sees that he's unshackled the prisoner, her eyes widen and she lurches backward, almost as if he's slapped her.

230

She's holding a glinting object in her hand, which she points at him. He wonders for a second how she got bullets past the explosives scanner when he realizes she's handing him a radio.

"Oye! Listen!" she hisses.

He takes it from her.

"...*tactical nuclear weapon of some sort has been detonated,*" a voice on the radio shouts. "*It's not clear if there are any survivors! I can't imagine how anyone could have lived through an explosion of that magnitude...*"

"Quickly," Doña Guerrero says. "Quickly!"

She picks up a whip and lashes the chino across the face with it. He screams in agony. Bloody tracks appear across his left cheek.

Edgar grabs hold of her forearm when she tries to take another swing. "I'm putting an end to this. Enough!"

She drops the whip.

"*Albany has been obliterated. And now the question is how the President will respond to this brazen...*"

"Albany?" he says. He releases Doña Guerrero. Mami. Carmela. He clutches the radio so hard his hand shakes.

The bruja gasps for air. She picks up the whip and strikes the chino again. He's now curled in the fetal position. She draws blood from his back, his ribs.

"*Because of you, Edgar,*" she gasps. "Because of your actions, people have died today. Dios mío, what were you thinking?" Her lips are trembling as if she's about to cry. She slaps Edgar's face. Then she stoops down, her hands on her knees, as she struggles for air. "Without my husband... I can't do this alone. For three hours, every morning, every afternoon, every evening, you must make it suffer. Terribly. Like the cubanos suffered. Like all dominicanos suffered."

"You're not... He's a human being. An americano..."

"Stop thinking that way! This is no game we're playing, Edgar. The stakes are too high! What we do here is what's keeping us safe from the terroristas."

231

"I never agreed...!"

"None of us chooses the burdens that God gives us to shoulder." She places the whip in his hands and closes his fingers around it. "One man suffers. *Millions* live safely. You can do this."

She raises his arm.

But he shakes her off and throws the whip to the ground. "I can't."

"Then we will all suffer."

The message light is blinking on Edgar's answering machine. When he presses the button it's Mercedes.

"Listen, hijo de puta! I don't know what the fuck kind of game you're playing, but I did what you asked. I went to your fucking building, even called the fucking policía because I thought you were in trouble!" There's a long pause and when she speaks again she's crying. "Why did you lie to me, Edgar? There were no stairs! No cellar! No fucking chino in the basement! I can't believe I was so stupid to believe a single word of what you said. The cops are taking me down to the station later today to answer some questions. Just stay away from me, okay?" Another pause. "I thought we were friends."

He paces back and forth, his hands on his head. Something snaps. He lifts his painting of the Dominican seashore and throws it to the floor. He tears up the pages of his sketch pads and slams a chair against a wall until he's holding two legs that he uses to smash a mirror, then he pulls open the door and runs down the hall, past Faruq, through the entranceway to the icy sidewalk. Mami. Carmela. The snow has turned to rain, and he's shivering and crying. The nightmare won't end. It won't end. Mami. Carmela.

Faruq stands at the doorway and shouts at him: "Precipitation today is Code 4! It's not safe out there!"

Edgar turns and heads back to the building, the warm raindrops streaking down his face. He walks past the explosives scanners half-hoping that the stairwell to the basement will be gone again, erased from his memory for good. But it's there. And he remembers. Why had he ever seen them to begin with? Why had he seen the viejo rising through the floor that night? And then it dawns upon him.

His azabache. He removes the necklace and the stairwell vanishes into the shadows of the long, dark hallway. He squeezes the onyx stone and the steps reappear, becoming clearer or fuzzier depending on the strength of his grip. His head is spinning.

He descends and enters the antechamber, pushes aside the hanging mirror, and steps into the basement. There's no sign of Doña Guerrero.

"Is someone there?" the hooded prisoner says. "Is it you again? Help me. Please help me."

Edgar picks up the whip. His hand is shaking. He holds it over his head.

And brings it down across the chino's already-bloody back. The chino shrieks.

He strikes him again.

The scream is louder, more high-pitched.

He has to protect the city.

He whips him again and again, until the sound of the whip is drowned out by the wails, though he can't tell whether it's the chino's shrieks or his own.

He never hears again from Mercedes, but he believes deep in his soul that she's still alive, that she's been spared.

Edgar picks up the brush and paints the red sky with a flourish. How many years has it been since Doña Guerrero disappeared, since he relieved her of her burden?

"Tu sufrimiento is what protects us. You understand, don't you?" Edgar keeps the chino gagged and blindfolded to avoid listening to its lies. Desperate lies about itself and its family. So that it won't beg. So that it won't look at him.

Edgar hears an emergency siren in the distance. No!

He throws down the brush and picks up the hose.

The chino's naked, scabbed body is tied to a wooden slab in the center of the cellar. It's missing an arm. The table is inclined so that its feet are slightly above its head. Edgar grabs the hose that extends from a faucet on the wall and holds the nozzle over the prisoner's head, blasting water through the gag and into its nostrils. After a minute, the chino chokes and its body spasms over and over until it lies immobile. Edgar pulls out the gag and slaps the face until it spits up water and gasps. The chino is missing a left ear. Its face is one big, purple bruise. Edgar turns up the water pressure and shoots water into its nose and mouth causing it to inhale water again.

The siren fades.

"You see? You see?"

Edgar slips a hood over the chino's head and turns back to his mural.

He considers turning on the radio again, but thinks better of it. There had been reports of an alliance between the gringos and the Chinese government to stop the rebels once and for all. "Because of us, chino. We're safe because of us! ¡Por nuestro sacrificio!" Edgar still has nightmares about what he did to the chino on the day they made the announcement.

Edgar stares at his blood-stained hands and then rubs them together rapidly.

The chino's breathing is labored. Doña Guerrero was wrong about their endurance. After the last one died Edgar had to head down to Canal Street to find a replacement before the terroristas could strike again.

Edgar stares at the mural of the red-sand beaches, the red-leaved palm trees that line the shore, the crimson waters stretching into the horizon. Something is missing from the mural. Something.

And then he remembers.

He bends down to where the blood trickles from the chino's bandaged ankle-stump into the wash basin and dips his brush.

And then he speckles the sky with precipitation. Snow. Red snow that occludes the orange sun.

"We're safe," he says.

Sleeping with the Anemone

Floating above the desk, a muscular masked man wearing nothing but a thin, silver ankle bracelet moaned loudly and thrust his pelvis into the Daffa's foliage-filled midsection. Its long, delicate stems splayed and its green leaves fluttered, twigs and appendages crushed under the human's weight.

Lanny Pacheco stared, slack-jawed. In all his years as a director of holo-films – even during the throes of his recent vibe addiction – he had never seen anything like this.

"You are watching the most profitable movie in our company's history, Lanny," said Juanita Vasquez, President and CEO of MacroHard, Inc., her eyes sparkling with flecks of green.

Lanny creased his brow and cocked his head sideways, trying to grasp what he was seeing. The human snapped off one of the Daffa's stems and the creature shuddered, its buds flowering. A chlorophyll-like substance seeped out. Scooping up some of the blue-green ooze, the actor rubbed it onto his white mask, moaning ecstatically as he did so.

"Xenophililia is proving to be more popular than we could ever have imagined," Vasquez said, squeezing a set of red rosary beads. Although her voice had the detached, analytical tone of a successful businesswoman, her eyes darted from side to side when she spoke, as if she suspected the authorities might burst out of the office closets at any moment.

"How can you...? I mean, how did you arrange –"

"Distribution of the xenoflicks?" She leaned forward and switched to a conspiratorial stage whisper. "Through the subsidiary of an affiliate of an off-world shell corporation untraceable to MacroHard." She leaned back in her chair, flicking the rosary beads from her right hand to her left and back.

Lanny hesitated, trying to decide whether to pose the

obvious question. "Isn't this... Code-barred?"

For a split second she seemed to glower at him, but then her expression morphed into a thin smile. "I suppose it depends on how literally one chooses to read the Galacti-code. Legal's opinion is that xenoflicks are in total compliance with the *spirit* of the Code. We're supposed to have amicable relations with our interstellar neighbors, no?"

Lanny nodded.

"Well, what could be more amicable than this?" She pointed to the close-up of the man's slime-covered face, a puff of yellow pollen swirling about him. His cold, blue eyes rolled up into his head; he shook a brown leaf between his teeth.

As a bead of sweat trickled down the arc of his receding hairline, Lanny realized that coming here might have been a mistake He was still a recovering vibe addict, after all. And even this – this *xenoflick* – triggered that familiar tickle in his temple.

Lanny squinted and cocked his head to the left, still trying to make sense of the mishmash of flesh, stems, hair, and petals.

Vasquez hit a button on her desk and the image faded. Lanny straightened out his head. He shifted his focus to the surrounding MacroHard corporate office, resplendent with its high ceilings and decorative holo-bookshelves. Trendy throw rugs made from Taurian skin sheddings swathed the white-marble floors. The window behind Vasquez's desk stretched from floor to ceiling, framing the city skyline.

She stood up from behind her desk, its blotter barren save for a single sheet of paper held down by a six-inch statuette of the Virgin Mary, arms outstretched. Walking over to the bar-counter-turned-altar lined with candles shaped like crucifixes and gold-framed pictures of human and alien saints, she genuflected.

This was no surprise. Vasquez, like most corporate bigwigs, held deep TransCatholic beliefs.

Reaching behind the altar, she pulled out a bottle of Absolut. As she mixed her drink, Lanny tried to decipher the upside-down writing on the sheet of paper she had been staring at so intently during their conversation. Titled 'Quarter-to-Quarter Results' it read:

Simian Spanking	-2.0%
Straight/Gay	-.05%
Anolillia	+.07%
Interdimensional Diapering	+1.2%
Underwater cross-species	+2.2%
Xenophililia	+128%

He shifted his gaze back to Vasquez as she plunked ice cubes into her drink. She looked nothing like the glamorous holo she projected in teleconference calls and other public appearances. Squat. Cocoa-skinned. Platinum-dyed hair pulled back into a tight bun. Lanny couldn't help but contrast her light-brown skin to his own pale pallor, her petite rotund figure to his own gaunt and gangly frame. In her loose-fitting yellow pantsuit and navy-blue blouse she seemed every bit the CEO of a major corporation: thoughtful, careful with her words, suspicious of everything.

Her holo had appeared to him the day after his release from Lunar Rehab, inviting him to this job interview. And since recovering vibe addicts could hardly expect gainful employment, he'd recognized this as an opportunity he could ill afford to ignore. .

"Let's cut to the chase. I'm familiar with your work." She sipped her drink. "Your romantic comedies were quite engaging, though commercial debacles."

He paused. "Thank you?"

"I also know about your difficulties." *Difficulties.* He'd heard that word used before to describe his vibe habit. "Nonetheless, I think you're an ideal candidate to replace our director."

"You're changing directors? Why?"

"Creative differences." She waved her hands dismissively. "Also, an incident with an angry Daffa grove... Nothing you need concern yourself with. MacroHard wants a director who can *humanize* sex with the inhuman. I think you can be that director, Lanny."

Lanny's mind reeled. While he'd allowed himself to hope that there might be some opportunity available, he'd never dreamt it would be anything like this. Directing pornographic features was the Big Time, exponentially more lucrative than mainstream pictures. With the amount of money he stood to make working on a MacroHard project he could afford to move back here to Earth, maybe even see his son and ex-wife again now that he'd recovered, now that he'd actually started to care about his life again. But sex with *plants*? *Alien plant-beings*? And yet... these were consenting sentients looking for mutual pleasure. Surely he could come up with something.

The intercom buzzed.

"Yes, Milly?" said Vasquez.

"Holmes Davies is here, miss," the AI drone purred.

"Send him in."

The office door slid open and a tall, well-built man swaggered in wearing a white fur coat, denim jeans and a cowboy hat and boots. Lanny recognized him immediately from his icy blue eyes: the actor in the xenoflick.

"Holmes! Fashionably late as always, dear," said Vasquez, kissing him on each cheek. "I'd like you to meet Lanny Pacheco, your new director. Lanny, superstar Holmes Davies."

Holmes seemed to size Lanny up before extending his hand. "Pleasure," he drawled in an Australian accent through a wide toothy grin.

"I was just telling Lanny about the growing ranks of xenophililiacs out there," Vasquez said, walking in front of her office windows and surveying the city stretching out below her. Under the darkened cloudy skies, the sea of neon-lit New Zealand skyscrapers stretched into the horizon. She spoke while facing out the window, holding her hands behind her back. "The bottom line, gentlemen: xenophililia is sizzling hot. Earth's economy – not to mention our average stockholder – is looking to us for leadership. God willing, we expect to beat the analyst's profit forecasts." She turned. "And to do that," she said, switching to the stage whisper again, "we need another xenoflick in production and on the UnderNet before quarter's end."

"This quarter? In two months?" Lanny said. He stood up. "But it takes three months to even get to Daffa space. I've never even –"

She held a finger to her mouth. "Anemone space is less than three weeks away via wormhole-stretch."

Lanny arched his eyebrows and glanced over at Holmes, who sat with his legs stretched out in front of him, crossed at the ankles. A slight grin crept across his square jaw.

"Did you just say Anemone space?" Lanny asked. "*Anemone* space?"

Like everyone else, Lanny had only seen videostream of the 'Anemone', so-named because of their striking resemblance to the colorful tentacled sea anemones of Earth, the only species ever permitted to join the Union without face-to-face contact. Renowned for their xenophobia, they communicated strictly through long-range transmissions, even attending legislative sessions via videolink. At their insistence, no alien species had ever set foot, hoof or root in their planetary system.

"You leave tonight, gentlemen."

Holmes Davies met Lanny at the lunar spacedock later that day, still wearing the same white-fur jacket. His apparel now seemed less eccentric to Lanny; Anemone transmissions had revealed an ice-blanketed water world.

Only the two of them would be manning the self-navigating spaceship for the twenty-day trek, the first eighteen days to be spent in spacesleep.

"All aboard," said Holmes with a smirk, pointing to a lime-green, seed-shaped Daffa spaceship visible through the porthole. "It's a gift from my co-star in 'Behind the Green Spore.'"

"A Daffa ship?"

"If we're discovered and destroyed," he explained, "MacroHard doesn't want to be connected to this project."

"So we're framing the Daffa?"

Holmes shrugged. "Nobody'll be framed, mate, if we're not detected. These Daffa ships have topnotch sensor shields."

Lanny knew the project was confidential, but setting up the Daffa to take the fall if things went wrong seemed unwise given the already frosty relations between the two species. The Daffa, a gregarious species, had sponsored controversial laws aimed at forcing the Anemone either to open up their system to visitors or risk losing their seat in the legislature.

"Sleeping pods are on level two," Holmes said. "Nighty-night, mate."

Upon awakening from spacesleep more than two weeks later, Lanny discovered that the Daffa ship had a skewed carbon dioxide to oxygen ratio, hot and humid temperatures, blinding artificial sunlight and, worst of all, a sod-covered floor with an overwhelming stench of fertilizer.

He and Holmes made the best of the situation. They wore sunglasses, bathing suits, and rubber strips that pinched their nostrils together, and stretched out on towels beneath the ship's halide lights, which emitted UV rays, good for a dark tan – and leafy growth, if one happened to be a Daffa.

"How are you going to get an Anemone to agree to this?" Lanny asked, staring out into the blackness of space through the large, aft porthole. "I mean, don't they find us – all aliens – revolting?"

"I've a certain irresistible charm, mate," Holmes said, lowering his sunglasses. "You'd be surprised at how far a little sweet talk can get you. Tell them that you love 'em and next thing you know they're spreading their tentacles. And if that doesn't work... there's also this." He pointed to the silver bracelet on his ankle.

"Jewelry?"

Holmes chuckled.

"I guess I've got to tell you about this sooner or later." He pressed a button on the bracelet and it emitted a high-pitched hum.

Instantly, Lanny felt blood rush to his extremities. He felt a tickle in his loins.

"Trick of the trade." Holmes pressed the button again and the sensation ceased. "The Taurians and Daffa had no interest in me sexually. Hard to believe, huh?" he said. He flexed a bicep and pointed to it. "MacroHard developed this little gadget. Press of a button, and suddenly everyone's interested. Helps me raise the flagpole too."

Lanny breathed hard, composing himself. "You mean... you're drugging them?"

"Not technically. It's a neuropulse. Affects certain pleasure centers in the brain – in intelligent species, that is. Tried it on a dog once. Didn't work."

Lanny raised an eyebrow, mulled the last comment, and shook it out of his head.

The neurobracelet reminded Lanny too much of the vibe on which he had grown dependent. The vibe too was not considered a drug. Simply pushing a button on the metallic, banana-shaped vibe unleashed a torrent of orgasmic, pornographic, holo-images. Uploaded nanoporn downloaded directly into his cortex in unending ecstatic e-jolts.

"You're raping them!"

"Lighten up. Legal says it's not technically 'rape' as long as no drug is used and we're stimulating the alien's own sexual impulses. Heck, not only is it consenting, it's consenting with enthusiasm. And, depending on the alien of course, there's no 'penetration' since –"

Lanny held up his hands. "Let's get one thing straight, Holmes. I don't like this, this *xenoporn* business of yours. And I don't like you. In fact, I'm only here because I've had some... difficulties... and need the money."

"Right. Difficulties." Holmes smeared suntan lotion on his arms.

"I have a kid, almost five years old now. I haven't seen him since he was born. With my paycheck from this project, I can catch up on my back child support and alimony. Maybe even afford to move back to Earth."

"That's admirable, mate."

Lanny had trouble gauging whether Holmes's remark was sarcastic. "You live on Earth, Holmes?"

"Nah. Bought myself a little place just off of Lake Flynt with my earnings from the last xenoflick. You know. Northern Mars." Holmes took a sip from a flask and exhaled between clenched teeth.

Lanny was impressed. Only the wealthiest one percent of the population – genetically altered politicians, athletes, porn stars and puffers, for the most part – could afford to live on Northern Mars among its manmade lakes, luxury resorts and other... temptations. The underground vibe market thrived on the Red Planet.

"You must hate living on the lunar darkside," Holmes said. He pushed his sunglasses back up his nose, and put his hands behind his head. "Don't look so surprised. Vasquez does her research. She told me all about your vibe habit, mate. It's the main reason she hired you. That and the fact that we lost our last director. Ran up against an angry Daffa grove – nothing you need worry about though..." Holmes's voice trailed off. "Anyway, directors are cattle, but directors who also happen to be nanoporn addicts...? Who could be better qualified to give the public what it wants?"

He was right, Lanny realized. Vasquez reaching out to him did make some twisted sense.

Lanny decided to change subjects. "Still can't believe what you did with that Daffa."

"That's nothing. Have you seen my first xenoflick? Did the naughty with a Taurian."

244

"A Taurian?"

"What the hell, mate. Mammalian sex is mammalian sex. No different really than doing it with a farm animal."

Lanny raised an eyebrow, mulled the last comment, and shook it out of his head.

"You've done this long?" Lanny asked.

"Six years. These xenoflicks have given my career a second life."

"Don't you ever get... disgusted?"

"Doesn't matter. I'm a professional."

"Back when you were doing commercial porn, didn't you ever, well, feel anything for your screen partners?" Lanny asked. Lanny couldn't help but think about how, at least for him, feelings of protection and intimacy had inevitably flowed from the sexual act.

"You mean, like 'love'?" Holmes guffawed. "Stupid question. Don't much believe in love."

"No, I meant more like... an emotional connection."

"You're a funny bloke. Like I told you, I'm a professional."

Lanny believed in love at one time. But love had paled next to the vibe. It seemed only yesterday that Traci had lost interest in sex in the months following childbirth. He'd decided to try the illegal vibe, just once. His life since then had been a blur. Only later had he learned from his Lunar Rehab counselor how he'd given up leaving the house, how he'd stopped speaking and eating. With the vibe pressed against his temple, in a perpetual orgasmic state, nothing in the world – not his wife, not his baby, not his job – meant a thing to him. Now, after all of this time, he surely meant nothing to them. How had he let things come to this? To make matters worse, his counselor had urged him to stay away from all forms of pornography – yet now he worked for the largest porn producer in the galaxy. But if it meant that he could see Traci and Jeremy again, maybe get a second chance to be a good husband and father...

"Well, keep an open mind, Holmes. I know it sounds like

Psipod psychobabble, but I do believe that there's someone out there for all of us."

"Yep." As the grow lights began to blink, Holmes pulled out the umbrellas and handed one to Lanny. "It does sound like psychobabble."

They opened their umbrellas just as nutrient-saturated water sprinkled down from the ceiling nozzles. If not for the high glucose content, which made it quite sticky, they would've enjoyed the cool spray.

"Did you read my script yet?" Lanny said. He'd given him his latest version the day before.

Holmes sat up on his elbows. He reached beneath his towel and pulled out the e-reader. "How the hell am I supposed to remember all of this?" he said. "If I wanted to memorize things, I'd go mainstream."

Lanny stood up and left, returning a few minutes later with a videocam. "Go ahead, read the lines."

"I don't know..."

"Trust me! Read!"

Holmes reached into his bag and put on the facemask he had worn in the previous xenoflick. He cleared his throat. "'How can this be, Annie? How can love, even a forbidden love like ours, ever be wrong?'" He smiled and looked up. "'Annie', huh? Cute."

"Go on."

"'Annie, it'd be wrong if I ran my hand along your tentacles, so wrong if I pressed my lips to your blowhole. What do we care what the galaxy thinks?'"

"Good!"

"'Annie, your tentacles, they're so smooth, baby.'"

"Again, with more feeling!"

"Annie. Your tentacles. They're so smooooth, baby."

"I've been looking for you," Lanny said. "We're an hour from orbit."

Holmes sat on a Daffa 'chair', a tall pot filled with soil. He squeezed liquid gel from a yellow canister into his hands, rubbing it over his torso.

Lanny pulled up a pot. "What are you doing?"

"Liquid latex. Last thing I need is to get the alien clap. Here, take this, mate!" He tossed Lanny a stun gun.

"What's this for?"

"Just in case the rooting gets a little rough. Don't want my head bitten off or anything. You can never be too sure about these alien mating rituals. Let your guard down and the next thing you know, you're black widow meat."

Holmes reached into his duffel bag and pulled out a long metal tube that extended into a fishing rod.

"What's that for?"

"You'll see."

Holmes pulled out the neurobracelet, which he slipped onto his left ankle. "A little Spanish fly to get me and little Annie in the mood."

He popped a tablet into his mouth.

"What was that?"

"Breath mint."

"Shuttle transport is ready," the AI navigator said in a sing-song. "Departure should proceed immediately to maximize daylight operation."

"We've only got a one day window to get this right, Lanny. Shake a leg!"

Lanny hesitated.

"I guarantee you," Holmes said, "that MacroHard payment won't hit your account until the xenoflick makes it onto the UnderNet."

This was news to Lanny. But he'd come too far to back out now. Just one movie, he thought to himself. One paycheck and he could seek out Traci again, hold Jeremy in his arms, beg for their forgiveness, reclaim his life.

The purple-tinted Anemone home-world, the fourth planet in the system, teemed with white-capped mountains, frozen oceans, and wispy blue-white clouds that swirled in its atmosphere. The ship's sensors revealed frigid global temperatures and breathable air. They wouldn't need their enviro-suits.

They landed the shuttle in a snow-covered valley near the planet's equator, where the temperatures hovered near zero.

Less than a kilometer away, the telltale signs of civilization emerged from the floor-bed of the ice-covered lake: the electromagnetic buzz of technology, radio signals, television sitcom transmissions. Holmes had used the ship's sensors to hone in on this underwater village, selected for its remote location, far from the sprawling metropolises that lined the planet's ocean floors.

They slipped into their skin-tight rubber hotsuits, fur coats and snow boots, then donned the visors that would protect them against the stinging winds. It took them most of the day to trudge several dozen meters across the frozen tundra, with the lights and heaters, to the ice-lined cave their sensors had detected.

Lanny and Holmes stood atop the blue-green icepatch at the edge of a waterhole. Lanny tried to hold his videocam steady while shivering. He recorded the towering mountains covered with bluish snow, the patches of exposed light green water in the ice-capped lake. If only he could get footage of the underwater city; viewers would certainly want to see that Given their time constraints, MacroHard's computers graphics department would have to lend an assist.

Holmes hooked the bracelet onto the end of his fishing rod and pressed the button. Lanny felt an electric current buzz in his loins. Holmes dropped the fishing line into a hole in the ice. The feelings of arousal subsided as the line sank deeper into the lake.

It took only several minutes before the line jerked and pulled taut. Holmes reeled it in.

"Well I'll be stuffed!" he shouted. "It's a big one!"

Lanny grabbed the pole and dug his boots into the ice.

"Hope we got ourselves a female," Holmes hollered into the wind.

"How can you tell?"

"You can't, but it's the principle!"

They dragged the Anemone into the cave. A dark blue bile spilled out of the gash where it had been hooked.

"Shall I activate the first aid drone?" Lanny asked.

Holmes sat on the floor pulling off his boots. "No time for that." He shrugged off jacket and unzipped his rubber suit. "Where should I do it?"

"But – it's injured."

"Doesn't matter. We have to kill it when we're done anyway."

Lanny gasped.

"Just like the Daffa and the Taurian. Don't play stupid. You didn't really think we could let the creature go, did you? It could identify us. MacroHard wants this kept quiet."

"But when the xenoflick is released –"

"Only Earthers will see it! And no one will know Annie here didn't volunteer for this gig."

"I don't know about this..."

"Do you want to be the cause of an intergalactic incident?"

He shook his head.

"Then get behind that camera!"

Holmes was right. It was too late. If the Anemone detected them, they could launch a full-blown military response. While the Anemone themselves wouldn't get their tentacles dirty, their cyberdrones could devastate any targeted planet. He and Holmes had to do their job and get out as quickly as possible.

Holmes dragged the creature by its tentacles towards the cave wall under the lights.

"Earn that paycheck, dammit!" he screamed.

Lanny grabbed a limb and heaved. The Anemone's body left

a wet blue trail.

Holmes shucked off the last of his clothes. He pulled on his mask, bent down and activated the neurobracelet.

Lanny stared.

"You can stand there and get off on this yourself, or you can do your job and get the galaxy off."

Lanny picked up the videocam.

Holmes threw himself on top of the creature, which remained flaccid, like a dead, translucent octopus. He ground his midsection into it. With each thrust, the Anemone's skin glowed brighter, first a pale yellow, then screaming oranges, tangerines, reds. "It's female!" Holmes shouted. How he knew this, Lanny didn't know. Its tentacles swayed below Holmes, pulsing, shifting from bright lavender to dark violet. There seemed to be even more tentacles emerging from the Anemone's torso now. Tendrils extended out from tentacles.

The bracelet worked its magic. Holmes humped furiously.

"Talk to it!" Lanny shouted, remembering his role as director.

"You like it, baby, don't you?" Holmes moaned.

"C'mon! You can do better than that!"

The Anemone's turgid tentacles grew longer and, in an eyeblink, flipped Holmes onto his back.

"Yeah, Annie, I like it rough, baby," he said to the camera, just a trace of fear in his eyes. The Anemone's moist, spherical trunk moved over him now, pinning him to the floor under its weight.

Lanny stared through the camera, intensely aroused.

"They're telepathic, Lanny," Holmes said evenly, dispassionately. "She says... She says that she loves me."

The Anemone's tendrils had now coiled around Holmes's outer extremities. Its colors were going crazy, shooting across the spectrum. Holmes's arms and legs appeared wrapped in layers of psychedelic, blinking Christmas lights.

"Tell her... tell her you love her," Lanny directed. Sweat

poured down his brow in a dazed, lightheaded ecstasy.

The Anemone and Holmes now positioned themselves on their sides. Holmes lay several feet away from the trunk, still held in its grip, though no longer underneath it.

Lanny zoomed in on the scores of pulsating colorful tendrils waving against Holmes's body like legs on a giant, wet cockroach. As if on cue, a thin tendril wrapped around Holmes's erect penis and skittered into his urethra.

Holmes's eyes bulged. He strained and managed to pull an arm free. He punched the button on the ankle bracelet, stopping its humming, deactivating it.

"Stop! Cut! Cut!" He opened his mouth to scream and two tendrils whooshed past his teeth down his gullet. A few seconds later, the two tendrils emerged from his nostrils. The long strings moved in and out, in an out, of his nose.

Despite the deactivation of the neurobracelet, Lanny still inexplicably found himself riding the edge of a powerful orgasm. "Yeah, nose-fuck him!" he muttered under his breath, zooming in on Holmes's nose, which breathed bright red spaghetti.

Tendrils had now worked their way into Holmes's ears. His bloodshot eyes pleaded with Lanny. He looked over at the stun gun lying on the ground by his feet, near the equipment bag.

Sheer bliss froze Lanny in place.

One of the Anemone tentacles spawned another tendril, which skittered across the floor and wrapped itself around Lanny's ankle.

Ecstasy consumed Lanny. Every fiber of his being wanted this.

A threeway with the Anemone.

Lanny shook his head. He stared down at the tendril snaking around his ankle. Hundreds of tiny pores opened and closed. They expelled a gas.

Pheromones.

Paralyzed, Lanny realized escape was impossible.

Holmes' face had reddened to match the color of the

Anemone's tendrils. The alien's torso had settled on a bright ruby-red glow, its body heaving, convulsing.

Lanny stared into Holmes' eyes. They bulged, bulged as if on the verge of erupting out of their sockets, as if tendrils were about to wiggle out of the gaping holes.

Then Lenny remembered the advance treatments from Lunar Rehab, the cutting edge techniques in which he had been trained to fight off the overwhelming urge for the vibe. He closed his eyes and held his breath. He thought of baseball scores and old people. He did mathematical equations in his head and bit the inside of his cheek.

He blinked. He could move.

Lanny snatched the stun gun and fired at the tendril around his ankle, which retreated. When he looked up to fire at the Anemone's trunk, lust overwhelmed him again. He shook his head and raced to the cave's mouth, grabbing his fur jacket without losing a step. As he reached the entrance, he stole one last glance over his shoulder. Holmes no longer struggled. He wore a mask of pure pleasure. It resembled death.

Powered by his pounding heart, Lanny ran through the blue snow banks in the direction of the shuttle.

Three weeks later, Lanny burst through the doors of Vasquez's office. She spoke with an aborigine woman who wore a skin-tight, black leather outfit and a spiked dog collar around her neck.

"I'm sorry, ma'am," the receptionist crooned. "He wouldn't stop."

"That's okay, Milly." She stood behind her desk. "I've been expecting you, dear."

"Do you have any idea what you've done?" Lanny shouted.

"Before you say another word, allow me to introduce you to holofilm star Teeza Jamison. Teeza, superstar director Lanny Pacheco."

The tiny woman, wide-eyed, popped up from her seat and extended her hand. "I can't believe it! The director of 'Sleeping with the Anemone'!"

Lanny stared down at the proffered hand.

"I've seen 'Sleeping' three times since it started airing on the UnderNet last week! It will be an honor to work with you, sir."

"Would you excuse us for a minute, Teeza?" Vasquez asked.

"Of course." As she exited, she stopped at the bar counter/altar and bowed her head.

As soon as the door shut, Lanny raised his voice. "'Sleeping With the Anemone'? What is she talking about? I dropped the videocam, left it on the Anemone home-world while I ran for my life. You told me it was consensual! You told me –"

"Every image you filmed was transmitted to the Daffa vessel in orbit. The ship, in turn, relayed the images to MacroHard's interstellar transceivers. We needed a failsafe, after all, in the event we lost both of you.

"Using those marvelous rehearsals you had with Holmes, the scenery shots, the footage of the encounter, our staff spliced together 'Sleeping with the Anemone' and released it in time to meet our third-quarter deadline. It's been wildly successful, Lanny."

"And that's supposed to justify –" He turned his head. "What do you mean, 'wildly successful'?"

She counted on her fingers. "One, MacroHard exceeded its earnings forecast. Two, 'Sleeping with the Anemone' has doubled the take of 'Behind the Green Spore.' Three, we deposited into your account the contractual amount we negotiated, with a substantial bonus. Four, I'm –"

"Wait a second! Holmes died making this xenoflick. Don't you even give a damn about...?" His head swiveled towards her. "A bonus?"

"Oh, that reminds me," she said. "Holmes Davies sent you a message several weeks ago."

"Message? You mean – he's alive?"

She pushed the button on her desk.

A fuzzy holo of Holmes Davies appeared, naked save for a

cowboy hat and a band-aid over his left nostril. Half-dollar-sized water blisters covered his body from head to toe. The Anemone stood next to him, glowing a healthy red. He held one of its tentacles in his hands, his pheromone-glazed eyes aglow with glee.

"Hopefully this videocam is still transmitting, Lanny. If you're getting this, I just wanted you to know that I'm man enough to admit when I'm wrong. You were right about love, mate. It's out there just waiting for us to find it. And with Annie, here, I finally have. I've never met anyone like her. She's loving, has a tremendous sense of humor, and she's a terrific homemaker. I mean, just look at what she's done with this place." He pointed to the barren, ice-lined cave walls.

"Also, I wanted you to be the first to hear the good news." He lifted the moist tentacle to his mouth and kissed it lightly; a trace of slime dangled from his lower lip. "Annie and I," he said, staring lovingly at the Anemone, which was now human-pink, "we're expecting. We're having seventy-two babies." He pointed to the blisters on his body. "Now Annie, I know she's gonna be a fine mom. And I aim to be the best husband and dad in the galaxy. Thanks for setting me straight, mate. Take care. And don't give up on love!"

He raised his hand and waved goodbye; the Anemone lifted a tentacle and it waved too. The picture faded.

"Well, there you have it," Vasquez said. "Happy ending."

"But – but… For God's sake, he's drugged!"

"Careful, Lanny. Legal has advised us not to set any unfortunate precedents by making such a claim. Technically, the pheromones merely triggered his own subconscious longing for love, wouldn't you agree?"

"*Seventy-two babies?*"

"Well, yes. MacroHard Medical believes that the seventy-two implanted eggs will hatch very soon." She paused, seeming to consider whether to continue. "The staff's best guess is that Anemone hatchlings, uh, devour their hosts." Vasquez looked at the pictures of the saints and crossed herself.

Lanny lifted his eyebrow, mulled over the last comment and shook, shook, *shook* the thought from his head.

"In any event, as I was saying, we'd like you to direct our next xenoflick."

"And what if the Anemone find out about this? What if 'Annie' spills the beans? It could be war!"

"The movie transmissions were already intercepted by the Anemone."

Lanny's jaw dropped.

"Relax, they loved it! They've just signed an agreement with MacroHard for future distribution rights. As long as we keep our arrangement confidential and don't go near their space again, they've even agreed to send a representative to participate in our next xenoflick."

Lanny's jaw dropped even farther.

"Don't look so surprised. If there's one thing we've learned from our encounters with intelligent alien species it's that, for all our cultural and physiological differences, we all share one universal trait, one commonality that cuts across the species divide."

"Porn," they both said at once, nodding their heads in unison.

"So you're making another Anemone picture?" Lanny said.

"Well, a simple human-alien sexual encounter has been filmed now three times. We don't want to repeat ourselves. MacroHard is a company of *vision*. For our next project, we want to think *bigger, grander*." She waved her hand skyward toward the horizon. "I'm talking, Lanny, about an interextraterrestrial orgy."

"Huh?"

"Just imagine: Taurian, Psipod, Daffa, Anemone and human, 'together' for the first time! This time we'd provide nose-plugs of course to protect against the Anemone pheromones. And saddles and sponges for the Taurian."

Lanny shook his head and laughed. "Do you really think that

I would continue after everything that's happened? Holmes told me about the other flicks, how he killed those –"

"Please!" she shouted, placing her hands over her ears and turning her back to him. "I'm not interested in hearing about the rogue activities of a disgruntled ex-employee."

"*Rogue* activities?"

"Your stock as a director has risen considerably, Lanny, and with the Anemone market now open to us, we have more money to reinvest in our xenoflicks. We'd triple your pay for the next movie."

He froze at the doorway. *Triple your pay.* The words hung in the air.

With that kind of money, it dawned on him, he could not only afford to live on Earth, but the luxuries of Northern Mars beckoned. Just one more movie. One more xenoflick, his grand finale, and then he could walk away from all of this. He could go to Traci and Jeremy in a few months, he supposed, after the completion of this next project.

"Would I have total creative control?" he asked.

"Absolutely, dear!"

He walked over to the altar, genuflected, and lit a candle for Holmes Davies, then one for himself.

"What can I say?" Lanny finally said after a long pause, the vision of Mars and its forbidden pleasures still lurking in a distant corner of his mind. "Where do I sign?"

Answers from the
Event Horizon

Q.   If our probe had the power to traverse this event horizon and enter the white hole, what would we find?

A.   A universe very much like your own. While there are an infinite number of realities beyond your cosmological horizon, each with its own unique physical properties, this conduit could only exist between superjacent dimensions in the transreality-froth. Passage is, in fact, possible if you could download an individual consciousness into a neutrino-flik and sail it across the event horizon at the correct angle.

Q.   What is the origin of life?

A.   Biological life as you know it originated in your universe 13½ billion years ago in the heart of heated comets. Heat and cosmic radiation bombarded the carbon dioxide, methanol and ammonia they carried. As they neared their star during their elliptical orbits, the comets' frozen cores thawed, allowing those chemicals to interact in a semi-liquid medium and form rudimentary organic compounds – proteins and amino acids, the building blocks of life. As they streaked by the six worlds of this solar system, they rained down those organic compounds in dust that settled in each planet's atmosphere and, eventually, onto its surface. On those planets with a heat source and a liquid medium, these compounds formed lipid membranes that facilitated the formation of self-replicating cells. These evolved into bacteria that over eons developed into simple bio-organisms, the first step in the slow, inexorable climb toward complexity. This process has repeated itself countless times throughout the cosmos over billions of years. This is why your universe teems with biological life.

Non-biological life incubates in the cool ether of dark matter shaped by processes beyond your current level of understanding. However, if our experience is any indication, in time you will come to know such life forms and recognize them as your brothers. In every universe we've explored, biological and non-biological life forms inevitably join together and lift each other to magnificent new heights.

Q.   With the data-file we provided detailing our biology, can you advise us how to cure the diseases we identified?
A.   *File attached.* This is not the most efficient use of our limited time together since you're already on the threshold of mastering the genome, which will allow you to resolve these matters yourselves. Genetic engineering will also provide the means for you to create life better suited to explore your universe.

Q.   Does God exist?
A.   Everything in existence has a creator, *ad infinitum.* Before the Big Bang there was neither time nor space nor matter, but consciousness. Formless. Eternal. Contemplating *its* creator. And contemplating others like itself that might exist across the infinite bubbles of reality. Since time did not exist, we cannot say whether this omniconsciousness existed for a millisecond a millennia or an eternity. But it jabbed with its thoughts at the weathered fabric between realities and poked an infinitesimal hole. And the entirety of a neighboring universe – endless space and matter – flooded through that pinhole in a spectacular cosmic eruption. The omniconsciousness found that matter gave it form, and reveled in its multitudinous shapes. It discovered that matter – molded by the flame of time and the winds of evolution – could eventually give rise to self-aware components, part of the omniconsciousness yet separate from it. It delighted in each of

the quadrillions of consciousnesses that flickered into and out of existence. It no longer knew loneliness. Time, space and matter continued to expand – prodded into acceleration by the omniconsciousness – hoping in vain to fill every crevice of infinity. This has happened in every bubble of the transreality-froth we've explored.

Q. Can you describe a clean source of unlimited energy that we can utilize?
A.   *File attached.* You were already on the verge of discovering this for yourselves. We were very much like you at one time, distracted by the mundane. You're capable of accomplishing more than you can imagine.

Q.   What is the nature of reality and what part does quantum physics play in it?
A.   You have a fundamental misunderstanding of quantum phenomena: particles briefly effervescing into existence, waves of probability collapsing into a particular reality, the entanglement of photons without regard to distance. The reason you can't reconcile these quantum events with the physical laws of your universe is because they are sparks of a superjacent reality in the froth, where the veil of your universe is worn thin. Eventually you too will be able to peer past that veil, if only for a limited amount of time, as we do now during this exchange.

Q.   How can we maintain our cultural and military superiority over those who would seek to undermine our way of life?
A.   You've wasted much time in our prior two exchanges with questions like these. You're better than this. If this is to be our final communication before the fissure closes, you should endeavor to make it more productive.

Q.   What question should we have asked you that we didn't?
A.   We wish you would have asked us about something

important. About love. About compassion.

We weren't always sure we'd be able to overcome our own primitive aggressive impulses. Our species evolved from an apelike mammal on a blue waterworld circling a yellow sun and, like you, we engaged in countless meaningless wars during our infancy. This is a familiar pattern, part of the growing pains all sentient species experience. So we take these final few seconds to urge you: imagine the inconceivable, strive for the impossible. The cosmic path is clear; you're on your way. And it's going to be an amazing journey, we promise.

About the Author

Mercurio D. Rivera burst onto the science fiction scene in 2006 with "Longing for Langalana," his moving tale of unrequited alien love that won the annual Interzone Readers' Poll for favorite story and created his Wergen Universe. Since then, he has published more than twenty stories in various markets such as *Asimov's Science Fiction, Interzone Nature, Black Static, Electric Velocipede, Abyss and Apex, Murky Depths, Sybil's Garage* and elsewhere. His work has appeared in original and reprint anthologies, including *Solaris Rising 2*, edited by Ian Whates (Solaris 2013), *Year's Best SF 17*, edited by Hartwell & Cramer (HarperCollins 2012), *Unplugged: The Web's Best SF and Fantasy for 2008*, edited by Rich Horton (Wyrm Publishing), and *Other Worlds Than These*, edited by John Joseph Adams (Night Shade Books 2012).

In 2011, Rivera was nominated for the World Fantasy Award for his dark fantasy/near-future SF tale of torture, "Tu Sufrimiento Shall Protect Us." His stories have been podcast at *Escape Pod, StarShipSofa* and *Transmissions from Beyond* and translated and republished in Poland, the Czech Republic and China. He is a proud member of the Manhattan writing group Altered Fluid (www.alteredfluid.com), featuring some of the rising stars in the field of speculative fiction. Altered Fluid subjected Rivera's story, "The Fifth Zhi," (then titled "The Fifth Daniel") to a live, on-air critique on the New York City radio show "Hour of the Wolf" (WBAI 99.5). His story "Dear Annabehls" was recorded and broadcast on the Maine radio show "Beam Me Up" (WRFR 93.3).

Rivera has lived in New York City his entire life, owns no pets and enjoys baseball, bad 1970's sitcoms and all things genre-related. He can be found online at: mercuriorivera.com.

Story Honors and Accolades

Longing for Langalana
  *Winner of Interzone's Annual Readers' Poll
  *Long-listed for the British Science Fiction Award
  *Honorable mention in Dozois's *Year's Best SF*
  *Translated into Chinese and published in *Science Fiction World*, China's largest science fiction magazine*Translated into Czech and published in *Ikarie Magazine*

Snatch Me Another
  *Selected for *Unplugged: The Web's Best SF and Fantasy for 2008*, ed by Rich Horton (Wyrm Publishing)
  *One of the Top 25 SF stories of the year – *Locus Magazine* Poll
  *Podcast at *StarshipSofa*
  *Broadcast on Maine radio show "Beam Me Up"
  *Honorable Mention - StorySouth Million Writers List
  *Honorable mention in Dozois's *Year's Best SF*

The Scent of Their Arrival
  *Second place in Interzone's Annual Readers' Poll
  *Podcast at *Transmissions From Beyond*
  *Translated into Czech and published in *Ikarie Magazine*
  *Honorable mention in Dozois's *Year's Best SF*

Dear Annabehls
  *Selected for John Joseph Adams' *Other Worlds Than These*

anthology
*Broadcast on Maine radio show "Beam Me up"

The Fifth Zhi

*Critiqued live on New York City radio show "Hour of the Wolf" by Manhattan writing group Altered Fluid
*Podcast at *Escape Pod*
*Honorable mention in Dozois's *Year's Best SF*

Dance of the Kawkawroons

*Translated into Czech and published in *XB-1 magazine*
*Honorable mention in Dozois's *Year's Best SF*
*Placed 6th in Interzone's Annual Readers' Poll

Missionaries

*Translated into Czech and forthcoming in *XB-1*

Tu Sufrimiento Shall Protect Us

*Nominated for the World Fantasy Award
*Translated into Polish and published in the anthology *Steps into the Unknown*
*Honorable Mention by Ellen Datlow in *Year's Best Horror*

CHRIS BECKETT
THE PEACOCK CLOAK

The Sunday Times named Chris Beckett's novel *Dark Eden* the best science fiction novel of 2012. This came as no surprise to anyone who has read the book or indeed any of Chris' work. After all, in 2009, Chris' first short story collection *The Turing Test* won the prestigious Edge Hill Prize, becoming the first, and to date the *only*, genre collection ever to manage this.

In doing so, the book triumphed over a very strong shortlist, including collections by one Booker Prize winner in Anne Enright and two authors who have been Booker shortlisted in Shena Mackay and Ali Smith (the latter a winner of the Whitbread Prize).

When announcing the result, one of the judges – James Walton, journalist and chair of BBC Radio 4's *The Write Stuff* – said, "I suspect Chris Beckett winning the Edge Hill Prize will be seen as a surprise in the world of books. In fact, though, it was also a bit of surprise to the judges, none of whom knew they were science fiction fans beforehand."

NewCon Press are proud to unveil Chris' second collection, **The Peacock Cloak**, and, we can promise you, it's just as good as the first.

Imaginings
The Way Ahead

A series of collections, each volume featuring the work of a single selected author, *Imaginings* brings together the very best of that author's previously published but uncollected short fiction plus pieces wholly original to the book.

Each volume is released as a signed and numbered hardback edition, strictly limited in number, plus an e-book version. There is no paperback edition.

The hardback editions are available to buy via the NewCon Press website, priced at £19.99.

Or... *Imaginings* can be purchased via **subscription.** The advantages?

- Reduced price. Four volumes: £74.00, inclusive of shipping within the UK (reduced shipping costs if overseas).
- Subscribers 'buy' a number within the limited edition run, which remains theirs exclusively until subscription lapses, at which point it will become available to others.
- In addition to the numbered hardback, subscribers receive a free copy of the e-book (kindle and e-pub).
- Subscribers are guaranteed a copy of a very limited book likely to sell out rapidly and become highly collectable.

Volume 1, January 2012:   Tanith Lee
Volume 2, April 2012:   Stephen Baxter
Volume 3, September 2012:   Tony Ballantyne
Volume 4, December 2012:   Lisa Tuttle
Volume 5, April 2013:   Nina Allan
Volume 6, July 2013:   Pat Cadigan
Volume 7, October 2013:   Steve Rasnic Tem

www.ingramcontent.com/pod-product-compliance
Lightning Source LLC
Chambersburg PA
CBHW030105260626
47156CB00008B/2524